RULE BREAKER

MIXED MESSAGES BOOK 1

LILY MORTON

Warning

This book contains material that is intended for a mature, adult audience. It contains graphic language, explicit sexual content and adult situations.

"Love is a fire. But whether it is going to warm your hearth or burn down your house, you can never tell."
Joan Crawford

CHAPTER ONE

To: Dylan Mitchell

From: Gabe Foster

Do you have the Houghton file to hand, or should I tell Mr Houghton that I'll be activating my crystal ball today?

I want to kill my boss.

It has become an absolute truth that a small portion of my time every day, is now taken over with creating increasingly inventive ways to murder him slowly. Take today for instance. Today I'm debating whether to hang him out of the tenth-floor window tied to the conference table, or disembowel him with the cake knife from the tea trolley. This is all done while taking diligent notes at the meeting that he's forced me to sit in. Never let it be said that men can't multitask.

It's a grey, overcast afternoon and the wind has picked up, throwing rain and hail against the windows like scattershot. This should, in theory, have made the interior of the small conference room at Harrison, Bernett, Farmer and Foster warm and cosy. However, the atmosphere is currently more akin to Siberia, as Hugh Kendall, one of the junior partners, sweats and mutters excuses, while my boss Gabe stares at him over the top of the tortoise shell, hipster glasses that he wears so well.

In all honesty, Hugh needs to find a decent excuse and quickly, because the mistakes that he has made are elementary ones that most interns would have second guessed. Now, his tardiness in completing the contracts for a takeover of a hotel chain is going to cost our company a fortune.

However, it's his fondness for Tracy from the Reprographics Department that seems to have overtaken his good sense most lately, and I know that my boss is well aware of it. There really isn't much that goes on in this firm that Gabe Foster doesn't spot.

"I'm sorry, Gabe," Hugh mutters, his forehead glistening with sweat. "I know that we missed the deadline, but there was simply too much work for such a small group to get done in time." He essays a faux, confident smile, as if he and my boss are brothers. "To be honest, the men I was given weren't exactly the brains of Britain. I mean, you know Murray Phillips – tell me I'm wrong." He gives a dismissive snort. "I know I should have alerted you to this, but I've just been so swamped with the work myself that I never found the time."

Gabe smiles. It isn't a nice smile, and there's something slightly wolfish about it, making me want to shout *abort abort* at Hugh. Unfortunately, he misconstrues the smile on my boss's face and tries a slightly lopsided, cocky grin back at him.

"Listen, Gabe," he mutters, leaning forward. "Let's say no more about this. Give me a bigger team and better people, and I'll get the work done by the end of the week."

I give a sort of half-strangled groan which Gabe kindly ignores, instead focusing his laser gaze on the poor unfortunate in front of him. Then he nods gracefully, and reaches over to pat Hugh on the shoulder. "I totally understand," he murmurs. "You need more people, so of course you'll have them."

Hugh instantly relaxes, lounging back in his chair and picking up his water to sip, and it's like watching a car crash in slow motion. "Yes," Gabe continues in a slow drawl. "I think the first person that I'll put on your team is Tracy from Reprographics." Hugh immediately spits his water all over the table and Gabe's suit.

My boss hardly reacts. He just brushes the moisture off, while staring intently at Hugh. It's the look of a lion toying with its prey. "Yes," he continues. "I think you really need her and it's past time that we made her position more formalized. My only query is which position?" He shoots a quick glance at my pen scribbling over the paper taking notes, before continuing. "Should we say missionary, or reverse cow girl?"

My pen scratches across the page tearing a big hole, and Hugh opens his mouth to say I don't know what. However, Gabe is now speaking in a faux, concerned voice. "Really Hugh, at first when I saw the two of you heading upstairs together at the Dorchester, I briefly considered that we had a problem with our photocopier and you were using theirs. However, the third time that it happened, I managed to dismiss the worry that had kept me up all night. Luckily the problem wasn't our machine, it was ... you."

Hugh is now so white that he seems to be in danger of fading back into the paintwork, but Gabe continues remorselessly. "Our problem was trusting a man who couldn't keep his dick in his trousers for long enough to finish a project. A man who decided to foist all the blame onto the rest of his team, who as far as I'm aware weren't indulging in quickies in Room 204 of the Dorchester with Tracy from Reprographics."

I decide to err on the side of caution and stop writing. Unfortunately, this means that I now have to sit as a hideously embarrassed bystander for the next twenty minutes, as my boss fires Hugh as cleanly and coldly as if he was a surgeon cutting through scar tissue.

When Hugh leaves, sheet white and shaking, silence falls over the room. Finally, Gabe stirs and stretches, giving a heavy grunt which makes my dick twitch, despite the loathing I feel for its incomprehensible attraction to the man at that moment. Then he stands up, pushing his chair away.

"Did you get all of that?" he murmurs, giving me a keen glance from under his slanting, black eyebrows.

"Most of it," I return, standing up and gathering my stuff together. "Although I'm not *totally* sure where you want the bit about Tracy from Reprographics performing reverse cowgirl on Hugh."

He smirks and strolls out of the conference room. "Maybe leave that for the severance card."

I follow him. "Wait. There's a severance *card*? How is it that I've worked for you for two years and never even got a Christmas card, yet you're handing cards out willy nilly to anyone that you sack?"

He gives a rough chuckle that still manages to catch me low in the stomach, even after two years of basically hating him. "Willy nilly?" he questions, as we stroll down the corridor to the elevators, both of us steadfastly ignoring the two secretaries who had been standing talking, but have now hurled themselves into the stationery cupboard to get out of his way.

I wonder whether this happens so much to him that he simply doesn't notice it anymore. An image pops up in my head of cab drivers hurling themselves from still moving vehicles, and chefs throwing pans out of the window to tuck and dive away from him, but then I dismiss it. The man misses nothing. He's like a bloody machine.

The elevator arrives and we enter, but not before he stands back to let me through first. I'd hated this politeness from him at first. It had made me feel a bit girly, like I was going to let my hair down in the lift and he'd do a double take and say, 'Why Dylan, you're beautiful'. Then I'd realised that it was just the way that he was made.

He's an extremely well-mannered man even to those that he's sacking. After all, he had just said thank you to Hugh, and stood up when the man stumbled out of the room, not to mention asked after his wife's health. I snort at the thought, and he looks at me with one supercilious eyebrow raised. I sigh inwardly because anyone else would find that gesture charming and sexy. Instead, it just makes me want to poke a pen in his eye.

"Something funny?" he mutters, one long finger pressing the button for our floor.

"Just thinking what's next in your diary today. I can't work out whether you've got kicking abandoned puppies, or the appointment to send small, orphaned children up the chimneys."

"Very funny," he drawls, unable to help the quick quirk of his lips. He lifts his hand to run it through the dark waves of his hair and inadvertently gifts me with a blast of his spicy orange cologne. I subtly inhale, while pretending to myself that I'm just sniffing. "What *is* next?" he asks, returning to seriousness immediately.

I sigh and look down at my tablet. Clicking through a few screens, I draw up his diary. "You've got the two o'clock meeting with Mr Pullman, and of course you've got the four o'clock appointment to explain to Hamiltons why their contracts aren't ready to exchange."

He sighs heavily, and when I look up, he's taken off his glasses and is rubbing his eyes wearily. When he lowers his hand, he blinks at me owlishly. "I'll look forward to that," he mutters.

For a second I forget myself and feel a pang of sympathy. "Well look on the bright side, at least it's not a root canal."

He stares at me, his glance seeming to get snagged on my smile, and then he looks away. "Anything else, or have you got your afternoon shift at the comedy club to get to?"

My second of sympathy is extinguished. *It was nice while it lasted.*

"No sir," I say facetiously. "That's tomorrow. Today I'm going to just settle for taking the minutes while you eviscerate a few more members of staff."

He straightens up as the elevator pings, and the door opens. "You can't be sympathetic to Hugh. The man is an incompetent idiot. Show some discretion."

"I wasn't talking about him," I mutter to his back, as he steps out, and immediately staff scatter left and right.

Ignoring it blithely, he saunters to his office. "What else?" he throws over his shoulder.

"You've got the black-tie function with Fletcher," I throw back to him, adding in a lower voice, "I'll look forward to *his* visit to the office."

He turns sharply. "*What?*"

"I said that I'll look forward to his visit to the office. I absolutely *live* to see his smile."

For a second I'm sure that he smiles, but then he grunts, "Bull-shitter!"

I move around my desk which guards the entrance to his office, subsiding into my comfortable, leather chair with a sigh of satisfaction. "I don't think I quite caught that, Sir."

He pauses at the door, looking at me intently. "Yes, you did. Nothing gets past you. You're the most astute man that I've ever met."

He vanishes into his office, leaving me in silence for a second, as I try to process the thought that Gabe has just paid me a compliment.

"Where the hell is my spare suit?" comes the roar from the office, and I make sure that he hears me sighing heavily.

"It's in the cupboard where it normally is." I come to a stuttering stop at the sight that greets me. His wet jacket is gone and he's shirt-less, with the wide, hairy expanse of his chest visible. I swallow hard, trying not to look at the tanned skin stretched tight over his hard, abdominal muscles, the visible v of his pelvis, and the way that his trousers hang from the swell of his backside as he turns around.

"Earth to Dylan," he gripes, snapping his fingers at me. "Where's my suit? It's not in the bloody cupboard where it should be."

"Do you want me to find it, or do a flamenco dance?" I ask sharply. "Because I'm sure that's the only *possible* reason that you could have for snapping your fingers at me."

"Or maybe I just want you to come to heel," he says wickedly, looking at me closely with his eyes full of malicious amusement.

"It'll take more than a couple of fingers to do that," I counter under my breath, turning to rifle through the cupboard where he keeps his spare clothes. The man is such a workaholic that he had once slept at the office for a whole week when there was an important deal going on, hence the need for spare clothes. "Here it is," I exclaim triumphantly, as I pull out his navy blue, Hugo Boss suit. "It was behind your coat, which you never noticed, as you tend to look for things at a distance of three feet away from anything with your eyes closed." I turn to find him watching me closely, his eyes seeming darker. "What?" I ask.

He shakes his head impatiently, as if dismissing what he had been thinking. "You're very pert all of a sudden."

I stare at him for a second. "Well, it's not every day I get a compliment like you just paid me." I pause. "Actually, it's not every *year* either."

"I compliment you," he says crossly, shrugging into his shirt and covering that chest to my secret dismay.

"'Why the hell does it take four hours to get my coffee? Are you actually grinding the beans with your feet?' and 'Did Dopey the third dwarf type up this contract?' are not compliments," I say patiently, standing with his jacket held out so that he can slip into it.

He snorts. "The thought of your face when I said that still has the power to make me laugh." I shake my head at him and he grins, his teeth white in his tanned, angular face. "No really, I was at a business luncheon with one of the senior partners the other day, and it made me laugh out loud."

"What did he say?" The senior partners are not known for possessing any sort of sense of humour.

"I had to pretend that someone had fallen and broken their leg."

I throw my head back laughing, but when I recover and turn back to him, he's staring at me intently again. "What?"

"I know I don't give you a lot of compliments," he begins slowly.

I lean forward eagerly. "Yes?"

"But I just want to say -"

"Are you ready, Mr Foster?" comes a nervous voice from the door. It's James, the new intern, or victim, depending on what you want to call the young men who enter Gabe's office arrogantly and then shortly afterwards race back to university with their tails between their legs. "You said to meet you here, and that you'd walk down to the meeting with me?"

I put up a hand. "No, he isn't ready yet, James. He was just about to give me a compliment, and as I'm sure that Margaret Thatcher was the Prime Minister the last time that happened, the meeting can wait."

Gabe laughs and bats my hand down almost playfully, making James and I look at him like he's grown two heads. "Sorry," he says, moving towards James, who promptly straightens as if he's standing in front of the firing squad. "Senior partners wait for no man's compliments. Grab the forms from Dylan, James, and I'll meet you at the elevators." Buttoning his jacket, he saunters off, amusement written all over him.

Silence falls, and I look up to see James staring at me in what looks like awe. "What?" I ask, gathering the folder with the papers that Gabe needs from my desk, and holding them out to him.

"*You?*" he whispers, coming to get them from me. "I can't believe how you talk to him, Dylan."

"What do you mean?"

"Last week I heard you tell him that never mind getting another degree, he ought to go back to primary school and learn how to write properly."

I laugh. "Well, he should. His notes look like a five-year-old did them."

He shakes his head. "Why aren't you scared of him like everyone else? He can be so utterly vile."

I sober instantly. "No, he isn't," I say sharply. "He's one of the fairest men that I've ever met. All he expects is for people to put one hundred percent into their work, the way that he does. He didn't make the youngest partner in the firm's history without being driven. He gives everything to the company, and all that he expects back is hard work and diligence. If you give him that, he'll respect you."

I can't let his criticism go. Gabe might be a complete bastard, but I sort of think of him as *my* bastard, and I don't like other people criticising him.

My message might have gone in more if Gabe's voice hadn't snapped behind him at this point. "Are you ready, James, or would you like me to make you and Dylan a cup of tea so that you can continue your cosy chat? Maybe you could plait each other's hair, and do your nails while you're at it."

James jumps about a foot in the air, before muttering apologies and rushing past Gabe. I shake my head disapprovingly, but Gabe just stands there for a second, staring at me with an inscrutable look on his face. Finally, he speaks. "You forgot to mention loyalty." I raise my eyebrows questioningly. "What I value most amongst employees, what stops my wrath, is loyalty."

Not saying another word, he turns and silently vanishes down the corridor, leaving me staring after him.

Finally, becoming aware that I could potentially catch flies with my open mouth, I slide down into my chair and switch my computer on. However, instead of doing the work that is piled up on my desk, I find myself remembering my interview for this job two years ago.

I'd heard about the job through an old boyfriend of mine, who had warned me that the man was an absolute slave driver, and went through staff like water. However, as my job as an administrative assistant at a theatre had come to a close, I'd ignored the warning and sallied blithely off to my interview.

Two hours of searing questions and cheesy role play situations with Verma, the dragon from HR, and my patience had finally run out. I'd attempted to answer everything that she'd thrown at me with good grace, but it had been hard to concentrate with my awareness of Gabe, or the Adonis as I had thought of him then. He'd been sitting back against the wall with his legs crossed, elbows resting on the arms of his chair, and his hands steepled.

He'd said nothing, but Verma and I had still heroically persevered in including him in everything that we'd said. I'd thought that the interview was going well, until unfortunately Verma had enquired about my ability with languages. Two hours of torture had made me want this job more than I probably would have done normally, so I'd lied.

"Oh yes, I can speak French and Spanish," I'd said firmly. In reality, I could order a pizza and breakfast in French, and ask where the toilets were. I spoke no Spanish at all.

Unfortunately, that was the point at which Gabe chose to join in with the interview. He said something quickly in a beautiful, fluid accent. My brain told me that it must be Spanish and that he looked gorgeous speaking it, but unfortunately it couldn't come up with anything else that was useful.

"Erm," I'd said, and the silence grew as Gabe calmly uncapped a bottle of water and took a drink. Very aware of the glee filling Gabe's face I'd wracked my brain again, and a long-forgotten memory of a phrase surfaced. "Donde esta el hombre con fuego en la sangre?" I rattled off happily.

Silence fell again before Verma stirred, looking impressed. "Well, Mr Mitchell, that sounds very -"

I never found out what it sounded like, because Gabe interrupted. "That's the opening verse from 'Mi Chico Latino' by Geri Halliwell," he said, his voice choked with laughter.

I'd looked at him and considered many answers, but finally

settled for shrugging. "Everyone's a critic. If only more people listened to Geri, the world would be a much better place, *and* we'd have more Latin men around."

Verma had been stunned into silence, but it had been broken by a strange noise which turned out to be Gabe choking on his water, before letting out a great guffaw of laughter. I'd stared at him, mesmerised by the beauty of his face when it relaxed into laughter. I'd been so taken aback at the notion of working with such a good-looking man, that I'd failed to realise that it would be the last time that I'd see him laugh. Verma had worked there for fifteen years, and I'd be prepared to bet that it was the first time that his face had ever cracked a smile in front of her.

I'd spent my first week in a horny daze, drifting around and staring at him whenever I thought I could get away with it, which, looking back, probably meant never. Luckily, after I'd sat through him firing three people, delivered a new Fleshlight to his boyfriend of the time, and picked up the special lube that he bought at a specialist shop in Soho, my crush had vanished.

I'd been amazed to find that I didn't follow it out the door, but instead I had stayed, because I found that the work stimulated and stretched me, as did Gabe. His humour was subtle at first, hidden under several very deep layers of bad temper and grouchiness. However, the longer that I stayed, the more I started to respect his mile a minute brain and canny scepticism. The more I proved myself, the more he appreciated it, until gradually we'd started to become a partnership.

He felt free to criticise and grumble, and I felt equally free to snark back, offering a sunny disposition. When that failed, I would use sarcastic comments, and even on occasion direct disagreement with him. He'd seemed surprised at first, but then he seemed to settle. Now he actually appears to enjoy working with me. He definitely trusts me, which puts me in a very small minority of people.

I'd managed to push my attraction to him away into a little box, but occasionally it still surfaces, and I have to acknowledge how very gorgeous he is. He's tall - six foot three to my six foot, with dark, wavy hair, gorgeous silver-grey eyes, and a perfect level of stubble which makes his high cheekbones look even sharper.

However, when that heat hits me deep in the belly, I take great care to remind myself of his boyfriend for the last year. As if on cue I hear a melodious voice. "Ah, it's David, isn't it? Is Gabe around?"

"It's Dylan," I say patiently, for what must be the hundredth time. "No, he isn't here. He's still in a meeting. Is he expecting you?"

"No," Fletcher says carelessly, slumping down onto one of the leather sofas in the waiting area in front of my desk. Even slumped he manages to look gorgeous, which shouldn't be surprising as he's a very sought-after model. He's slender and toned, with shoulder-length, blonde hair, full, pouting lips, and a pair of cheekbones that you could slice bread with. However, to my mind he's nowhere near as gorgeous as my best friend and flatmate Jude, who is also a model. Jude lacks Fletcher's perfection but makes up for it with a quirky beauty, and a lively, interesting face.

Fletcher interrupts my thoughts by snapping his fingers under my nose. "Earth to Dylan," he sneers. "Does Gabe know how much time you spend daydreaming?"

"I'm not daydreaming. I'm just thinking about Gabe's timetable for today," I say tightly, resisting the urge to grab his fingers and break them. It doesn't escape me that his boyfriend had done something similar to me a few hours ago, and lived. However, when Gabe did it, it didn't have the mean, derogatory edge that Fletcher gives his.

I don't feel like playing into Fletcher's hands and losing my temper. Fletcher has always hated me, and would love to cause a problem for me. He's one of those people who are deeply suspicious of anyone who orbits their partner, imagining themselves so fabulous that everyone is looking for a piece of their life.

I also personally think that those people who are so possessive of their partners are quite often up to something themselves. Either that, or Gabe has strayed before. Neither of them seem to have that happily settled air about them. However, I wouldn't like to test that if

Fletcher ever demands my sacking. I would imagine that empty balls top diligent workers every time.

"You call him by his first name. I've always meant to mention it. That's unusual for a boss and his employee, isn't it?" he sneers slightly.

"I've worked for him for two years," I say quietly. "He told me to."

He shrugs petulantly. "Oh, who cares, Dylan? When is he coming back?"

I check my tablet. "In about half an hour if the meeting ends on time."

"Boring," he sniffs, picking up a snow globe from my desk with a little, jolly Santa on it, and shaking it. "How twee." I smile calmly and watch his face as the snow stops falling to reveal the Santa baring his buttocks. It had been a gag gift from Jude from the airport when he was travelling back from one of his jobs. Fletcher shakes his head dismissively, tosses it back onto a stack of papers on my desk, and then gets to his feet. "I'll wait in his office."

I stand up. "I'm sorry, Mr Newton, but I can't let you do that. Gabe's instructions are very clear that no one goes in if he's not there."

"I'm not *anyone*," he says through clenched teeth. "I'm his boyfriend."

"I know," I say faux apologetically. "But there are confidential documents lying about."

"I'm not interested in shit like that." His voice is rising, and I sigh. He bores the crap out of me, and I really, *really* want to tell him that I know there's no risk of him reading any of the papers, as none of them have pictures.

However, I manfully keep my mouth shut and settle for shrugging insolently. His clenched teeth show that I haven't calmed him. Either that, or he's noticed the smirk that I can't quite hold back.

"Now listen to me, you little shit," he says, coming towards me.

Yes, it's the smirk. I draw myself up to my full height, which as it's a full couple of inches above him, makes him stop.

"Yes sir," I say helpfully, knowing and relishing the fact that this politeness is really winding him up.

"You are nothing, do you hear me? You can't tell me what to do. Now, I'm going to go and sit in his office and wait for Gabe, and do you know what?" He leans forward and smiles. "I might wait for him naked and lubed up. What do you think about that?"

"As long as you're not getting the documents sticky, I'm fine with it."

"Like I believe that," he jeers. "You hate the idea that he's with someone. You'd like him all to yourself."

I tense slightly, because he's hitting close to the bone with this. The truth is that yes, a bit of me does hate the fact that Fletcher is with him. It bothers me more than I like that Fletcher sleeps naked next to him, and is fucked by him, because I'd bet my rent check that Gabe is a top. However, I won't admit that fully to myself, let alone to a dipshit.

I open my mouth to say who knows what, but we're interrupted by a deep voice at the door.

"What the hell is going on in here?" Gabe looks at me, his eyes seeming almost concerned for a second. Then without looking away, he says sharply, "Fletcher, what are you doing here?"

"Waiting for you," Fletcher says smoothly. "I was just debating clothed or not." He shrugs, pouting prettily. "I'll leave that to your decision."

Gabe's eyes instantly darken, and I can almost hear the snap as his attention is broken from me. He strides past me, unconsciously adjusting the bulge in his suit trousers. "Get inside," he says to Fletcher, in a dark voice that makes me swallow. "Hold my calls," he orders me dismissively, barely glancing at me now.

"Yes, Dylan, hold his calls. I'll hold something else," Fletcher calls, laughing triumphantly.

The door slams behind them, and I can't help flushing at the sound of a body hitting the door. The door is thick, but it isn't quite thick enough, so I make sure to shut the outer door to my office. I finish my work to the faint soundtrack of grunts and deep groans filtering through, as I remind myself once again that the rare, nice moments don't compensate for the dismissive way that he usually treats me.

I hate him I tell myself repeatedly. *I fucking hate his dismissive, perfect arse.*

CHAPTER TWO

To: Gabe Foster

From: Dylan Mitchell

Mr Simmonds rang for you. Due to the strange noises coming from your office since Fletcher came to visit, and a strong desire not to have to bleach my eyes, I took a message.

Two hours later, I virtually fall through my front door. The journey home had been horrendous, with strikes on the tube making a simple journey something more akin to a Greek odyssey. My day is almost complete, when I step forward and promptly fall over a suitcase lying on the floor.

"Fuck!" I ease up to a sitting position, viewing the offending article which is spewing clothes left, right, and centre. "Jude," I bellow. "Why the fuck can't you put your bloody stuff away?"

I hear footsteps, and he appears, naked apart from a white towel wrapped around his waist. As normal, he looks utterly gorgeous and camera ready. He's all long legs, dark curls, and olive skin, with a heart-shaped face made older by the addition of a new beard. "Dylan," he says delightedly. Then his face creases in concern. "Why are you sitting on the floor?"

"Because I didn't see your fucking luggage," I grumble, putting out a hand for him to haul me up.

"You should really look where you're going," he says primly, making me laugh reluctantly. "That's better, you've got a face like a wet weekend. What the hell happened to you today?"

"Boss Man," I say grimly, and when he looks at me, I shake my head. "Don't ask. It's been a long day."

He smiles at me. "A long day spent with His Gorgeousness. I don't know how you stand it."

"I don't know how I stand it either, but I doubt it's for the same reason as you."

He stares at me for a second. "*Really?*" he asks, with a lively scepticism. "I doubt that, Dylan. You've got eyes in your head."

"Yes, but unfortunately, I've got ears as well, which means I have to listen to him all day."

Ignoring his sceptical expression with the ease of practice, I make my way past him and collapse on a sofa with a sigh of relief. "Fucking hell, that was a hideous journey home." I roll my head back to look at him as he settles opposite me. "When did you get home?"

"Lunchtime." He settles back on the opposite sofa with a sound of contentment. "I'm glad to be home. Helsinki is fine, but nowhere feels like home."

I snort. "Yeah, I feel your pain. Poor you in the five star hotels, eating out every night with pretty boys."

He shakes his head chidingly. "I'm not after casual pieces of ass anymore. I told you that."

I flash a grin at him. "I know you *said* it, I just didn't really believe it."

"Well, believe it. I'm a reformed man. I want something serious. I've taken a leaf out of your book."

I grunt. "Take the whole fucking tree, Jude. It's never done me any good."

He shakes his head. "I know you've had a bit of bad luck in the romance area."

"A *bit*? You do remember Jason, don't you?"

He snorts. "Okay, a lot of bad luck."

"Jesus, he brought a suitcase of his clothes over the first night that we fucked."

He bursts into laughter. "And then there was Robert."

"Laugh it up you giant wanker, but you were fucking scared of Robert."

"It wasn't so much Robert, more his unhealthy interest in the occult."

I sigh. "I think he's a high priest now." I twist my head to look at him. "And you want some of *that*? Are you mental?"

He sighs. "I don't want your own personal brand of looney tunes per se. I just want someone that's mine, and who's loyal."

"Good luck with that," I say morosely. "Men like that are rarer than rocking horse shit."

"What about Boss Man?"

I close my eyes and groan. "How many times do I have to tell you that I fucking hate him?"

"Once more than your voice dipping low every time that you mention his name."

I want to glare at him, but settle for raising my middle finger at the twat. "How long are you back for?"

"About a week, then I'm off to Fiji."

"Of course you are," I mutter. "So, what's on the agenda for this week?"

He looks at me and bites his lip. "Well, I'm glad you asked, Dylan, because I have a piece of fantastic news."

"Oh God," I groan. "I know that look. What is it?"

He shakes his head. "No need for that tone of voice," he chides. "Really Dylan, you've got awfully cynical since you went corporate." He pauses, and says with a flourish, "I've only got free tickets for Haunt."

"Really? Isn't that *the* place to be seen now?"

"Oh, that superior tone of voice. How I've missed that."

"What?" I laugh and then relent. "Okay, it's a gay club, isn't it?"

"It's not just *any* gay club. It's *the* private club at the moment, and it's extremely selective about its members. I've heard all sorts of famous people go there because they're guaranteed complete discretion."

"Ah, the closeted celebrities. So I take it that you want to go and ogle them like they're in a private zoo?"

He sits forward. "Of course I do, babe, and you're coming with me."

I sigh and rub my eyes. "Okay, when are we going?"

He checks his watch. "In about an hour?"

I sit up abruptly. "What the *fuck,* Jude?"

He holds up his hand. "Save it, Dylan. I know that you're tired, but go and have a long shower and I'll pour you a drink." He looks at me. "Okay, I'll leave the bottle with you." He laughs as I flip him off. "Sorry that was low, but come on, Dylan. We haven't gone clubbing in bloody ages, and I miss you, you staid fucker." He reads the surrender in my face and smiles. "Go and shower, and I'll find you something to wear."

I stand up and stretch. "Okay, but nothing too tight, Jude." He casts me a look, and I shake my finger at him. "I mean it. I need my circulation. I'm still a young man."

"A young man with the soul of a sixty-five-year-old at the moment," he returns, as I move past him. "Now hurry up and get your club on."

An hour later we pull up outside the club. Emerging from the taxi, I pull petulantly at my black, muscle-fit, long-sleeved t-shirt.

"Fucking hell, Jude. You can see how cold my nipples are in this, and these black jeans are so tight that if I take them off there'll be an imprint of my dick on them."

He laughs and slaps my arse. "Well hello, Sister Dylan. How nice to meet your puritanical self."

I follow him, still pulling at my shirt. "Is it puritanical to not want to tell the general public that I've been circumcised?"

A blonde in the queue for the club turns around and looks me up and down. "Oh baby, that's not puritanical, that's damn right charitable showing those eight inches off."

Jude laughs, and pushes me past the long line of people standing waiting, their breaths white on the cold air, until we get to a red rope blocking the way. He flashes his invitation card at the massive bouncer dressed in a tux on the door, and ignoring the cat calls, we gratefully escape into the toasty warmth of the foyer.

As Jude joins the coat check line to hand in his jacket, I look around curiously. The foyer is relatively small for a club, indicating a place that doesn't make its patrons wait around. It's panelled in walnut, and is bright and warm. There's a big door to the left through which people are entering, letting out the deep, bass thump of music. Unbidden, I feel a stirring of excitement.

Jude comes up behind me, and taking one look at my face, he laughs and slaps my back. "There's my Dylan. I haven't seen him in far too long."

"Shut up," I mutter, and then grab his hand, dragging him to the door. "Come on. I want to drink my weight in alcohol, and get on the dance floor."

We fight our way to the bar ploughing through groups of people, and it's immediately apparent that this isn't a routine club. Everywhere looks expensive, from the bright white and silver decor which makes everything look light, to the massive dance floor made of varnished planks. The huge bar is made up of onyx and silver, and festooned with low hanging, warm, white lights. Raised plinths are scattered around the room, on which dance, or rather writhe, scantily clad men.

Finally reaching the bar, Jude immediately secures the attention of the barman, simply by standing there and smiling. I briefly contemplate whether this would work with Gabe, imagining me just smiling and cocking my hip while he shouts for me to take down a letter. I snort out a laugh because the high likelihood is that he would think I'd had some sort of breakdown.

Jude catches my eye and hands me a shot of something dark red. "What's this?" I shout.

"Cherry vodka shots," he shouts back. "Nice and warm like you, my little sweet cheeks."

"Fuck off," I groan, and on his signal, we shoot them down. The burn is instant, and I lick my lips, capturing the sweetness there. "Another," I shout in his ear and he grins, motioning to the bartender for another three shots apiece.

While he's occupied, I look around idly. The place is packed, but not to the claustrophobic proportions that I've seen in other clubs, and I watch the dancers writhing and grinding, enjoying the anticipation that has always filled me in a club.

I love to dance, and I'd always found nightclubs exciting, ever since the first one that I'd snuck into aged fifteen with Jude. I think then it was the sense of anticipation of a hook up, and the not knowing what might happen. Now, I secretly know that the anticipation comes from the chance that I might meet someone special. I sigh. *Jude was right. I am an old man.*

He comes up from behind and nudges me, handing me the shots as I laugh. We shoot them quickly, enjoying the warmth, and then I pull him onto the dance floor.

We stay there for the next couple of hours, dancing to nearly everything, and breaking only to get another shot. After two hours I have a decent buzz on, and I'm starting to get thirsty.

Leaning up, I shout to Jude that I'm going to get some water, and he nods, smiling as he watches a particularly beautiful man circle him as if he's chum in the water. Patting him on the back, I leave him to it, secure in the knowledge that it is highly possible his vow to find fidelity might take a battering tonight, as will his hole. I laugh out loud at that and push my way to the bar.

It takes me slightly longer to get served than it did Jude, as I lack his startling beauty. I know I'm considered good-looking, with brown-blonde hair, a thin, square-jawed face with green eyes, and an olive-coloured complexion. I'm lean and muscled, but more like a runner than Jude's gym-honed physique. However, I have never really seen myself as anything special, probably because I've had a lifetime of standing next to Jude.

I order a couple of bottles of water when the bartender finally sees me, and then push away from the bar, deciding to lean against the walnut balustrade to watch the dancers and cool down.

I've only been standing there for about a minute when I feel a body lean in next to me. Turning I see a good-looking blonde man who looks vaguely familiar, staring at me.

"Hi," he shouts, leaning close enough for me to feel the warmth of his breath wash across my neck, which makes me shudder slightly.

I smile back. "Hi, yourself."

"Have you been here long?"

I shrug. "A couple of hours maybe. How about you?"

"Same. Have you been here before?"

I've found in the past, very good-looking people quite often don't bother to develop the fine art of chat up, and Mr Pretty is obviously no exception. Inwardly sighing, I shake my head. "No, first time."

He smiles widely. "Ah, a club virgin."

I laugh, settling my back against the balustrade, and telling myself to relax and enjoy the tentative steps of the light flirtation. I have a feeling it will turn heavy soon enough, which is fine with me. "Not sure about that. Are you a member?"

He smiles and nods, coming in a bit closer under the guise of making himself heard. "Yes, I know the owner. He's done a good job with it."

I suddenly realise where I've seen him before, which is on the cover of a fashion magazine. He's a model, and I'm sure that Jude knows him. I become aware that he's still talking. "Are you a member?"

I shake my head, half wishing we could just go and fuck in the toilets like normal people, rather than make all this polite conversation. "I came with my flatmate. He got the tickets." I point Jude out, who is currently grinding against his next conquest, and he jerks in recognition.

"You know Jude Bailey?"

I nod. "I've known him since we were in nursery together. Why? Do you know him?"

He scoffs. "Of course. *Everyone* knows Jude."

I straighten, not sure that I like his tone. "What do you mean by that?" I ask, my voice deepening with aggression, and he puts up his hands.

"Sorry, he's your friend."

"I thought I'd made that patently clear, mate."

"I didn't mean anything by it. It's just that I worked with him on the Levi's job last year. He's a nice guy, but it was an absolutely shit shoot."

I relax now that he's lightened up his tone. "Why?"

"Jude and the photographer famously didn't get on. They spent the entire week bitching at each other like an old married couple until finally, the photographer asked him to bend over, and Jude told him to buy him dinner and to at least warm the lube first."

I throw my head back laughing, and he leans even closer, running his hand down my arm. "You're fucking gorgeous," he murmurs. "Have you ever considered modelling?"

I shake my head. *Why did men always think that was a come on?* "Not since Jude made it sound like the next best thing to a gulag."

He twists until he's leaning into me, and I let out an involuntary moan as I feel his hard cock pressing and digging into my thigh. "How about we move this somewhere private?" he says into my ear, taking the opportunity to run his tongue along the shell of my ear. He grips the lobe lightly with his teeth before suckling it. A shiver runs down my spine, and I press into him harder. My ears have always been an erogenous zone, and just breathing onto them can make me hard.

He grunts, grabbing my hip and rubbing briefly against me. "Do you want to go somewhere quiet?" he asks, standing back and offering me his hand.

I look at him considering, and really, what am I waiting for - Prince Charming? I've not met him yet, and the chance of a hard fuck with someone who won't expect anything of me sounds extremely good, especially when my life is spent at someone else's beck and call.

For a brief, insane second, an image of Gabe comes into my head, but I push it determinedly away. He might rule my working life, but he doesn't rule my head or my personal life. I smile at the man in front of me. "Why not."

He smiles triumphantly and stands to one side as I twist to place my water on the low table by my side. It's as I straighten that I see Gabe, and I'm struck dumb as if I've conjured him up just by thinking of him, rather like the villain in a bad film.

He's standing to my right, leaning against the balustrade with his arms folded just like I'd been. However, while I'd been jostled about, it's like an invisible force field surrounds him. I send my eyes down his body, dimly aware that the model is still standing behind me, but enjoying the opportunity to ogle Gabe without him knowing.

He's wearing dark jeans and a sky-blue shirt, with the sleeves rolled up to his elbows, showing off his tanned, muscled forearms. Simple clothes, but on him, they look like haute couture. His hair is tousled rather than beaten into submission as it is when he's in the office, and his devilish eyebrows are quirked, giving him an air of caustic humour. I can see several men watching him avidly, but he isn't paying them any attention at all.

Instead, he's concentrating on something on the dance floor. I follow his gaze, eager to see what holds him in rapt attention, and then I jerk slightly as I see Fletcher. Not a total shock, but what is surprising is that his blonde partner is twined around a dark-haired man like poison ivy. I watch, my mouth hanging open, as Fletcher runs his fingers over the man's lips, before lowering his head and fitting his own lips to him. They kiss avidly, tongues visible as the two men grind against each other in total tune with the music.

I look back at my boss expecting I don't know what, maybe rage. Instead, he's watching the two men closely, running his tongue slowly over his full, lower lip as if tasting them. I feel my cock stiffen involuntarily, and I can't tear my eyes away, dimly registering movement behind me.

The song ends, and a slower one starts, and I see Fletcher look up and motion to Gabe to come to him. Gabe stands back however, and raises one long-fingered hand to motion Fletcher to him. His boyfriend grins up at him, and then he leans in whispering something to the dark-haired man. The man looks up and sees Gabe, and then grins back at Fletcher, saying something which makes him throw his head back and laugh.

Someone comes between me and my floor show, and I hiss impatiently, moving to stand by a pillar where I have a view of the unfolding scene. Fletcher and the other man have reached Gabe by now, and I watch like a voyeur as Fletcher reaches out, and with a finger through the button hole on Gabe's shirt, he draws him to him. Gabe comes, his face impassive apart from that wickedly arched eyebrow, and when he's close, Fletcher grabs him and pushes his hands into Gabe's hair, drawing him to him and kissing him deeply.

They kiss for what feels like ages, and there's something about the scene that turns me on beyond anything that I've ever experienced. I'm a twenty-seven-year-old gay man. I have had many partners, although not in high figures. I consider myself relaxed sexually and open to anything, and because of this I've seen and done a lot.

However, nothing has prepared me to see my boss in an intense lip-lock with his boyfriend.

Against my will, my cock rises from a semi to a full-on erection so quickly that it almost makes me dizzy, and I absentmindedly palm it as I watch the dark-haired man move to stand next to the embracing couple. He stands there for a second, and then runs his hand down Gabe's back, tracing the muscles and wide shoulders, moving down his body until he reaches his tight arse.

At first, I think that Gabe will turn on him. Instead, he lifts his lips from Fletcher's and reaches for the other man, drawing him close, before lowering his head and taking the man's mouth. He goes deep instantly, and I can almost feel the man's moan on the air.

Fletcher watches for a second, his eyes bright. Then he twists until he and Gabe are sandwiching the dark-haired man, Gabe still kissing him, while Fletcher thrusts against him.

I'm amazed at the openness of the act, but then I suppose that this is a private club, and one that the senior partners of the firm are unlikely to attend.

I watch them for a long second, feeling a peculiar mix of feelings. I'm amazed at Gabe being so obviously accustomed to being part of a threesome. I'm not naïve. I've taken part in them myself, and although they were hot as fuck, they weren't for me, requiring far too much attention to work out the logistical fairness of the act. A lot of men I know do them, and a few of my friends are in open relationships, and it works for them.

What bothers me is that I've somehow read Gabe's character wrong. I'd seen him as a possessive man, who held what he owned tight to him. I'd obviously been wrong, because the most personal of his possessions is currently having his arse felt up and his tonsils examined.

However, what bothers me most is that it's almost like a curtain has dropped from my eyes. For the first time since I'd met him, I'm now seeing him as a sexual man again, rather than just my boss. I'd pushed that initial awareness away for two years, knowing that I wouldn't be able to function in my job if I kept it. But now it's back front and centre, and I stand helplessly, my cock hurting in the tight confines of my jeans, as I watch the threesome.

It is then, with the worst timing known to mankind that Gabe looks up and sees me. He and Fletcher, almost by silent communion have stepped back gracefully and left the dark-haired man looking turned on and slightly confused. Fletcher is leaning forward whispering in his ear as he eagerly nods, but it's at this point that Gabe looks around and finds me there, staring right at him.

For what seems like an aeon we stare at each other, and a gamut of emotions race across his previously placid, unmoved face. Surprise, concern, anger and then a dark, fierce look which in any other man I would have classed as lust. I dismiss that thought immediately, clinging onto the sole blessing that he can't see my erection. God forbid that my boss should know that I had popped a stiffy while watching him and his boyfriend tongue fuck a complete stranger.

Something must have crossed my face though, because in contrast to his smooth, controlled movements so far, he makes a sudden, jerky lunge towards me, making me step back involuntarily into a stranger behind me.

The stranger curses, and in the flurry of apologies, I see Fletcher grab Gabe's hand and say something to him. Gabe shakes his head and lets Fletcher pull him and his friend towards the exit, and by the time I've fully turned back, they are all gone.

Remembering suddenly that I'd had a model about to fuck me, I turn around, only to find empty space. He had obviously fucked off while I'd stood gawping rudely at another man.

I slump against the pillar, groaning. *How am I going to get over this?* Gabe now knows that his personal assistant has stood and watched him and his boyfriend personally fondle a complete stranger into almost an orgasm. The only thing missing had been a tub of popcorn and a handful of tissues.

However, the main problem is that the ignorant scales have fallen completely from my eyes. How can I look at my boss the way that I always have, when now I have this bone deep knowledge of his face when he's aroused?

I groan again. "Fuck my life."

A man standing next to me laughs. "Rough night, darling?" he asks, and I shake my head morosely.

"It's going to be more than just a rough night. I can feel it."

CHAPTER THREE

To: Dylan Mitchell

From: Gabe Foster

I have logged onto Amazon and purchased you a dictionary, because even auto correct seems unable to cope with your erratic spelling.

A week later I dump my messenger bag onto my desk and hang up my coat. Switching my computer on, I wonder what new tortures Gabe has devised for me today.

The morning after the club I'd sat at my desk, picking at my nails nervously and wondering how we were going to get through the oncoming conversation. An hour later I knew, and the answer was complete avoidance of any subject matter that might bring it up.

Gabe had strolled in dressed in a black suit with a black and tan polka dot tie. He'd looked cool and collected, and nothing like the tousled, turned on version that I'd seen the night before. His outer appearance, however, was matched by a bone-deep coldness that didn't invite any conversation.

He'd then spent the entire week in an icy shell, levelling scorn at anything I'd done, his tongue more cutting than it had ever been. It had been like the first week that I'd worked for him, as if we were complete strangers.

Initially, I'd understood his need to get us back into our clear compartments, with no chance of overlap. However, I'd grown steadily angrier with him until finally, I'd lost my patience yesterday. I had snapped, and I snort under my breath at the thought of his face by the end of the day.

In the morning, I had examined his diary with forensic attention, and then systematically moved his appointments around until there wasn't even a minute's break between them. I had switched his usual strong coffee that you could stand a spoon up in, for a hazelnut blend from the staff room. Smiling happily, I'd then spent the day patching calls through to him from the very people who were on our tacit list of *'no fucking way will I ever talk to them again'*. After that, I swapped the cards on the two bouquets of flowers that he wanted to send out. His mentor's wife had therefore got a card thanking her for a fantastic night between the sheets, and Fletcher had got the one congratulating him on his pregnancy.

At that point, I had taken the coward's way out by leaving for home after putting Fletcher through to him. Giving him a cheery wave, I had manfully ignored Fletcher on the speakerphone demanding to know if Gabe was trying to say that he had put on weight. Pretending not to notice the look of apoplectic doom on Gabe's face, I had sallied home. Jude and I then spent the following couple of hours drinking beer and plotting fresh new tortures.

Becoming aware of the ominous silence from his office I sigh, feeling distinctly too hungover to deal with whatever retaliation he has planned. Squaring my shoulders, I run my suddenly damp hands down my dark grey, skinny trousers. I've teamed them with my v-neck black jumper, worn over a white shirt and grey and black striped tie. The clothes make me feel good, and I need the pick up today.

Taking a swig of my green tea, I knock on the open door and stick my head around, only to come up short when I see that the room is empty. There is no sign of occupation at all. You can normally tell when Gabe has been in his room, as his coat is usually flung on the sofa, and his chair will be pushed sharply back as if he'd stood up in a massive hurry. Books and papers are usually everywhere, along with half empty coffee cups. Even when he isn't there, he has a way of filling his room with a thrumming energy.

Not today though. Today it's completely silent. Pursing my lips, I pivot and go back to my desk, grabbing my tablet to access his diary. I'm sure he has an eight o'clock appointment, and he's usually in the office an hour before them as he likes to be prepared. There is every chance that he's cancelled it on the calendar that we both have access to, as he's done before. However, when I check the appointment, it's still green lit.

Dismissing it, I head for the kitchenette attached to my office and start up a pot of the sludge that he calls a hot drink. His guests will have the more palatable stuff from the staffroom. Once done, I'm just about to get the paperwork out of my files for the meeting when my phone rings. Picking it up, I see to my amazement that it's Gabe. He usually prefers to text me, saying that there is less chance of my arguing with him that way.

Clicking the button, I offer a hesitant, 'hello'.

There is silence for a second, which is enough time for me to wonder if he's arse dialled me. He'd done it once before, and I'd been treated to the audio of him fucking Fletcher somewhere. I'm ashamed to admit that I didn't click end for a good couple of minutes, and the sounds had entered my spank bank for quite a while.

"Hello," I say again, more loudly. "Gabe, can you hear me? You've arse dialled me again."

The only answer is very heavy breathing, so I try for humour. "Mother, is that you? I've told you not to do this in work hours."

"Very funny," he grouches, and then I tear the phone away as a terrible hacking noise comes through.

When it finishes, I say hesitantly, "Gabe, is that you?"

"Well, of course it bloody is," he says grumpily, but it's so hoarse it's hard to understand. "Who else would it be ringing you on my fucking phone - Gary Barlow?"

"Hmm, I'm thinking that might be a better option. Gary looks like he might be a very charming boss, unlike some people." I draw my head back as he makes the noise again, and I realise that he's coughing.

"Gabe, you sound bloody awful. Have you got that nasty virus that's doing the rounds in the office?"

He sighs heavily and then coughs again. "I think I must have it." He sighs again, and then says morosely, "I feel absolutely terrible."

"I take it that you're not coming in. Do you want me to cancel your meetings?"

He coughs again, making me wince at the awful sound. "Yes, please."

"Why don't you go back to bed, and I'll handle everything here, and clear the diary for a couple of days."

"I won't be ill for a couple of *days*." He sounds so horrified that it makes me smile. The man resents even having to take Christmas off.

"I think you will," I say cheerily. "It seems to be a forty-eight-hour thing." I hesitate. "Is Fletcher there? He might need to keep an eye on your temperature. Maureen from Accounts said that her husband's temperature spiked so badly he ended up in hospital."

He sighs with a rattling murmur. "Fletcher's not here."

"So you're on your *own*? How long for?"

"The week probably. Listen, Dylan. I hate to ask, but if I'm going to be cooped up here today I'm going to need the Roper file. The meeting's on Friday and I'm not ready for it."

"You can't possibly be thinking of working today!" I sound embarrassingly like Hattie Jacques from 'Carry on Nursing'.

There's a silence and I prepare myself for an earbashing, but instead, I hear what sounds like a snotty sigh. "Please," he finally says, and my heart melts slightly because he sounds grumpy and vulnerable. It's a combination I never would have thought would work for me, but obviously it does.

Relenting, I sigh. "Okay, I'll be round in a bit. Give me time to clear your diary, and take notice because I'm clearing it for *three* days."

I wait for the argument, but it's a sign of how bad he's feeling that I only get a low 'thank you' before he hangs up.

A couple of hours later, I emerge from the tube at Highgate Village. The tube had been almost pleasant outside rush hour, and I suppress a wish to work part-time with the knowledge of the pay packet that accompanies it. That, and the fact that Gabe likes me at his beck and call far too much to deprive himself.

I look around curiously. I like Highgate. When I first moved to London, I'd spent a happy day with my boyfriend at the time, tramping around the wonderfully gothic cemetery, peering at the gravesites of its notable occupants including Karl Marx. We'd spent a less happy evening splitting up over his dislike of Jude, but it hadn't spoilt my fondness for Highgate. I like its funky mix of leafy green streets and red brick Victorian houses with their village feel, interspersed with stunning buildings like St Joseph's Church with its eye-catching, copper dome.

As I walk along the High Street, a row of shops with Georgian facades catch my eye. I hesitate outside the chemist, before sighing and going in. I snag a basket and start to chuck Lemsip and various other cold remedies into it. Gabe might be a bastard, and more so this week, but I'm unable to ignore that he's ill.

To further my stupidity, I then go into the next shop, which is an artisan deli that caters a lot of our events. I buy a load of his favourite foods, along with some bits that he'll be able to eat if his stomach is upset. I've only been to his house once, but I still remember opening one of the kitchen cupboards to look for a glass. I'd found them and enough alcohol to set up as an upmarket bar, but that was it, and the fridge had been bare of everything apart from takeaway boxes.

Finally, laden down with carrier bags, I make my way up the street to Gabe's home, enjoying the odd stunning glimpse of London laid out like a magic carpet before me. Eventually reaching his house I look up, paying more attention to it than I did last time.

It surprises me now, just as much as it did then. I'd expected him to live in a converted warehouse, full of stark, designer pieces of furniture and modern art. The reality is dramatically different, in that his home is a three-storey, red brick, Victorian house. It sits comfortably on a quiet, tree-lined avenue, its bay windows gleaming in the sun. It's unusual because it's still a house, rather than having been converted into flats, which has happened to a lot of these big, old properties in London.

I'm drawn from my musings by the navy-painted front door opening and Gabe appearing. "Are you coming in, or hovering outside like a tourist?" he asks grumpily, and I immediately regret my purchases.

My carrier bags burn a red flag in my imagination. I imagine them calling out, '*Look what he's done now. You asked for a folder, and you got Nurse Dylan and a metric ton of snacks*'. The worries die away, however, as I walk up the front steps to him, and notice how he's leaning against the door for support.

He holds the door open and I edge past him, trying to ignore how very fine he looks in the navy and white checked pyjama shorts and white vest that he's wearing. They show off the sleek, muscular lines of his body and his olive skin.

Once I'm inside, I put down the carrier bags with a thud while he closes the door. I look at him with concern. "Jesus, you look a very funny colour, Gabe." Ignoring his muttered objections, I put my palm on his forehead. "And you're really bloody hot."

"I know," he mumbles, and to my alarm he sways slightly. "I know I'm hot, because I'm me."

"*Okay.*" I elongate the word, and he shakes his head wearily and holds out his hand.

"Never mind me. Have you got the folder?"

"I have," I say calmly, bending to gather the carrier bags and moving past him in the direction I remember the kitchen being. "But you're not getting it."

His mini explosion is completely spoiled by a massive coughing attack, which follows me as I make my way down the long, Milton tiled hallway, catching glimpses of a large, airy lounge to my right. Finally gathering his breath, he comes after me, standing in the doorway of the kitchen as I deposit the carrier bags on his central island. I step back with a sigh of relief and try to massage the feeling back into my fingers.

"What are those?" he asks cautiously, pointing at the bags.

"Some medicines and some food and bits." I take off my grey, wool pea coat and fling it cavalierly onto a bar stool, before looking around appreciatively.

The room is part of a big extension on the back of the house. It's full of sunlight as one wall is completely filled by bi-folding doors, giving a glimpse of a green, leafy garden. A long table sits by these doors with enough chairs to seat ten people, and there's also a huge, central island that doubles up as a breakfast bar, if the steel bar stools are anything to go by. The kitchen units themselves look extremely expensive. They're made of a white gloss lacquer, and have been matched with a black granite work surface that sparkles in the light from the low hanging pendant lights.

The flooring is made of wide, white wood planks, and the whole effect is sleek, modern-looking, and expensive. However, to me, it looks sterile and empty, like a film set. It's crying out for a pop of colour, and in my mind's eye, I picture one wall painted a deep, hot pink with a big sofa in front of it. I could just see myself sitting there with a cup of tea in the morning. Shaking my head clear of thoughts which are perilously close to imagining him with me in that scenario, I turn back to him.

"Jesus, Gabe. This kitchen is bloody lovely, and completely wasted on you."

He snorts slightly which develops into some more of the hacking coughing, and I wait him out patiently while trying to hide my concern. He's a putty colour with red flags of colour over his cheekbones. When he finishes and is wiping his forehead, I move over to the kettle and switch it on.

"Have you seen a doctor?" I throw over my shoulder, and he scoffs.

"For a *cold*? No, I bloody haven't."

I sigh. "It's not a cold. It's a virus, and it's nasty. Bernard from Acquisitions had it, and he said that he'd never felt so bad."

"Touching as these stories are about my co-workers, and much as I want to know how you can possibly know all that you do about the people that we work with, I'm actually more interested in what you think you're doing."

He's making a valiant attempt to be his usual irascible self, but failing due to his white-knuckled grasp on the counter. I smile at him. "Exactly. The people we work with. The operative word being *with*. They're people and very interesting. You could maybe try a conversation one day. That's if you can manage to catch them before they employ their ninja strategies to get out of your eyesight."

He scoffs. "I know all that I need to know about them because *you* tell me. It cuts out the middleman business."

"Ah, that pesky middleman business, usually called conversation. How it does interfere with everything," I say lightly.

A smile crosses his full lips as he sits down on a bar stool. However, it vanishes quickly, as he leans his head on his hand and sighs heavily.

"Seriously, Gabe, you look awful. Where's Fletcher? Is he on a shoot?"

He looks down at the counter. "No, not a shoot. I presume he went back to his flat."

"Why?" I don't even try to stem my interest. I have to grab these titbits of information when I can.

"Well, because I'm sick. He can't be catching it. He's on a shoot next week."

I'm flabbergasted, and it must show on my face. "But you're *ill*."

He shoots me a sidelong glance, rubbing his back absently. "So? I've been ill many times in my life. I've never needed anyone to hold my hand before."

"Gabe, were you listening about Maureen from Accounts, whose husband was taken to hospital?"

"Yes, I found it hard to rest after that, with all the concern flooding through me."

"I'm ignoring your attempt at sarcasm, because the moral of that story is that he might have been seriously ill if he hadn't had someone with him. Shall I ring Fletcher and he can come back?"

He shakes his head, a move he obviously immediately regrets, judging by the white knuckles that he massages into his temples. Then he looks up, showing red-rimmed eyes and wild-looking hair. "Fuck no, don't ring him. I really don't need that, on top of being ill. He'd drive me mad. Then I'd end up having to do something to appease him, and then feel worse. It's easier being ill on your own."

I can't believe what I'm hearing. *Who doesn't want their partner around when they're ill? It's nice to have someone look after you.* Shaking my head, I open a few cupboards before finding the mugs. Taking a large, silver-coloured one down, I upend a Lemsip packet into it and then pour hot water over it. Stirring the bright yellow mixture, I push it across the counter to him.

"What's this?" he asks suspiciously.

"Lemsip. It'll bring your temperature down, and help with the aches in your back and your headache. Drink it while it's hot, and then you can go back to bed."

He seems almost surprised that I've noticed his aches and pains, and when I catch his eye I nod at his mug determinedly. Looking at it suspiciously, he brings the mug to his lips and takes an experimental sip, before screwing his face up like a little boy. "Ugh, it's really fucking sweet."

"Well, it's not a dirty martini or a whisky sour, but it'll do the trick." I reach into the carrier bags. "I've bought you some Lucozade and some lemon barley water because it's important to keep your fluids up." I pause and then smile. "Now I *know* you're really ill when you can't make a remark about fluids."

He shakes his head tentatively, still taking disgusted, little sips of the drink. "I thought of it, but the idea of semen just makes me feel sick."

I laugh, and while he drinks, I drag more items out of the bags, as he watches me with a sort of feverish apathy mixed with a little interest. I look up at him. "I've bought some things from Harpers Deli that I know you love, like the stuffed bell peppers. You always make a beeline for them when they cater events. However, I think to start with, once you're hungry, you should have something light, like scrambled eggs. Are you hungry now?" He shakes his head immediately. "Okay then, I'll put everything away until you're ready."

I look at the cupboards, all concealing emptiness, and think back to the takeaway containers in the fridge, and a thought occurs to me. "Can you actually cook?"

He finishes the drink with a shudder and pushes the empty mug at me. "No, of course I can't. That's what restaurants are for."

"But this is such a gorgeous room."

He shakes his head. "Of course it is. I wanted the best, and this was it. The designer said it was a chef's wet dream." A salacious smile crosses his lips. "I don't know about a chef, but the designer gave me several wet dreams." He pauses. "And awake ones."

I shake my head and look around. I can't picture either him or Fletcher bustling around in an apron. Now myself, I would love it, because I like nothing better than cooking. I would rather have friends over for dinner than go clubbing. I feel suddenly sorry for him, because the kitchen seems evocative of his life – expensive, yet sterile and empty.

He must catch something on my face, because he says hurriedly, "I'm out too much to use the room. I make coffee in here, but that's about it."

I look at the ranks of glass bottles on one of the counters, all bearing the labels of expensive spirits, and I sniff. "And you pickle your liver in here too, I suppose?"

"Only in my off time." A smile crosses his face before he leans into his hand with a weary sigh.

"Come on," I say briskly. "Why don't you go and get into bed and try to sleep?"

He nods tiredly and stands up, but I exclaim as he sways worryingly. Rushing to him, I slot my shoulder under his arm and prop him up. "Okay, that's decided me. I'm going to help you upstairs and into bed, and then I'm going to stay for a bit until I'm sure that you're alright."

"You can't do that," he immediately, and predictably argues.

"Yes, I can. Gabe, you're sick, and as much as you're a shithead sometimes, I've trained you to be a fairly acceptable shithead to me. If you died, I'd have to go to all the effort of training someone else."

"If I died, maybe you should consider a change of career into the nursing profession. With your lovely bedside manner, you'd be a shoo-in."

I snort out a laugh, and we somehow manage to bump our way up two flights of stairs to the top floor, then down a hallway to the open doorway that he indicates.

"Jesus, I'm sorry," he says hoarsely, as he loses his balance and shoves me sideways into a wall with his weight.

"Don't apologize," I wheeze. "You can't help being ill."

"I could help smelling like this," he mumbles. "Good grief, I stink."

"You don't smell at your best," I admit, thinking of his normal spicy orange scent. "But I repeat, you are ill." I pause. "Do you want to have a shower? I think if you could manage it, it might make you feel better to be cleaner, and you'll sleep better if all the sweat's off you."

"You are not giving me a bed bath," he mutters in a very alarmed way, and I sniff haughtily.

"You should be so lucky, Gabe." He huffs what sounds suspiciously like a laugh, but then coughs again, so maybe not.

We make our way into his bedroom, and I stop briefly to appreciate what a gorgeous room it is. In the old days, the top floor of these houses was usually set aside for servant's quarters, but he's knocked all the rooms into one big suite. Two walls are painted navy blue, the others a bright white, and the oak floorboards have been refinished and varnished.

It's full of light from a big window, and sunbeams play over the massive, oak bed which is set back against one navy wall. It's made up with pure white sheets and a thick, blue and white patterned comforter. The other side of the room is a seating area with a large leather sofa and a coffee table on which I can see a mass of papers. Through one door I can see a dressing room fitted with light oak shelves, and I inhale the citrus scent which seems to be embedded in the walls.

Then I look at him. "Shower?"

He nods determinedly, moving towards a door that I presume leads to an en-suite bathroom.

"Leave the door open," I say sharply. "I need to hear if you need me, and don't hesitate, Gabe. If you fall over, you could really hurt yourself." I pause. "That would make my day a *lot* harder, having to pick you up."

He pauses at the door and gapes at me, his grumpy exterior not hiding the smirk that he always gets when I snark him. "You know, illness brings out a real Nurse Ratchet side of you."

I raise my eyebrow. "You have no idea."

He moves into what I can see is a gleaming white bathroom with blue, metro tiles and modern oak cupboards. I try really hard to avert my gaze as he lifts up his tank, showing off that amazing, hairy chest and six-pack. He has always lacked modesty, and I've seen him half-naked more times than I want to count, as he changes in his office regularly. This explains why he doesn't even try to close the door, as he drops his shorts. I swallow hard at the sight of his bare buttocks, tight and high and drool worthy, before he moves out of sight.

Turning around I look at his bed which looks like he's fought World War Two in there, with the sheets and duvet wrinkled and tossed about and the pillows dented. Shaking my head, I roll up my sleeves and start to strip it.

A search of the immediate area locates a tall airing cupboard full of spare sheets and towels, and when Gabe comes out, it's to find me smoothing out the duvet cover and plumping the pillows in their soft, navy cotton.

"You didn't have to do that," he mutters, and I exclaim as he sways slightly, going white.

"Yes I did. It's horrid to get into a sweaty bed. Gabe, you look really bad. Get into bed now and do as I say."

I put out my hands to help him if he needs me, but then freeze at his next faint words. "I've imagined you saying that a few times, Dylan, but never when I feel this crap."

I shoot a glance at him, trying to analyse what he means, but it's useless as I'm not sure that *he* even knows what he's saying at this point. "Get in the bloody bed before you fall down."

He accedes to my urging and slips under the duvet I hold up for him, settling into the fresh sheets with a throaty murmur of happiness.

"This feels nice," he says sleepily, smiling at me. His thick black eyelashes flutter on his cheeks and make him look young and vulnerable for a second.

"Of course it does," I soothe, as his eyes grow heavier. "Sleep now, Gabe. I'll be here when you wake up."

His hand suddenly shoots out and grabs mine, but his grip is lax. "You promise?" he says, opening his eyes and looking up at me.

I'm confused, and trying very hard to ignore the sparks I feel in my wrist under his warm clasp. "Promise what?"

"Promise me that you'll be here."

"Of course I will," I say softly, giving in to the crazy impulse to stroke his hair back from his forehead as he falls asleep. It's warm and heavy, and feels like rough silk on my fingers. I want to move away, but something stronger keeps me static by his side, stroking his hair as he falls asleep with a small smile on his face.

It's only the threat of him waking up his normal grumpy self, and demanding to know what the hell I'm doing, that makes me move at all.

CHAPTER FOUR

To: Gabe Foster

From: Dylan Mitchell

Mr Thorpe wanted to know today why I don't call you *Sir,*
and you nodded in agreement. It feels a bit Fifty Shadish to
me, but I'm willing to give it a go. Just don't make me put the
words *ball gag* with it.

Leaving him asleep, I make my way downstairs and back into the
kitchen to make myself a coffee and put the food away. I take my cup
and wander over to the wall of glass, sipping the steaming drink as I
look into the garden. There's a big flagstone patio with expensive-
looking wicker patio furniture.

Like most gardens with these houses, it's long and thin, but it
looks well cared for, with established bushes and a large apple tree at

the bottom. I can only presume that Gabe employs a gardener, because I can't envisage Fletcher and him standing out there with their truckles and secateurs.

I settle down at the kitchen table and retrieve my phone and tablet from my bag. It's time to do some work.

A couple of hours later, Gabe's diary is cleared for a few days. I've remade some appointments, cleared a lot of the little jobs that have been niggling at me, and now the silence is beginning to creep me out. I need noise around me, even if it's just a radio playing, so I decide to go and put the television on in Gabe's lounge.

Gabe has avoided any attempt to keep the house period inside. Instead, he's opened up the interior downstairs so that the lounge stretches the whole length of the house, and is therefore bathed in sunshine. It's a beautiful room, and I have to reluctantly admit that the bastard has good taste.

A huge, comfortable-looking sectional sofa in a stone-coloured fabric is filled with big cushions. Large, rustic-looking lamps sit on corner tables, and magazines are stacked on a low coffee table.

The décor is a bit too beige for me, but it's relieved by the modern art pieces which fill the walls. The one that draws the eye most is a beauty that dominates one entire wall. It's six feet tall, and is a bold rendering of some tropical flowers on a white canvas, the oranges and pinks looking so vivid that they almost invite touch. I look long and hard at that one with my lips quirking, because I know the artist.

The walls to either side of the fireplace are covered with book-shelves, filled to overflowing with books. I spy a very expensive stereo in a cabinet, alongside media shelves filled with CDs and vinyl, and I crouch down to nosily rifle through the music to see his tastes. I'm probably overstepping many, *many* boundaries, but it's likely to be the only opportunity that I'll ever have to find out what makes the man behind the grumpy twat. I'm surprised to discover that we share a lot of similar tastes. I'm a huge fan of the 80s, and he has a lot of the classic albums of the time, along with a lot of blues and jazz.

I stand up and browse the bookshelves. He has eclectic tastes, so thrillers and historical tomes share space with battered poetry books which indicate a softer side. I try to imagine him declaiming poetry to Fletcher with them both wearing smoking jackets, but it's actually easier to imagine him fucking him over the sofa.

I shake my head, because when I think about it, I can actually picture Gabe stretched out on the sofa in front of the huge fireplace, reading with a glass of wine. When my thoughts start to include me pottering in his kitchen, I back away hurriedly.

There's a huge, flat screen TV over the fireplace, and finding the remote control, I switch it on and find an old episode of 'Friends'. Leaving it playing, I look around the room and realise what is lacking. There are no pictures anywhere. I have photos everywhere in my flat of my parents and siblings, and Jude and I with various groupings of friends. We also have a massive bulletin board in the kitchen with several layers of photos. It offers a pictorial record of the gigantic pissheads that we had been, or still are. Photos of gatherings dominate, always with a table piled high with empties, and morning after photos are obligatory.

However, Gabe has nothing. If he died and the police examined his house, they wouldn't be able to get a clear picture of the man beyond the history and poetry books, and the challenges to his liver in the kitchen. Shaking my head, I move on. It's time to get my snoop on. I feel no guilt. I'm going to be cooking for him, so it's a fact that he owes me knowledge.

I examine his study next, which is a small, cosy room painted a warm, light red. It has a desk and chair in front of the long window, and is filled with books again, to the extent that they are stacked on the floor around the full bookshelves.

The reading choices here are more professional, and centred on the tools of his trade. Gabe is a very successful lawyer, specialising in contracts and employment law, and seeing a row of battered books, I take one down and open it. I can see his name on the fly cover, written in a youthful version of the elegant, bold scrawl that I see every day.

I'm about to leave when I see a photo on the wall behind the door, and chuckle when I realise what it is. It's Gabe in a cap and gown, and is obviously the graduation portrait that everyone had done. Mine, thankfully, is in my parents' house, as I really don't want to ever again see the haircut I was sporting at the time.

I move closer and smile. Gabe had been utterly gorgeous even then, but he hadn't yet grown into his height, so he stood with a slight stoop, reminding me of my younger brother Ben who was six foot four by the time he was nineteen. Gabe's hair is longer in the picture than I've ever seen it, hitting his shoulders. It suits him, and makes him look a bit rockerish. He was also very skinny, unlike his muscled frame now.

I look around hoping to see other photos, and maybe a glimpse of his parents or family, but there is nothing, and I wonder why *this* photo is out. It's almost like he wants to remember that pinnacle of success, but at the same time the positioning of the photo out of general view, makes it seem like he's almost ashamed of that urge.

I shake my head in mystification, and then decide to get a move on with the prying, because I don't want him to find me snooping in his home office.

I move slowly up the stairs, and then keeping a sharp ear out for any signs of movement from his room, I poke my head through the doors leading off the first-floor hallway. I find three more bedrooms, all decorated beautifully, and a gorgeous bathroom decorated with sage tiles and a huge, claw-foot bath, set before a picture window looking down onto the garden. The angle of the window means that anyone could bathe looking out over the garden and a cluster of nearby houses, with no danger of being seen.

Everything about the place puzzles me, because despite the absence of photos, this is quite obviously a home decorated to his exacting tastes. It feels almost like a family home, albeit one that belongs to a family that loves beige. I would totally have thought to find him in one of the trendy areas of London, surrounded by designer furniture with martinis on tap, and not here in this soothing, warm house. I shake my head. The man is still an enigma, but now an enigma with a lovely home that I want.

Before succumbing to complete house envy, I lope up the stairs and peep into his room to check on him. He's sleeping soundly but has tossed the covers down, obviously when he'd gotten hot. His long, muscled body, clad only in a pair of sleep shorts, is stretched out with one arm flung to the side, and the other holding onto his pillow that he's buried his face in.

I smile because he sleeps with the utter, messy laxness of total oblivion, and it's so odd to see him like this. He's such a force of nature with the energy of ten men, and it touches me to see him so still and almost vulnerable. However, as I watch, he moves and moans fretfully as if looking for warmth, and I can see his skin pebbling with goose bumps. Without thinking, I stride over and pull the covers over him, tucking him in securely, and he nestles under with a low mumble.

I can't help but reach out and stroke his hair, but he comes suddenly awake on a rattling cough. Flailing slightly, he jerks at my touch, and I only just avoid ripping out a hank of hair from where I'm clutching it. He lifts his head coughing again, and then twists to see me hovering over him, probably looking a bit creepy.

"Hi," I say quickly. "You were shivering, so I pulled the covers over you."

He stares at me, but it's completely obvious he's still half-asleep, and his expression remains vague. Smiling, I pull the duvet back up, covering the bare shoulder he's exposed by moving. "Go back to sleep," I say softly, but as I turn to leave the room his eyes open fully, and a smile fills his face that I have never seen before on his grumpy visage. It's warm and clear, and so full of happiness that it ruins me. I would pay money just once to have someone look at me like that.

Then I stop dead as he says one word 'Dylan', before falling asleep again.

For a long time I stand immobile, staring at the sleeping man, but then I shrug and make myself move away. Delirious men are just that, delirious. I'd be mad to read anything into it. For good measure I make myself remember the other day, when he'd called me an incompetent imbecile because I'd spilt coffee on him. I smile and move downstairs. *Job done. Order restored.*

Gabe sleeps for the rest of the afternoon, so I do some more work, and then stretch out on the sofa to read on my Kindle. At about five o'clock I ring Jude and grandly instruct him to bring me some clothes and a takeaway, as I'm starving. He's reluctant to do so until I tell him where I am, and then he can't agree quickly enough.

I watch out of the window for him, so he doesn't ring the doorbell and wake Gabe. When I see him sauntering up the road, I quickly open the door and gesture him in.

"This feels quite clandestine," he remarks, smirking as he squeezes past me. "Almost like we're spies."

"You'd never go unremarked in that getup," I say, gesturing at his tight, royal-blue chinos.

"I'll have you know my little corporate whore, that this is a very fashionable colour."

"Only if you work at CBeebies."

"You're just jealous because you could never pull these off."

I look dubiously at how tight they are. "I sincerely doubt that *you* can pull them off unless you've got a chisel."

He snorts. "Oh, fucking lovely. I schlepp your shit all over London, and even stop off for Chinese, and you *still* can't stop insulting me."

"No, I can't, and you only did all those things to see Gabe's house."

"Yeah you might be right," he murmurs, following me down the corridor, his eyes everywhere. "Jesus, this is gorgeous. Why can't we find somewhere like this?"

"Because I am a lowly assistant, and you are a model, and together we *still* don't make what a partner of Gabe's status makes."

"Life's not fair," he huffs, and then spies the booze. "Oh, bingo!"

"No," I whisper sharply, snatching a bottle of vodka off him. "You are not getting blitzed in Gabe's house."

"Why are you whispering?" He snorts. "Is it because he hasn't realised yet that you've rather creepily moved in, while he's too sick to notice?"

"I have *not* moved in, and Gabe's ill."

"Oh, it's Gabe now, is it? Not Shithead Boss Man, like normal?"

"Oh, shut up."

Then we both jump about a foot in the air when a deep voice drawls from the door. "Shithead Boss Man, eh? You know, Dylan, I really lucked out in the assistant department. The other partners in the firm have ended up with someone *awful,* who soothes them, is at their beck and call and agrees with them *all the time.* I got one who is sarcastic, argumentative, scruffy, rarely where he should be, and calls me Shithead Boss Man rather than Sir."

Jude laughs at him, before reaching out and swiping one of the prawns from my carton of sweet and sour. "He'd call you Sir if you spanked him."

"For fuck's sake," I sigh, burrowing my face in my hands, and then raising it in surprise as Gabe bursts into laughter.

"I'll have to bear that in mind for his next appraisal," he chokes out, before succumbing to a massive coughing fit which racks his body.

"For fuck's sake," I snap. "Why are you out of bed?"

He gradually gets control of his breathing, as I run him a glass of water. "Because I needed to walk around. I've never slept so much in my life."

"Well, you needed it. That's why I put you to bed."

Jude snorts. "This is like a regular Saturday night, listening to Dylan having this conversation. Only the recipient is usually a tad more eager."

"Jude, shut up," I hiss, and when Gabe looks at me with one eyebrow raised I shake my head. "He's lying." I hand him his water and reach out, laying the back of my hand over his forehead. "Jesus, Gabe, you're burning up. Let me call the doctor."

He leans into my touch for a second, then steps back shaking his head. "I just need to get over it. I'll have another of those shitty, yellow things that you made earlier."

"You mean Lemsip?" I say patiently.

"Yes, that's the one, but it might be improved by adding whisky."

"Only if we wanted to add accidental overdose of drugs and alcohol to severe virus on your hospital admission sheet," I snipe, turning away to put the kettle on. "I'll make you a virgin Lemsip and then you can go back to bed."

For a second I'm sure that he's going to argue, but then he sighs and nods. He settles heavily down onto a bar stool, and accepts with a thankful smile the throw that I snag from a chair when I see him shivering. Pulling it around him he looks at Jude who is busily eating my Chinese. "So, you must be Jude?"

Jude nods. "You've heard of me then?"

A wry smile crosses his face. "How could I fail to have heard of you? I'm treated daily to the other side of your conversations with Dylan. I like to start my morning with a strong coffee, and listening to the retelling of both of your exploits from the night before. It's better than 'The Archers'."

"Oh God," I groan, as Jude laughs. "I didn't realise you were listening. I'm sorry, I'll try to keep it down."

He smirks. "I notice you didn't say that you'd stop. I like that." He pauses and looks hard at me. "I like it anyway. It's interesting and occasionally humorous." He pauses. "And sometimes quite pitiful."

Jude laughs. "That'd be him, not me."

I hand Gabe his Lemsip. "There. Drink that. Do you need anything else?" He shakes his head slowly. "Okay then, go back to bed." When he doesn't move, I make shooing motions. "Say goodbye to Jude. He's just going, and won't *ever* come back."

"Oh no, do feel free to stay," he says to Jude. "Dylan's been *so* kind and stayed here, forcing himself on me, completely beyond my wishes or instructions. It would be nice for him if he had company in his home invasion."

Jude bursts into laughter, and nods. "I'll stay for a bit. Thanks, Gabe."

He nods, and then looks at me where I'm still making shooing motions. "Dylan, I am neither a dog, nor a farmyard animal, so it is beyond my comprehension why you are making those gestures at me."

"You're certainly not trained at all," I say briskly, and walk behind him as he moves towards the stairs.

"Why are you doing that?" he asks hoarsely.

"In case you fall backwards."

"Well, stop it. It's making me uneasy. Go and sit with your friend."

I ignore him, shadowing him to his bedroom where I settle the covers over him, noting with anxiety how ill he actually looks when he isn't bantering. His hair is wet with sweat, and his skin has gone sheet white. There is also a visible tremor in the hand clutching the blanket.

"Go to sleep, Gabe," I say gently, straightening the duvet so that it sits neatly over him. "The only thing that really works with this virus is rest, according to Sheila from the canteen."

I wait for another acerbic remark about our co-workers but get nothing as he's asleep before I even leave the room.

When I get downstairs, I remove Jude from my takeaway forcibly and fall on the food with a groan of happiness. "Thanks for bringing this. I was so hungry, and there's fuck all to eat in this house." Silence greets me, so I look up to find him staring at me. "What?"

He shakes his head. "What was all that?"

"All what?"

"All *that* - the tender touches, the snarky conversation. It was almost like foreplay for sick people."

I choke on a prawn. "It was *not* foreplay for fuck's sake. That's the way I always talk to him."

"Well in that case, I'm surprised he hasn't got you bent over his desk every spare minute that he has."

"Oh my God, stop."

"No, you stop. I'm feeling overly warm because there was so much sexual tension in here. And that was despite him being ill."

"There's no sexual tension, don't be a prat. You're seeing things."

"I am not. I see things very clearly, clearer than you that's for sure, because what was with the touching?"

I push my plate away, suddenly losing my appetite. "Stop it, Jude."

He bends forward, and behind the humour I see concern. "No, you stop," he whispers. "I've never seen you together. All I've ever known is your complaints about him. From that, I formed a picture of a cold man, albeit a fucking funny one. I live for the putdowns he gives you. But now I've seen you together, I have to admit that I'm worried."

"Worried? Why?"

He reaches out and grabs my hand. "You're more closely involved with him than I'd thought. Seriously, Dylan, be careful, because you're a giving bloke. If anyone needs anything, you're first in the queue to provide it. Don't choose someone who will never appreciate that gift. Don't give to someone who will take it and never give back." He looks towards the stairs. "I've got a horrible feeling he's one of those people. There's something very closed off about him."

"But that's just me. I don't know why you're so worried. I've been concerned about people before."

"And it never combined well with when you started fucking them." I draw back as if stung, and he shakes his head quickly. "That's not the whole reason that I'm worried, Dyl."

I relent at the childhood nickname. "Why, then?"

"Because he's not immune himself. I'd write it off as unrequited attraction from you working in close confines with him, but he's interested in you too. That's as clear as your reflection in that very expensive mirror over there."

I protest but it falls on deaf ears, and when he leaves after a couple of hours I try again, but he shakes his head. Drawing me into a tight hug, he whispers into my ear, "Be careful, Dylan. This has disaster written all over it. He's not someone you can have a safe crush on. That man is dangerous and damaged. I know it."

I wave goodbye, but an hour later as I lie on the sofa watching a repeat of 'Casualty', I can't help picking at his words like worrying a sore tooth.

Gabe's voice draws me from my thoughts. "Has your friend gone?"

"Jesus!" I jump. "I swear you need a fucking bell on you."

He smiles, and then to my surprise, he settles down on the edge of the sofa next to me, subsiding against the cushions with a weary grunt.

"How are you feeling?" I ask softly, the lateness of the hour seeming to ask for secrets.

"Shit," he mutters, "but slightly less shit than before." He shudders violently, and I throw the blanket that I've been cuddled into, over him. "Thanks," he mutters, and then groans. "God, that's so warm from you."

I feel my dick twitch at that throaty murmur, and try hard to think of things like tax returns and scabs until it settles down. I look up to find him looking hard at me, and my dick's condition isn't helped by the heavy-lidded face and wild hair. If he wasn't so ill, he would look like he'd just been fucked.

Pushing those thoughts aside and trying to remember Jude's warning, I sit up. "Are you hungry?"

He's silent for a second and then nods. "I am a bit. I don't think I've eaten since yesterday, but I don't feel like much." He pushes the blanket off. "I'll go and have a rummage and see what treats you bought me."

I reach out without thinking and push on his hard chest, and for a second, time seems to stand still. I have touched him of course, but over the years they had been casual touches to maybe get his attention, or to hold his jacket. This, however, is in a low-lit room at a late hour, and my fingers have never felt before the hard ridges of his muscles, and the springy wiriness of his chest hair. We both stare at each other before I quickly clear my throat and jump to my feet.

"You'll sit there and rest," I say quickly.

"Okay," he says hoarsely, and then clears his throat. "Where are you going?" The latter is said with a hint of panic, as if he thinks I'm going to leave.

I stare at him. "I'm going to make you some scrambled eggs on toast."

There's a new flush on his pale cheeks as if he's blushing, and he shifts awkwardly then protests. "Oh, no, there's no need to do that. Seriously, Dylan, you don't need to cook for me. You've done enough."

I pad to the kitchen, aware that he's collected his blanket and is loping after me, the blanket wrapped around his shoulders and head like a refugee. "I don't mind," I say, as I flick the lights on and gather the ingredients together. A long search later, and I manage to find a saucepan.

I shake my head at the state of the kitchen and then become aware that he's staring at me. "What?" I ask, as I put the pan on the burner and add a knob of butter. I slide the bread into the massive Dualit toaster that looks like it's never held any form of bread since it came out of the box, and look at him.

He shrugs awkwardly. "I'm just not used to people doing things for me."

I pause in my whisking of the eggs, to add salt and pepper to the bowl. "Well, that's a bit sad. Anyway, you're used to me doing things for you. I do them every minute of the day."

"That's in work hours," he mutters. "When we both know our jobs."

I pause before emptying the eggs into the pan. "Oh my God, I'm so sorry, Gabe. Is it making you uncomfortable me being here? I was just worried about you being on your own."

"I'm not on my own," he says indignantly, and I raise my eyebrow looking around the empty house. "Well, I am now, but that's my choice. If I wanted, I could have someone here in a second."

"I'm sure you could," I say in a low voice. "My question is do you want me to go?"

Indignation bleeds from his shoulders, until he slumps, staring at me like I'm an unidentified species that he's found in his kitchen. I put the whisk down with a clatter, and he puts his hand out quickly.

"No, I don't want you to go. Please stay, Dylan."

I stare at him for a second, seeing the tightness that looks almost like worry around his eyes. "Okay," I say calmly. "I'll stay."

He seems to relax immediately, making me wonder what is going through his mind. I'll never know, as he's tighter than a clam with his feelings. I pour the eggs into the pan with some chopped peppers. The toast pops up, and I look at him as I butter it. He's staring at me in fascination, as if he's never seen anyone make food before.

"You said you weren't used to people doing things for you," I say abruptly, and he jumps slightly, returning his gaze to my face from where it seemed to be transfixed by my hand holding the knife. Then he catches my words.

"I'm not."

"But you must have when you were a kid?"

He looks out over the kitchen as if looking at something fascinating, and when I see the flush on his cheeks, I relent. This is obviously an uncomfortable subject for some reason, and I'm just about to change the subject when he speaks.

"Not really." He shoots me a glance heavy with an undecipherable emotion. "I was brought up in the foster care system."

I put the knife down with a clatter. "Oh no, Gabe. How? Why?"

He smiles at my garbled questions. "My parents died, and my grandmother was the only family that I had left, and she was too ill to take me in."

"How old were you?"

"Five."

"Jesus, Gabe."

"It was alright," he says quickly, signs of his prickly personality trying to come through, and then he gives up. "Actually no. It was horrible and at times horrific, but I came through it, and as soon as I was eighteen, I was out of there. School was an escape for me. There were a couple of teachers who really believed in me, and I spent as long as I could there where it was safe." My heart hurts at the word *safe,* but he carries on, speaking blithely now. "I had my parents' life insurance money which I got when I was of age, and my grandmother left everything to me, including this house. At that time it had been empty for years and was very dilapidated. I moved in when I was officially released from care at eighteen. I used the money to restore it, took on a shit load of student loans, and rented it out while I went to university." He looks up, startled, as if he's said more than he intended. "It was a good investment," he finally says stiffly.

This is my answer to why he lives here. He's obviously been looking for the home he never had. This is his sanctuary. I feel pain in my hand, and realise that I've been digging my nails into my palm. Wriggling my fingers, I busy myself with plating his meal up, giving him time to get his equilibrium back.

When I place it in front of him, he looks up. "How about you? Do you have family?"

I nod, fetching my tea from the side and putting a glass of milk in front of him before sitting down on the bar stool opposite him. "I do. They all live in Devon."

"Why don't you?"

I shift. I feel awkward talking about this to someone who has no family. "I love them to death. My mum and dad are brilliant, and I have two brothers and one sister. They all live on our farm. My mum and dad have the main house, and my sister and older brother have houses on the property. My youngest brother's away at university."

He looks at me, curiosity alive in his face, and I notice he's eating with great appreciation, wolfing the food down in big bites.

"Is that okay?" I ask, motioning to the supper, and he nods.

"It's bloody great, Dylan. I've never tasted eggs like this."

I smile. "It's not Michel Roux, Gabe, it's just scrambled eggs. It's the cayenne pepper in them that spices them up a little bit."

He waves his fork at me. "Go on with your story. You haven't explained why you're not there too."

It occurs to me how weird it is that this *isn't* weird. We are sitting at a table in a cosy room, talking about personal things, when I'm not convinced he even knows when my birthday is. Every time I've tried over the years to get to know him, he's dismissed my questions as flim-flam devised to delay work.

I give in when he gives me the big eyes. He'd hate to know they're like Bambi's eyes, and particularly cute today as they're surrounded by all that wild, tousled, Stig of the Dump hair. Repressing a smile, I carry on. "They're all a bit mad. My mum's an artist and very eccentric. My dad's the only sensible one. He's a typical farmer, very stoical, but you need that when you encounter the rest of the family."

"Were they good to you? What did they think when you came out?"

I look up, startled at the personal question, but then shrug. I make no secret of my sexuality, and neither does he. "Oh God, yes. My mother believes *fervently* that everyone should be free to love whoever they want. She's a big fan of individuality and nonconformity. I think my brothers and sister disappointed her a bit, as none of them really got into trouble or had any crisis of sexuality. A couple of them are even Tories, much to her horror." I smile. "Unfortunately, that left me, and after my zillion lectures on gay rights, I'd had enough. University was a blessing because otherwise I might have had to alienate her by joining the Young Farmer's Association."

He smiles. "Did you meet Jude then?"

"No. I've known Jude since we were in nursery together. Our mothers are best friends, and he's always been part of the family."

He runs the tines of his fork down his plate. "And you weren't ever together?" His voice is low, and he doesn't look at me.

"No," I say softly. "Never. We kissed once, and it was so horrifying we vowed never to do it again. He's enough like my brother for that to have been worrying."

He huffs out a laugh, and I'm relieved that his earlier awkwardness and sadness seem to have gone. He looks much more like himself, and I sigh inwardly, because God help me, but I like the vulnerability that he's shown me far too much. Jude was right to be worried because I'm in far more trouble than I'd thought. That prickly exterior of his has always challenged me to be better, but the real *him* attracts me beyond comprehension.

Shit, I think morosely. *I'm fucked.*

CHAPTER FIVE

To: Dylan Mitchell

From: Gabe Foster

When you have finished your totally, fascinating account of who did what in a public toilet, do you think that you could possibly descend back into the mundane world of work with me?

Over the next few weeks, Jude asked me repeatedly about the situation, and I reassured him that things had gone back to normal. Gabe had got better quickly, and was soon back in the office, throwing his weight around and issuing dictates left, right, and centre. I was lying.

I should have been relieved the first time he called me a moron, but I wasn't. Things weren't the same, and something had changed in our relationship. The same way an earthquake erodes the foundations of a building, the underpinning of who we were was shifting, with previously firm stones breaking up and rolling away.

It's a rainy afternoon in late November when I give up on trying to decipher Gabe's handwriting. I throw my pen down on the desk and stare blindly into space.

The trouble I'm beginning to think, is me. I have changed from the person who had coped with his sarcasm and pickiness and thrown everything back at him, because now I feel that I know something more about him. Now, when I look at him, I don't see the arrogant shithead. Well, I do see that, but I also see the man who needs a home but can't seem to let himself have it. I see the vulnerable, grumpy man who isn't used to having anyone look after him.

However, I don't think the whole blame rests on me, because underneath the sarcasm and caustic tongue, Gabe is different too. The sarcasm is a little less biting, his tongue a little softer, and although the first couple of times I caught him staring at me from his desk I'd dismissed it as coincidence, the third and fourth time it happened, I couldn't.

I sigh and then jump as Gabe breezes past me dressed in a grey, three-piece suit. "I'm glad you've decided to take up part-time fly swallowing, Dylan, but maybe concentrate on your full-time job for a bit."

I rise to my feet and trail after him into the office, taking the briefcase he shoves at me. "Why are you back now? I thought the meeting wouldn't finish for another hour?"

"We just blitzed through everything. It was amazing, like one of those days when you're driving to work and it's green lights all the way."

"I wouldn't know," I say morosely. "There are no green lights on the tube, only red lights and interminable delays."

"While I'm always glad to hear about the little people's problems, maybe not now," he drawls, a smile tugging at his lips as I huff indignantly. He shrugs out of his jacket and flings it on the sofa, so I make sure he hears me sigh heavily as I hang it up. His full mouth quirks.

"Can I do anything for you at this moment, beyond picking up the detritus that appears to follow you around?" I ask.

He looks up at me as he loosens his royal blue tie, and rolls up the sleeves of his white shirt. "Yes. Look, do you want to sit down?"

Trying to avoid staring at his tanned forearms, I lower myself gingerly into the chair opposite his desk.

"Why are you hovering like you've got fucking piles?" he asks curiously.

"Well, you don't always invite me to sit down, Gabe."

He looks at me, flabbergasted. "Yet your arse always seems to make its way to that seat."

"Hmm yes, but that's my usual response to your orders. It's not normally a *request*."

He stares at me. "So, you're telling me that you obey *all* my orders, because honestly, that would be news to me."

"I always obey your orders," I say indignantly. "I am quite possibly the best assistant in history."

"That would certainly be true, if you were the *only* assistant in history."

I huff. "When have I *ever* disobeyed a direct order?"

"Let's be charitable and call them polite requests." I stare at him, and he smirks. "Okay, let's not. Hmm, let me see." He rests his elbows on the desk and steeples his fingers together. "How about the time when I specifically told you to book a five-star hotel, and because you had a few drinks at Samuel's leaving party, you did what?" I mumble something, and he puts his hand to his ear. "I'm sorry, what was that?"

"I booked you into a youth hostel."

"Yes," he purrs. "That was a very interesting experience."

"Why?"

"Well, I spent twenty minutes outside the place waiting for the valet parking." He pauses, and then suddenly laughs out loud. "Oh my God, but Fletcher's expression when he saw the bunkbeds was priceless, I have to give it to you."

"My verbal warning when you got back was a similarly hilarious occasion," I say sourly, which makes him laugh even harder. I can't help but smile at him, because Gabe's laugh, on the rare occasions that it happens, is seriously contagious. Deep and booming, it seems to come from deep inside him, and when he looks at you with his eyes creased in amusement, it can make you feel like you've won an Olympic medal.

"Well, I didn't realise that work was such a happy, jovial place, Gabe." We both jump and turn to see Fletcher leaning against the door with a very sour expression on his face. "I had gained the impression from your daily list of complaints about Dylan's work rate and constant cock-ups, that work wasn't particularly enjoyable at the moment."

He saunters into the room and rests his arse against the back of one of the leather sofas, crossing his arms and regarding us in a very hostile manner.

I shake my head, a wry look on my face. If he thinks that Gabe hasn't made me aware of any cock-ups, he's very wrong. It does sting to think of him going home and complaining about me, because I really am very good at my job. However, I've experienced enough of Fletcher's passive aggression, or just plain aggression, to not lose my temper.

Gabe however, isn't subject to the same control, and I stare at him in amazement as his face clouds over angrily. "Fletcher, that's fucking out of order. I have never, *ever* complained about Dylan to you, and you know it. He's the best assistant that I've ever had, and I'd be lost without him, because he goes above and beyond what's expected of him."

I turn to look at Gabe, my mouth open in amazement and a warmth filling my chest, but he's staring hard at Fletcher with a look that could kill. I check Fletcher. *Damn, it hasn't worked.*

Fletcher glares back. "Yes, he does go above and beyond. I think we all know that. I mean what secretary stays at their boss's house, and nurses him back to health?"

"I'm not a secretary," I mutter, but I'm shouted over by Fletcher.

"I mean that's true dedication, Gabe."

"I appreciated it," he says stiffly.

Fletcher's expression instantly morphs into one of faux sympathy, as he does an abrupt volte face. "I know babe, but it just blurs the boundaries. At the end of the day, he's an employee. You don't want to take advantage of someone's good nature, and I know that when you were better, it worried the hell out of you in case he got the wrong idea about you and him."

"Still here," I say clearly, wanting to punch him in the face and break his fucking nose. Gabe's face has lost all traces of the earlier laughter, and now he looks vulnerable, as if Fletcher is stepping on a nerve that none of us can see. I hasten into speech. "And I was quite happy to help my boss. I'm *fully* aware that he is my boss. If I wasn't, the day that he came back and called me a clumsy twat would have reminded me."

Gabe doesn't even break a smile. "I'm actually embarrassed, Fletcher. You have completely embarrassed both yourself and me. I presumed my conversations with you were private, not something to throw in the face of a member of my staff. Especially when that member of staff has never done anything to deserve such treatment. I'm actually very ashamed of you."

His face is cold, and both Fletcher and I shift in our chairs awkwardly. Although it's spectacular to see Fletcher get a bollocking, it's still embarrassing in front of me, and I know Fletcher will get me back for it.

Fletcher, however, seems unperturbed. "Oh Gabe, I'm so sorry," he says softly, pinning a sweet smile on his face. "You're totally right. It was out of order, and I'm sorry, Dylan." The last bit is thrown over his shoulder at me, and then he stands up and goes to hug Gabe. "I just felt bad because I didn't stay to help you. I was worried about you all week."

I rub my fingers over my lips to stop the words tumbling out. I'd bet he didn't worry at all, seeing as Jude saw him at a club on the same night I had stayed at Gabe's house.

Gabe remarkably seems to swallow it, and his frame relaxes slightly. "Okay, that's fine. Why are you here?"

Fletcher perches on the arm of Gabe's chair, and leans against him. "I came because I had a fantastic idea."

Gabe looks worried, which is justifiable. Fletcher's ideas are rarely fantastic, such as the time he decided to give up taking taxis and bought a mountain bike to get around London. He'd found out too late that he didn't have a great deal of balance, and had been involved in a heated war of words with a taxi driver, when he stopped to take a phone call in the middle of the road.

I jerk out of my thoughts as Fletcher carries on. "I was thinking how jaded you've looked since you were ill, so I wanted to make you feel better, and I decided ..." He pauses dramatically and I sigh a bit too loudly, earning me a glare from Fletcher and a quirk of Gabe's lips. Fletcher turns back to him. "How about going away for a few days skiing?" Gabe looks like he's going to argue, so Fletcher hurriedly carries on. "We could rent a chalet in Verbier, and get away from everything. The snow's fantastic at the moment, so we could ski all day and then exercise *all night*." He waggles his eyebrows lecherously at Gabe, which makes me want to throw up in my mouth a bit.

"Babe, that sounds wonderful, but I can't go at the moment," Gabe interjects.

Fletcher jerks and pouts. "But why?"

"Because I have the conference to prepare for." Fletcher looks oblivious and Gabe sighs. "The one in Amsterdam next week. I'm the keynote speaker, and I haven't got anything ready yet."

"Oh, for God's sake," Fletcher whines. "Gabe, you're clever. You can rustle that up in a couple of hours today."

Gabe and I share a look because it's going to take a few days' worth of work to get this ready. He still hasn't written his speech, and I have a thousand things that need arranging.

Fletcher catches the look, and it seems to make him angrier. "For fuck's sake, Gabe. We need this. *I* need this. We haven't seen much of each other lately, and I don't want that to carry on and damage us."

Gabe stares at him. "You've booked it already, haven't you?"

Fletcher sags. "Yes. We're booked into Tommy's chalet in Verbier."

There's a long silence. "And I suppose that Tommy is joining us, is he?" Gabe asks in a cold voice.

"Yes, but it'll be brilliant," Fletcher says imploringly. "I know you don't get on, but it is his chalet, and it was his idea. Please, Gabe, it'll be great, and it'll give you the chance to get to know him better."

"Fletcher, I would rather get to know Slobodan Milosevic better."

Fletcher is instantly diverted. "Is he the new Abercrombie model, the dark-haired one?"

I snort and then cover it brilliantly with a cough, or at least I thought I had until I look up and find Gabe staring at me, a dark look of humour in his eyes. Still staring at me, he speaks to Fletcher. "So, when are we going?"

"Thursday."

"For how long?"

"Four days."

"I see." Fletcher stares at him, and Gabe gives a small smile that instantly makes me nervous, as it never presages anything good. "So, it's just you and I and Tommy?"

Fletcher looks nervous. "And Will and Jamie."

I look up because I know that Gabe hates these people. I've heard him on the subject many times through his door. I'm amazed, however, to find instead that half-smile playing on his lips again, and he looks at Fetcher challengingly. "Well, Tommy's chalet is big, so Dylan and I will fit in nicely."

My incomprehensible gabble of shock is drowned out by Fletcher's *what the fuck,* and Gabe leans back, a pleased smile playing on his lips. "Fletcher, I explained I have work to do that can't wait. You took it upon yourself to book me out of the office, and I've given in with good grace. The problem is that my work will have to come with me, as will Dylan because he assists me in my work."

"Erm I'm really not sure -" I start to say, but he shakes his head fiercely at me and I subside, albeit with a glare on my face that I make sure he can see. As normal any sign of rage from me is treated by Gabe as if I'm putting on his own personal show to entertain him, and I see him suppress a smile. He is the most contrary man that I've ever met.

Fletcher rises to his feet. "So *he's* coming with us, is he?"

"That's what I said," Gabe says slowly and clearly, making me want to laugh. Fletcher opens his mouth, but Gabe beats him to it. "I will go skiing with you and do some of what you want, but the simple fact is that I have to work and Dylan is a part of my work." He pauses and then says silkily, "I presume I am paying for this trip anyway?" Fletcher flushes, and Gabe smiles coolly. "Then it will be no problem if I add Dylan to the bill, will it?"

I dig my fingers into my arms to avoid asking him angrily if I'm a pound of bananas that he's added to his trolley, or an actual person, but manfully stop myself. Although from his expression, I know he's guessed what I'm thinking.

Fletcher steps back with one of his complete changes of mood, that manage to make me dizzy within just five minutes of his company. "Okay, then it's decided." He cups Gabe's face. "We'll have a fantastic time, babe. Do you remember the last trip away with Will?" He lowers his voice, but I hear the last comment because I'm meant to. "My ass was so sore I couldn't sit down for most of the holiday." He grabs the lobe of Gabe's ear in his sharp, white teeth, making Gabe shudder, and me want to gag. "Don't forget to let Dylan go out at night though," he says softly. "You can't monopolise all his time, and at night you're mine."

Gabe stares at him, and I take the opportunity to mutter an excuse and leave the room, resisting the urge to slam the door off its hinges.

Ten minutes later, he finds me as Fletcher leaves, giving me a poisonous glare that Gabe misses.

I tap away on my computer, ignoring Gabe completely. He shifts from foot to foot almost nervously, before perching his arse on the corner of my desk. "Dylan," he says softly. I switch the pencil I'm chewing on to the other corner of my mouth, and keep typing. "Dylan," he says a bit louder. "I know you can hear me."

If I wasn't so angry, I would want to smile, because he hates to be ignored. He's like a small child in that regard. Finally, a minute later, he loses patience, and reaches over and switches off my monitor. "That's better," he says. "Now you can talk to me."

I swivel to look long and hard at him, and he squirms slightly. "Oh, you want me to *talk?*" I say in a tone of amazement. "That's a surprise. I wasn't aware you needed any sort of input from me anymore."

"Dylan, *please*," he groans. "I know you're a bit angry."

"A bit?" I hiss. "I'd be a *bit* angry if you put olives on my sandwiches. This is beyond that."

"You'd really be angry about the olives?" he says, trying to be charming. "Good grief, I wasn't aware that you took lunch so seriously."

"I don't, but you know what I *do* take seriously, Gabe?" He swallows and tries hard to maintain eye contact as my voice rises. "I take managing my own time seriously. I take the ability to say yes or no to a request very seriously. I mean, what's next? You'll be telling me how to fucking shave or put deodorant on next."

He looks at my stubble. "Well, that might not be out of the ball park."

"It's not funny," I hiss. "I'm bloody furious. How dare you, Gabe. I actually imagined that you thought more of me than to use me as a tool in your argument with Little Lord Lubeship."

"Who?" he asks, with a gleam of absolute hilarity.

"Never mind," I say quickly, unable to believe I've let Jude's and my nickname for Fletcher slip out. "I'm serious, Gabe," I say sharply, standing up and grabbing my jacket from the hook, and my bag from beside the desk.

"Wait, where are you going?" he asks anxiously, jumping to his feet.

"Home."

"No, wait."

I walk past him, and he takes the opportunity to grab my arm, staying my progress and sending sparks down my arm so quickly I can't help but gasp. Immediately his expression darkens, as he looks down at his hand as if feeling it too. I'm unable to stop the shudder that runs through my body, and suddenly we're closer than we had been, with our chests almost touching. He sucks in a sharp breath.

"Jesus," he says hoarsely. "Jesus, Dylan." He reaches up slowly, as if the gesture is beyond his control. Time seems to slow as he grabs my other arm, bringing me into him, but a sudden bang from the corridor outside the open door makes us both jump back.

Gabe stares at the open door, as the post boy walks in with his arms full of envelopes.

"Afternoon," he says cheerily. "How are you, Dylan?"

"Hi -" I stop and clear my throat. "I'm fine. How are you, Mark?"

"Great. Thanks for that tip about the college course. I -" He suddenly catches sight of Gabe. "Oh hello, Mr Foster," he stutters.

"Afternoon," Gabe says, turning to his side and showing a forced interest in a picture of a sailing ship on my wall. I stare hard at him, and then suddenly notice the reason he's moved is to cover a massive erection.

A shudder runs through me, and I'm glad of the concealing folds of my coat. Mark looks curiously between the two of us, and I rush into speech.

"Just put them on my desk, Mark. Thank you."

He hastens to do as I ask and hurries out of the room, leaving a silence loud with something.

I stack the envelopes for something to occupy my hands, wondering when he's going to look at me. Finally, he sighs heavily and turns back, his face once more wiped clean of expression, and not a sign of the heated, slack intentness of before.

Sighing, I grab my bag from the floor where it's fallen and go to move past him. "I'm taking the rest of the day off," I say coolly. "I'm sure that's okay with you, because you just decided that you would requisition my time for four whole days and nights."

"Wait." The thickness is still in his voice, but now he sounds nervous. "You're not leaving, are you?"

"Yes," I say patiently, and he whitens slightly. I catch his meaning and sigh. "I'm not leaving my *job,* Gabe."

He looks up too swiftly to totally guard his expression, which for a minute I could swear shows blinding relief, but he clears it quickly. "That's good," he mutters, thrusting his hands into his trouser pockets and rocking back on his heels almost nervously. I stare at him, wondering who this stranger is in front of me these days. He bears little resemblance to the man I've worked for, for such a long time.

Catching my gaze, I see a faint flush on his cheeks. "I'm sorry," he mutters.

"What did you say? Could you speak a bit more clearly?"

He looks at me crossly. "You heard me."

I lean back on the desk and cross my arms. "No, I really don't think I did. Repeat it. Pretend that I'm a moron, and you're dictating your letters *again.*"

"Bastard," he says almost admiringly. Then. "I. Am. Sorry," he says through gritted teeth.

I stare at him, seeing him squirm and enjoying it for a brief, joy-filled minute. "Okay," I say coolly.

His head shoots up. "What do you mean, okay?"

"I mean okay. Thank you for your apology." I lean forward. "But don't you *ever* think that you can speak for me, and make arrangements for me without my consent again. I'm not your boyfriend." He stares at me, silver-grey eyes locked on me in what looks like fascination. "I mean it, Gabe," I say sharply. "If you ever do that to me again, not to mention in front of people, I will lose my shit in a big way. And then I *will* leave."

He nods his head quickly and anxiously, then jerks as I move past him. "Wait, where are you going?"

"Out. I'm taking the rest of the day off, Gabe, and it will *not* be coming out of my holiday pay." His eyes threaten some form of retribution, so I make sure to fling my scarf around my neck with jaunty abandon. "After all, I've got to go and find some ski gear."

The last thing I see is the look of relief on his face as I leave the office, making me smile when I know he can't see me. However, when I get into the elevator, I lean back against the wall with a sigh. *What the fuck have I committed to?*

CHAPTER SIX

To: Gabe Foster

From: Dylan Mitchell

Would you like me to take dictation in the meeting? I'm sorry, I can't even type that without sniggering.

A few days later I ease out of the minibus that's brought us to the chalet Fletcher has borrowed. I look up at the building and shake my head. Chalet is really the wrong word for it. Monstrosity would probably be a better word, because it's huge, more like a mansion. It's traditionally built of wood with lots of balconies jutting out over the drive like raised eyebrows, and it's probably got more floor space than Buckingham Palace.

The others are laughing and mucking about as the driver removes their bags from the boot, so I take a welcome second to get away from them. I wander over to stand on the edge of the gravelled drive, looking at the stunning view of the snow-covered mountains. I breathe in through my nose, feeling the cold sharpness of the air fill my head and lungs. It's truly beautiful here, and normally I'd be in my element and raring to get on the slopes. However, normally I'd be with Jude, rather than the present company of idiots.

I shoot a glance towards the men now walking up the steps of the chalet. The journey here had been interminable, filled with inane chatter about nothing and was about as interesting to me as a lecture on waste disposal would have been.

The other men in the party consist of the friend Tommy, whose parents own the chalet, and who is seriously into Fletcher. He's a part-time model as well, and I get the distinct impression that it isn't a way to earn money, as his parents seem to pay for everything. He's undeniably gorgeous, with golden hair, pale skin and that skinny, almost frail appearance that's so trendy at the moment.

He and Fletcher look gorgeous together, but it's a false glamour. It's like looking at a picture in a gallery that everyone loves, but it just leaves you cold. However, his upper-class drawl and supreme confidence grate on me. He obviously looks down on me with my state school education and well-worn clothes, and he makes no secret of his disdain when I speak.

There are also two brothers called Will and Jamie. They're both dark-haired men who are also models, and they look sufficiently alike that I still can't work out which one is which. They are also eerily perfect, like they've rolled off a conveyor belt somewhere. I've inwardly christened them Topsy and Tim.

The only bright side of the trip is Gabe's friend, Henry. He's actually the only friend I've ever met who belongs to Gabe, and not Fletcher. I'd gathered from not too subtle prodding that he'd been at university with Gabe, with both of them studying law. He'd specialised in family law, but the two seem very close. He's gorgeous, with dark-red hair like the colour of a fox's pelt, and vivid, hazel eyes.

He isn't staying at the chalet with us, but rather with his brother who has a home here. He'd appeared at the airport to cadge a lift from Tommy on his parents' plane, and I'd brightened instantly when he'd stepped through the plane door. He'd always without fail, been polite and friendly to me when he'd called into the office to pick up Gabe for lunch, but truthfully, I'd have welcomed even Hannibal Lecter at that point. Anything to block out the unrelenting tedium of listening to four grown men recount tales involving men called Alexander and Trubbers, who are apparently too busy throwing up in the Ritz, to actually do anything productive.

Gabe had taken one horrified minute to listen, and had then buried himself in some of the papers I'd packed for him. He'd motioned for me to sit next to him at one of the small tables, and I'd seen Fletcher direct a poisonous glance at me and then lean closer to Tommy, saying something that had made the other man laugh and shoot me a cryptic look.

I'd stiffened my spine, but it was at that point that Henry had stepped onto the plane, and Gabe had greeted him with a wide smile, standing up and hugging him. I'd tried not to stare, but Gabe's smiles, although rare, are worth seeing as they fill his whole face, making his eyes crinkle, and his eyebrows arch wickedly. I'd been surprised when Henry had then reached out and hugged me, as I didn't really know him, but he'd seemed genuinely pleased to see me.

He and Gabe had then launched into a long conversation, trading war stories for the rest of the flight, as I tapped away on my tablet and made notes for myself of things that still needed to be done before Amsterdam.

It was very noticeable how apart from the others Gabe and Henry were. They wore wealth and success easily, but it wasn't in the louche way the others did. They had a palpable sense of energy about them, like even sitting still, they were poised to move. Their conversation was lively and funny, and I thoroughly enjoyed hearing them catch up. The others seemed to treat them as though they were a lot older; as if their successes meant a gain in age when both of them were only thirty-two.

I turn at the sound of crunching footsteps, as Henry strolls up and stands beside me gazing out over the snowy landscape. "It's so beautiful here," he says, taking a deep breath the same way I had done. He turns to me. "Have you skied before?"

"Yeah, loads of times. My friends and I come when we can during the winter." I look around. "Not in places like this though. Our getaways are much more budget appropriate."

He laughs. "Some of my best holidays have been like that. Gabe and I did some serious travelling around Europe in our uni holidays, on a shoestring budget. You should hear some of the stories I've got stored up on him."

I look at him with interest, but at this point Gabe comes up behind us, stretching with a heavy grunt that makes me shift my position quickly. "What stories?" he asks, flinging his arm around Henry's shoulders.

I stare at them. They look very striking together and I wonder if they've ever fucked. Gabe shoots a quick, dark glance at me as if he knows what I'm thinking, but then his gaze slides away instantly, the way it has done since that moment in the office.

Henry laughs loudly. "I was thinking about Rome," he starts, and Gabe immediately shakes his head.

"Fuck no, don't tell Dylan that. I'll never hear the end of it." I open my mouth, but he shakes his head fiercely. "Too much ammunition."

I snort. "As if you haven't got loads on me."

He strokes his chin, his face alive with amusement, and making my breath catch. "Yes, I do seem to remember last year's Christmas party."

"Oh my God, don't."

"What?" Henry asks, and Gabe starts to laugh.

"Dylan hates old man Bernard."

"Because he's so rude to everyone," I interject.

"Because he's so *rude* to everyone," Gabe parrots, and turns to Henry. "Anyway, Dylan had far too much to drink, and put a photocopied picture of his arse on Bernard's desk." Henry starts to laugh, and I groan. Gabe continues blithely. "I had to do a lot of talking to dissuade Bernard from his plan to have everyone drop their trousers and then sack the culprit."

"How would he have known?" Henry asks curiously.

Gabe laughs. "Because Dylan here has a birthmark shaped like Italy on his bum."

"Oh my God, you said you hadn't seen it. You bloody swore," I say indignantly.

Gabe starts laughing helplessly, balancing on Henry's arm. "Seen it. I'm using it as my work Christmas card this year."

"Oh, I call absolute bullshit." I pause. "You couldn't anyway. There's no holly on it."

"Or a prick," Gabe gets out, before giving a disgusting snort. He misses Henry giving him a startled look, but I notice him extend that look to include me.

We're interrupted by a shout of *Gabe* from the steps, and turn to see Fletcher with his arms folded.

"Oh dear the missus is calling," Henry says sweetly, and I laugh.

Gabe shoots us both a look, then hugs Henry. "Give me a call and we'll go out for a drink this week."

"With Fletcher?" Henry asks doubtfully, and Gabe smiles wryly.

"No, don't worry."

The two men clap each other's shoulders. "Okay, but make sure to bring Dylan," Henry adds, and Gabe gives him a startled look before nodding quickly.

"Of course, we'll be there."

He moves away, answering something that Fletcher shouts at him with a grunt, and I watch them before becoming aware of Henry staring at me. When I turn, he doesn't attempt to hide his study, but just looks at me before suddenly smiling. "I like you, Dylan," he says. "You're good for him."

"Who?"

He shakes his head and digs his hand into his pocket, pulling out a business card which he hands to me. "My mobile number's on the back, Dylan. Give me a ring if all this gets too much." He looks up at the house. "They're not a nice bunch of people."

I smile. "Oh, I can take care of myself, but thank you."

He shoots me an amused glance. "I know you can take care of yourself. Gabe's always been full of stories about you, so I know you're your own man." He stares at me, and says softly, almost as if not aware of muttering, "I wondered, and now I know."

"Know what?"

He shoots me a smile. "Oh, lots of things, and I have to say I'm very relieved and happy at the way that things are progressing."

I'm completely puzzled. "What things?"

He shakes his head. "Just something I've been nagging Gabe about for a couple of years. Nothing for you to be concerned about. It's a work in progress."

I nod. I'm not aware that they have any projects together, but I suppose I'll know soon enough when Gabe drops the work on my desk. I shake the card at him. "Well, thanks for this anyway."

"Not at all." He suddenly steps a little closer, and says in a low voice, "Don't let him work all weekend. Make him have some fun."

I laugh awkwardly. "I'm not in control of that. That's Fletcher's business, and I'm sure he'll pull him away from work when he needs him. I think I'm more cast in the role of Cinderella on this trip." He looks at me querying. "All work and no play."

He laughs lightly and claps me on the shoulder, before walking back to the car, throwing over his shoulder. "Don't forget what happened to Cinderella."

I shake my head at him, waving as the car moves off. *Yes, Cinderella won a real prize - a man who couldn't see her true worth until she fitted in the shoe properly.*

Making my way into the chalet, I find my suitcase abandoned and lying on its side as if someone has kicked it over. I look around for someone to ask where my room is, and just as I'm about to go and find someone, I become aware of raised voices coming from a room nearby.

Carrying my case, I pop my head around the door, only to realise that Fletcher and Gabe are involved in an argument. I catch the words '*he's in the way*', and I hastily go to pull my head back, but it's too late as Fletcher has spotted me.

"Oh, for Christ's sake," he hisses. "He's everywhere."

Gabe turns, his face full of irritation and anger at the interruption, and it catches me on the raw unexpectedly. Maybe because he's been so nice and funny lately, I'd forgotten how irritated he can get with me, and now it unexpectedly stings, especially in front of Fletcher.

"Sorry," I mutter. "I didn't mean to interrupt. I was just looking for someone to tell me where my room is."

Fletcher waves his hand dismissively. "There *is* a housekeeper, Dylan. I'm sure she can help you. I think Tommy put you somewhere on this floor."

I bite my tongue to stop myself saying something sharp and go to back out gracefully, but Gabe says '*wait*' sharply.

He turns to Fletcher. "Why the fuck is Dylan on *this* floor?"

Fletcher makes a dismissive motion. "I don't know. I presume Tommy put him here because he's staff."

"This isn't fucking 'Upstairs Downstairs', Fletcher. How fucking rude." He strides towards me. "Let's find the housekeeper and put this right."

"Oh yes, walk away, you fucking bastard. That's what you do so well," Fletcher shouts, which is wasted on Gabe who is patently not paying attention. He strides past me, and I swear under my breath and follow him, grimacing and dragging my case after me.

Gabe catches a woman he finds in the foyer, and talking swiftly in French, he must have asked her where my room is, because she smiles and gestures for us to follow her. She walks down the corridor past the room where Fletcher had been, but which now stands empty. We follow her until she reaches a door into what is obviously an annexe to the building, as it looks a lot more plain and functional than the rest of the house. Going through the door I can hear the sound of pots and pans coming from what must be a kitchen, and she takes us up a set of stairs to a corridor with about ten doors leading off it.

She walks to one and opens the door, gesturing for me to go in and patting me on the shoulder. "Welcome," she says in accented English. "I will give you time to unpack, and then someone will come and find you and show you the staff kitchen and the recreation room."

She takes a look at Gabe who is standing in the corner of the room with his arms crossed, and blanches at the look of rage on his face. Smiling nervously, she leaves the room and shuts the door behind her, leaving us standing in silence.

I take a look at the room which is tiny but functional, with a single bed, wardrobe, and a desk and chair pulled up to the window. I wander over to peer out of the window and look down on what looks like the garage. It makes me want to smile because Fletcher and Tommy couldn't have been clearer in their intent to make me feel my place. I'm obviously going to be punished for Gabe's decision to bring me here because they can't do anything to him. He's like a mountain, firm and inviolate with no weak spots.

I sling my case onto the bed and take a look at him. Actually, he doesn't look inviolate now. He looks bloody furious. "What on earth is the matter with you?" I ask lightly, unzipping my case. "You look like someone's pissed in your coffee."

He moves suddenly, lowering his arms and coming round to where I'm standing. "I wouldn't unpack," he says sharply, rage simmering under his voice. "You're not staying *here.*"

I sigh heavily. "Oh yes, I am." He starts to interrupt, and I hold up a hand, which has the effect of doubling his irritation level but actually shutting him up. "I *am* staying in here because I don't want a fuss being made, Gabe. This room is perfectly adequate for my needs." I look around. "Anyway, Jude and I have stayed in worse than this."

He looks around the room sniffing. "I sincerely doubt that."

"Well, you shouldn't. This room even has a window. Once, in Crete, we stayed in what looked like a broom cupboard."

He goes to the window and releases an angry sigh, his fingers clutching the sill so hard that his knuckles are white. "You might just as well not have one. You're looking out over the fucking garage."

I join him at the window, and playfully nudge his shoulder. "Yes, but it's a nice garage, and ooh look, snow."

His lip twitches as my voice gets high, and then he growls. "You are not charming me out of my rage. This is deplorable." I open my mouth, and he shakes his head. "This isn't right. You're with me. I asked you to come with me."

I raise my eyebrows, and he grins reluctantly. "Okay, I *told* you to come. But the onus was then on me to make sure you were comfortable on this trip, and not shoved in the box room and talked down to like you're little fucking Orphan Annie." I look at him, and he shakes his head. "You don't think that I've missed the jibes, do you? Believe me, they won't continue."

"Oh, please," I sniff. "As if the opinions of four people who have the IQ of snails, could bother me."

"It bothers me."

"Well, don't let it," I say sharply. "Ignore it, and I'm asking, no I'm *telling* you not to make a fuss about this room. I'll be comfortable in here, and I'm unlikely to spend much time in here anyway with the amount of work we've brought with us. Shall I ask the housekeeper to set us up in a room?"

He nods. "Fine, but I am very aware that you're changing the subject."

"I am, because as far as I'm concerned, the subject is closed. I'm working, not on holiday. Now, I'll see what I can organise regarding a room, and then we should be able to start tomorrow. Is that okay, or are you skiing?"

Something flickers over his expression too quickly for me to read at the mention of skiing, but I file it away for future reference. He shakes his head. "I'm not skiing until I've got all this sorted out. I can't rest until I know we're set up. They won't be bothered. Fletcher will be happy with their company until he needs me for the evening."

"Okay," I say doubtfully. "I'll see you at ten tomorrow."

"No, you'll see us for dinner tonight." He raises his hand to stem my torrent of excuses. "Man up, Dylan. If I've got to sit through it, then so have you. You may have won over the room, but you won't win over food. There's no fucking way that you're sallying off to sit with the staff, and leaving me alone. Okay?" I nod reluctantly, and he smiles. "See you for dinner. I'll send word."

"I'm sure you will," I say sourly, hearing him laugh as he leaves the room with his humour restored.

=✉

The next morning, I look up as the door to the library opens, and Gabe appears, looking distinctly hungover. "Morning," I say brightly and more loudly than I need to. Watching him wince with satisfaction, I then throw my arm out and gesture around the room. "Well, what do you think?"

Giving me a narrow-eyed stare, he looks around the beautiful, book lined room. "Lovely," he says faintly. "Have you got coffee?"

"Hang on a minute," I say indignantly. "I've been here for an hour making sure that everything is up to your gruelling standards. I need more than a pathetic *lovely*."

"My standards are not gruelling, and is this where you've been all morning? Have you had breakfast yet?"

I wave my hand. "Oh yes, I ate in the kitchen with Frau Gerber the housekeeper, and Bruno the chauffeur. Did you know that Tommy Senior has not one, but *two* mistresses from the village? He actually schedules them on different nights."

He sits down heavily at the desk in the middle of the room, a glimmer of humour showing. "You and your gossip grapevine. He must be taking his vitamins. Well, I suppose like father like son."

I give him an arch look, and before I can stop myself, the words come out. "So I gather. Well, I suppose you'd know."

He freezes for a long second, and I brace myself for the explosion, but to my surprise, he looks slightly shamefaced. "I suppose I deserved that. Did you know before last night?"

I shrug, straightening some papers unnecessarily. "Fletcher's not terribly discreet, Gabe, and I got the impression it was heading that way last night."

The dinner had actually been painful in a way I don't want to analyse, as Fletcher had spent half of it ensconced on Gabe's lap, flirting heavily with both Gabe and Tommy. Gabe had been drinking heavily, and when I'd made my escape, I had cast one look back and seen Fletcher kissing Gabe torridly, while Tommy leant over with his hand in Gabe's lap, stroking his obviously erect cock.

Gabe jerks and looks anywhere but at me. "Yeah, but that's not where it went for me," he says suddenly, catching my gaze and holding it with the force of a laser. "I spent the night alone in my bed."

"And Fletcher?" I can't believe that we're having this conversation, with me asking him such intrusive questions, and him answering me as if I have the right to know.

He shrugs. "With Tommy, I presume, although it could have been the twins. That wouldn't be the first time either."

"Goodness it's like a disturbed version of 'Dynasty'," I say lightly, and then shoot a look at him. "And you're okay with that?" My tone is far too startled, and not to my surprise he stiffens.

"I'm fine with it. We don't have the sort of twee, traditional relationship that you obviously look for, Dylan. We're adults, and if we want to add a third or a fourth, then that's our business. You should try it sometime."

"I don't think so," I say clearly. "That's not really my thing."

"That's patently obvious," he mutters. "Shall we get to work?"

So we do. And it's just like at the beginning - as if we're strangers working in the same room with no connection at all.

CHAPTER SEVEN

To: Dylan Mitchell

From: Gabe Foster

Margaret from Accounts rang. Could she please have her assistant back? He appears to have taken up residence outside my door, discussing the size of men's penises with you ... loudly!

That afternoon after lunch, I stir from my position on one of the huge, brocade sofas where I'd set up my part of the office. I wander over to one of the multi-paned, floor-to-ceiling windows, and stare out longingly at the snow-covered landscape. In the distance, I can see movement across the skyline as the ski lifts ferry people up the slopes and the coloured dots of people enjoying themselves on the runs.

I sigh and stretch, giving a low groan as muscles that have grown stiff with sitting too long, stretch and release. Lowering my arms, I turn and stop dead, to find Gabe staring at me intently through his tortoise shell glasses. His hand holding his pen hangs slack. "What?" I ask. "Have you found an error?"

He shakes his head absently, his eyes an almost dark, gunmetal grey. "No, no, it's all perfect so far."

I waggle my eyebrows, hoping to get a better and more normal reaction. "Well, don't hope for more. I'm sure you'll find something soon." I head back over to my laptop and activate the screen again. "Did you check your emails?" I ask, looking down at the screen. "Bob Parker needs a reply on the Saunderson deal, and Izzy McIntosh's assistant has emailed asking for a meeting as soon as we get back." Becoming aware of total silence, I glance up to find him still staring at me. "Hello. Earth to Boss Man. Are you okay? Do you want me to ring for more coffee?"

He jerks as if awakened. "No, I don't need anything." He pauses as if thinking something through. "Listen, Dylan, it's not fair for me to keep you locked up here when it's so gorgeous outside. Why don't you get your gear together, and head out to the slopes for the afternoon? I know you like skiing."

I straighten. "I'm not leaving you here to work, Gabe. That's not fair, and definitely not what you brought me here for."

He shakes his head. "You always work hard. I'm giving you the afternoon off, and I really don't care to discuss it any further."

I fold my arms across my chest and stare at him. "I'm not going." I pause, hit by an idea, and then follow in a rush. "I'm not going unless *you* come too. It *is* a beautiful afternoon, and it's perfect for skiing. Come on, what do you say?"

That funny expression crosses his face again, and he looks down at his hands. "No, I'm fine. I really have far too much to do to jaunt about skiing."

Something about the way he says *skiing,* as if it's a disease, catches my attention, and suddenly I'm hit by a blinding revelation. "Oh my God," I say slowly. "You can't ski, can you?"

"Don't be ridiculous," he says irritably. "Dylan, I swear your mind makes more fictional leaps than J.K. Rowling."

I shake my head. "Give it up, Gabe. I'm right, aren't I? You can't ski, can you?"

He shakes his head, and taking off his glasses, rubs his eyes. When he looks up, I'm still staring at him, and he laughs. "Oh my God, MI5 should employ you." I raise my eyebrow, and he shakes his head crossly. "Okay, I can't ski. Are you happy now?"

"But why didn't you say something to Fletcher when he booked this holiday?"

"I couldn't tell him *that*. It's too embarrassing to admit that I've never been skiing, or even ice skating before."

I can't fathom the relationship these two have, where to even admit the slightest weakness to their partner is almost a taboo. "Gabe, plenty of people can't fucking ski. It's not a required element for survival."

He stands up, pacing to the window and staring out. "It is in my circles," he finally says quietly. "You know the crowd that I hang around with."

"Yes, trust fund babies on the whole," I say disapprovingly. "They know how to do these things because they've probably been skiing since they could walk. Although personally, if I'd been Tommy's father, I'd have pushed him down a slope when he was a baby." Gabe smirks, making me happy as the embarrassment slowly clears from his expression. "What I'm trying to say is that I know from things you've said before that you don't come from that sort of background, and I personally think you're far more impressive for where you are in life."

He stares at me, surprise written on his face. This isn't the way we talk to each other. We use sarcasm and wit as our tools, not genuine kindness, but I carry on. "I'd rather have you around ski-less, than running the slopes all day with the fuckwit foursome out there." He snorts, and I laugh, but then I'm hit with an amazing idea. "Why don't I teach you?" In the process of sinking down onto the sofa, he freezes and looks at me dubiously. "Oh, come on, Gabe, it's a brilliant idea. You trust me, don't you?"

He nods his head. "Of course I do, but *you* can't teach me."

"Why not? I know I'm not a strapping ski instructor called Johannes, but I can ski. I've been going skiing every year with Jude since we were sixteen. We've single-handedly skied in some of the crappiest, most tourist-inundated areas in Europe. If I can ski those, I can definitely teach you." I pause before saying quietly, "And you know I won't use it against you, don't you?" He looks at me intently, surprise and something else running over his face. "I would never do that, and I won't tell anyone. We'll go on the nursery slopes in a quiet area. What do you think?"

He shakes his head. "Why do you want to do this?"

"Because it's you. You've taught me a lot since I've been with you. I would trust you with anything, and I hope that you feel the same. I know you're my boss, and you like to keep your distance, but maybe today we could just forget that. How about it?"

He stares at me for a second and then nods slowly. "Okay, you're on, but do not think that when we get back to the office, I won't make you redo the coffee when it's shit."

"Wouldn't dream of it," I say blandly. "My day wouldn't be the same if we didn't have the ritual, multiple refilling of the coffee pot for our cosy, little taster sessions."

"Smart ass," he says tartly.

"Yes I am. Go and get changed. We've got lift passes and boots and stuff, and you brought ski gear with you, didn't you?" I pause. "What were you going to do all day anyway?"

He shrugs. "I thought I might try and get some private lessons."

"Well, it's your lucky day," I say brightly. "I'm free."

"Yes, a free, uncertified ski instructor who lacks any coordination on a normal day, as opposed to a buff teacher called Stefan."

"Johannes," I say automatically. "Stefan teaches the ladies."

He smiles. "Of course. Okay, go and get ready, Johannes."

≡✉

An hour later, we stand on the road looking at the nursery slopes. The snow is thick underfoot, and the sky is a dirty-grey colour, promising more snow and soon.

I sneak a glance at Gabe and admire his appearance. He may have no experience at skiing, but he was born to wear the clothes. His wide shoulders, narrow hips and long legs look amazing in an Oakley grey and black, camo-patterned snowboarding jacket and black ski pants. His hair is windswept, his cheeks ruddy, and he's already attracting sidelong glances.

I look down at my own outfit, and I have to say that I don't think I'm letting the side down. Although I have my own ski gear, it's quite old, so I'd borrowed stuff from Jude, who has a shit ton of designer label gear after a photo shoot in Whistler. The gear had been wet and used, so the models got to keep it. I'm wearing black pants with a red and black checked snowboarding jacket. Seeing somebody staring at me I strike a jaunty pose, until I look around to find Gabe's Oakley sunglasses trained on me.

"What are you doing?"

I tip my sunglasses down to look at him. "Pretending that I'm a film star who's incognito."

"Why?"

I shrug. "It's something Jude and I do when we're away."

He shakes his head. "Sometimes I wonder how you manage to walk and talk at the same time."

"Hey, don't knock your ski instructor."

He looks me up and down. "Hmm."

"What's that supposed to mean?" I call after him, as he starts walking towards the start of the nursery slopes, his skis slung carelessly over his shoulder like he's done this millions of times. He even makes the walk in ski boots a thing of grace and beauty, unlike myself who always makes it look like I've shit myself.

He looks back at me. "Why are you walking like that?" he asks, a thread of laughter running through his voice.

"Oh shut up. These fucking boots always hurt my shins."

He shakes his head. "Okay, where do we start, Obi Wan?"

I nod approvingly. "I like that, my little Skywalker. Begin we shall."

I look around. The kinder classes have finished, and the adult classes have probably advanced to the beginner slopes, so the nursery slope is empty apart from ski instructors with private pupils. "We'll go over there," I say, pointing to a flat area and then following him to the designated spot.

We dump our skis on the ground, and I stand back. "Right, we'll get your skis on first. Stand to the side of the ski binding, and knock your right foot against the front of the binding to get rid of the snow. Then put your foot, toe first, into the toe cup of the binding." I watch him do it and nod. "Now push your heel down, and you'll hear a snap as the binding snaps shut."

Once his foot is secure, I place his ski pole to the side of him. "Okay, thread your hand through the strap from below, and then spread out your hand and grab your pole." I snicker, and he glares at me. "*What?* It's funny. I'm instructing you to spread your hand and grab your pole. In England, this would be a sexual harassment case waiting to happen."

He shakes his head, but a grin is playing on his lips. "Okay Master, I'm grabbing my pole."

"Please say that again, but make your voice go all husky, like on a Friday afternoon when you've been yelling all day."

"*Dylan,*" he warns, and I hold my hands up.

"Okay, okay. You're going to walk across the flat like you're on a scooter, using your ski poles and your free foot to propel yourself. That'll give you a good feel of the gliding motion."

Over the next twenty minutes I have him do this with the other foot, and then both feet. For such a tall man, he's very graceful. It doesn't surprise me at all because he moves very fluidly, even while walking down the street, being one of those lucky people who are always in control of his body. This is totally unlike myself, who could smack into a door frame just by walking through the door on my own.

What does surprise me, however, is how patient he is, and how, despite claiming that he couldn't tell Fletcher that he couldn't ski, he seems perfectly happy for it to be just the two of us.

Once I'm satisfied that he's moving easily, we tramp across the snow to a small slope. "God, I love that sound," I sigh, listening to the *krump krump* as we stride along. "And don't you just love the fresh cold? It feels cleaner here, and so bloody open. We're so hemmed in, in London." He looks at me sideways, shaking his head as if mystified by something. "What?"

"You're just so happy with simple things, Dylan."

"I hope you're not taking the piss," I say smartly, and he stops walking to grab my arm.

"No, I'm not," he says seriously. "It's a lucky character trait to be pleased with the plain things in life. There aren't enough people like you, and I like the way you make me feel it too. If I'd been with Fletcher and the others, we would have crammed into the ski lifts, with them talking incessantly all the time about rubbish. When we got to the top, we'd have come down, and we'd have repeated that until it was time for lunch at wherever the trendiest place is at the moment. No one would have pointed out the noise of the snow because they'd never have heard it over their incessant, fucking talking."

I shake my head. "I like peace. It gives me the energy to get through things."

"Like a Friday afternoon in the office?"

"Yeah, don't go too far. Quiet hasn't got miracle properties."

He laughs, and we come to the slope which is very much a gentle incline. I smile at him. "Okay, let's do this since you're ready for a descent. The way to climb a slope in skis is to go up sideways, lifting one ski at a time, and when you get to the top do a quarter turn. Then you're ready to come down the slope." I shoot a look at him. "Don't worry, it's gentle. It might feel a bit fast because you're on skis, but this is a very small slope."

I look at him, standing with the gentle breeze ruffling his hair and making the light pick out the coal-black sheen, and then clear my throat. "Posture is important, so don't ever lean back which is an instinctive reaction. Instead stand up straight, and then bend your knees slightly forward so you're leaning slightly." He looks at me and I grin. "Think about when you're fucking a short man." He shakes his head but adjusts his posture perfectly, and I laugh. "Excellent. I really should be a ski instructor. I'd be the best."

"I wouldn't use that particular instruction in the children's group though."

I laugh. "I wouldn't be teaching little *children*. I'd be teaching the good-looking men. Okay, leaving my fantasy of living here and being the best ski instructor, I have to say you should be feeling the strain in your shinbones. That's normal, but just don't lean back because it'll set your balance off."

He nods his head determinedly, and I know he'll be skiing well in a few days. He has the drive and the natural balance and grace to make a good skier, and it makes me stupidly happy to have been a part of giving him something that he'll love for the rest of his life.

I watch him over the next hour as he picks up speed and moves towards steeper slopes. I feel the cold on my face, and watch the wide, unconscious smile on his lips as he falls in love with the sport. A melancholy thought occurs to me that one day he'll find a partner, and the two of them will go skiing every winter together, laughing and happy. I wonder if he will ever pause on a snowy afternoon and glance at the nursery slopes, and see for a second the ghost of a man who was there the first time that he did this.

Looking up, I'm just in time to see him fall over, so I shake the wistfulness away for another day, and stroll over. "Even the most talented skiers fall over," I say as I get near. I pause. "Or so I hear. I mean *I've* never done it, but hey that's just me."

He sits in the snow grinning up at me, his teeth white in his tanned face. His stubble shines black against the pink of his wide lips, his hair is a windswept mess, and for a second I'm struck dumb by his masculine beauty. Then he shakes his head. "Okay Johannes, how do I get up?"

I show him how to position his skis parallel to the slope, and then dig his poles in behind him and use them to pull himself up, and as I do, the grey sky delivers its bounty, as great, white snowflakes start to fall from the sky. Within seconds the air is heavy and full of white.

"Brilliant," I shout, putting out my hands and lifting up my face to see the blurry wildness of the snow falling onto my face from above.

Gabe laughs at me. "You're a bloody, big child."

"No, come here." I gesture to him. "Put your head back and look up. It's wild, and it makes you dizzy because it seems even heavier when you're looking up at the sky."

Humouring me, he stands next to me and tilts his head back. I throw my arm around his shoulder, forgetting for a second that we aren't friends, but instead of pushing me away, he leans into me for a long, precious second. Then he seems to recall himself and stiffens and goes to move past me, but as he moves, his ski hits a rock and he half slips into me.

I throw my arms around him, bracing my weight so that we both don't go over. I start to laugh, but at that point, he looks up, our eyes meet, and everything falls away. I don't see the snow, or feel the cold, biting wind. I just see his eyes, and in them is everything I'm feeling - a sweet heat and desire, and almost fear.

"Gabe," I whisper, but he jerks back almost as if by instinct. My arms fall away, and for a second I think I see regret in those silver orbs before he shakes his head.

"Nearly falling over twice in a minute means I'm tired I think."

"Are you ready to go back?" I ask reluctantly. I don't want to lose this carefree, grinning man and see him return to his guarded self, but it's inevitable and I sigh.

My head shoots up, however, when he says almost hesitantly, "I don't want to go back. Do you fancy getting dinner and having a drink?"

"I'd love it," I say, perhaps a bit too vehemently. However, he kindly ignores it, and we set off down the slope, the snow falling around us like confetti.

We find a brightly lit bar down a side street, its outside lit by lanterns festooned with icicles, and it's a relief to duck into the lobby out of the heavily falling snow. We dump our skis and boots in the containers provided, and make our way into the toasty interior of the bar in our thick socks. We both sigh simultaneously in pleasure at the warmth that hits us, then laugh before stripping off our jackets and joining the other skiers enjoying après-ski.

The interior of the bar is dimly lit, with most of the light coming from candles burning in hurricane lamps everywhere, and the festoons of fairy lights which hang from the beams. Oompah music is playing, and the whole big, light-timbered room smells of something lovely cooking.

I straighten my grey, woollen hoody. "This was a *good* idea," I say emphatically to Gabe, and he laughs.

"I know. It's just rare for you to positively acknowledge any of my good ideas."

"That's because they usually mean a lot of work for me."

He smiles. "Not tonight. Why don't you grab that table that's just come empty, and I'll order some food and drinks. What do you want?"

I look up at the menu board over the bar. "I'll have a burger and chips and Glühwein, and you have to have that too, Gabe. It's tradition."

"Isn't tradition covered by things like Trooping the Colour and the Changing of the Guard?"

I shake my head. "Tradition comes from something being so brilliant and such a good memory, that you try to recreate it every time that you can."

Gabe stares at me, something complicated running across his

face, before a very soft expression settles. Smiling at me warmly, he runs his hand down my arm. "Okay, tradition it is. Go and grab the table."

I make my way over to the booth, which is set back from the main bar in a dark corner, lit only by the guttering flame from the candle on the table and fairy lights hanging overhead. I sit looking around idly, trying hard to ignore the tingles shooting down my arm from that big, warm hand.

Movement catches my eye, and I watch him move towards me, that big body clad in his ski pants and a thin, black, hooded fleece which clings to the muscular plains of his chest. His hair is wild around his face, and the dim light catches the sharp angles of his face, making him look dark and mysterious. I'm aware of a couple of men enjoying their view of him, and I'm filled with a sense of pride and misguided possession because just for this brief moment, he's mine.

Four hours later, we're officially and completely pissed. We'd eaten our food, and then downed Glühwein after Glühwein, graduating to shots of amaretto and cinnamon schnapps. We'd also chatted and laughed in a way we'd never done before, as the invisible barrier of boss and employee seemed to have melted away.

To have all of his attention focused on you, to make him laugh and see his eyes examining your face as he listens intently to what you say, is a heady, dangerous feeling, and I've never felt so happy and free. I feel stupidly like I'm one of those couples I've watched enviously before, who have this obvious connection and happiness in each other's company.

I can't deny to myself that I'm fascinated by him. He makes me laugh and challenges me, but it's fucking dangerous. I'm not his boyfriend. He's waiting back at the chalet, probably with a face like a smacked arse, ready to fire up the bed for another scorching-hot threesome. However, the alcohol has loosened my inhibitions enough, that I'm seriously doubting my ability to stop myself from throwing myself at him.

As if aware of my thoughts, Gabe suddenly stops humming and

swaying to the music and turns back to me. It's darker in our little corner, and his eyes seem almost black, but his high cheekbones are spangled by the pinks and gold of the fairy lights which make him look mysterious and almost magical. "I have such a good time with you," he says in a low voice. "Everything just always seems better when you're here."

The music and the noise in the bar dies to a distant hum, and all that's left is the almost visible attraction between the two of us which seems to shimmer in the air. "Gabe," I whisper, feeling myself almost fall into him, and then I gasp as he raises his hand and draws his fingers down my cheekbones. He traces a path which seems to leave glittery, fire blooms under my skin, and I hold my breath as his fingers ghost inward until they find my lips. I shudder as he traces one long, calloused finger over my lower lip.

"So beautiful," he whispers in a thick, hoarse voice. "These lips, so full and pouty." He groans suddenly, and the sound from deep in his throat shoots fire down my body, centering on my cock which stiffens immediately, rising and pressing against my ski pants as if waiting for his touch. Almost as if he knows it, he glances down at my obvious erection, jutting up and making my trousers bulge obscenely.

"Dylan," he says harshly. "Oh God, you feel it too."

I nod, and moan in the back of my throat, as the gesture drags his finger over my lips.

A rumble sounds in the back of his throat, and his finger moves, pushing my lower lip down slightly, dipping in and testing the moisture. "I dreamt about your lips last night," he whispers hoarsely.

"What was the dream?" I hardly recognise my voice, it sounds so thick and heavy.

"They were wrapped around my cock so tight. Then you looked up, and I saw your eyes and those full, red lips, and I woke up coming."

I make a hoarse, wild sound, giving his finger a catlike lick, and something in him seems to snap. Reaching out he grabs my head, sliding his long fingers into my hair, and before I can think, he brings my lips to his, and I taste Gabe Foster for the first time outside my incoherent dreams.

He tastes of the sweet spices of the Glühwein, and for a second he rests his lips against mine as if stunned that he's kissing me. Then a moan leaves his mouth and enters mine, and my lips open to his, and he takes. His thick tongue dances with mine, and I can feel his panting breaths heavy on my face.

One or both of us groan, and the kiss goes wild. In the warm gloom of our corner, he eats at my mouth as if starving, and I kiss him back frantically, sending my hands travelling over him to feel the wide width of his shoulders and the big, strong chest.

I rub my fingertips over the springing hair there, as he sucks my tongue into his mouth as if it's my cock. Then I find one of his nipples which is tight and raised, and I flick it with my fingernail.

A hoarse, rattling groan leaves him, and for one brief second his hand drops and I arch into it, as he grips my cock through the thin material of my ski pants and gives it one long, firm stroke.

However, that one action seems to wake him up. I feel his body freeze, and then there's only coldness against me, where before there had been the intense heat of his body. I open my eyes, the haze of lust still making me dopey, only to find him sitting back. The old familiar coolness has returned to his eyes, replacing the heated darkness that promised so much.

I want to grab him, to gather him against me. I want to be in a bed lying naked in the warm darkness, feeling his weight on me, and his cock filling me. Unfortunately, this trip away from normality has left me with so many other half-formed desires and yearnings, I can't list them in my head anymore.

All I know is that this man is special to me. He has the ability to make me feel more than any other man I've ever met. He makes me angry and challenges me, almost at the same time as making me laugh and filling me with a strong sense of protectiveness towards him. He makes me feel alive, the way that my mum had always promised me would happen when I met someone serious. But I know looking at him that I still mean absolutely nothing to him.

The sharp pain and chill from that thought is enough to make me draw back and take a second breath. I glance around quickly, suddenly concerned because we haven't exactly been discreet, but the action is at the bar, and no one seems to have noticed that my world has just spun on its axis.

Sadly, that includes the man who has done the spinning. I look over at him, and he swallows hard and says stiffly, "I'm sorry, Dylan. That should never have happened."

CHAPTER EIGHT

To: Gabe Foster

From: Dylan Mitchell

I have prepared the fourth pot of coffee for you to taste. I pray that this one meets your exacting taste buds, because I do actually have plans for the rest of my life.

One Week Later

I sigh and slump slightly before flicking the key card into the slot outside my hotel room in Amsterdam. The light turns green, and I walk in and lean against the door with a relieved sigh. It has been a truly fucking awful week, only topped by the last two days in Verbier which had been hellish.

We'd walked in silence back to the chalet the night of the skiing lesson, with the tension simmering between us. At one point, I'd slipped on some ice and he'd grabbed me, holding me close enough to see how dark his eyes had gone before shoving me away as if I had Ebola. That had been the last time I'd been close enough to touch him.

He'd conducted our work time in the chalet after this as if I was in another room. He was distant and cool, and when I'd met his eyes, it was like ice had flowed over him. There were no more cosy working sessions while the others went out. Instead, he'd gone out with them, leaving me alone to do what I wanted.

It had hurt to find out he'd told Fletcher that he couldn't ski. Fletcher had immediately booked lessons for him, which was probably something I should have done in the first place.

I'd taken to walking out by myself or skiing solo, taking the cable car up to the top of the mountain. I'd seen them all once when I was drinking a hot chocolate, prior to skiing back down. They'd been sitting out at a table with a fantastic view and the sun shining down on them. They'd looked rich and sleek, and more than one eye had been on the group, but I doubted anyone else watching Gabe slide a hand into Fletcher's hair and kiss him would have flinched the way that I did. I had put down my drink and left, and that night I hadn't gone to dinner. Instead, I had sat in the kitchen with the rest of the staff. He hadn't sent for me.

The situation hadn't improved when we got back, but it did ease somewhat because Gabe had vanished to help one of the other departments with a case, leaving me alone to finalise the arrangements for the conference.

It had always been customary for me to go with Gabe when he was giving lectures, as he needed my organisational help, and more often my social skills to get him out of whatever situation his high-handedness had got him into. However, for the whole week I'd half expected him to tell me that he didn't need me this time, but he'd said nothing.

He had, however, for the first time in our history taken an earlier flight on his own, telling me coolly that he was meeting friends for drinks in Amsterdam. I'd nodded numbly and tried hard to enjoy the luxury of business class on my own, but it was difficult when I was used to his acerbic commentary.

I shake my head. *Enough malingering.* I look up for the first time at my room and gasp. Surely there has to have been a mistake, because I'm in one of the nicest rooms I've ever seen. I look around. Strike that, I'm in a suite. It's decorated sumptuously with black and gold wallpaper, and has tall windows through which I can see lines of trees swaying in the breeze. The French oak bed is huge and made up with pristine, white bed linens, and through one door I can see a lounge area with purple, velvet sofas and a large, flat screen TV. Through another I can see a bathroom with an unusual copper, free standing tub under a Velux window. The whole suite looks like a set in a play.

I lean over to look out of the window at the charming, gabled houses lining the canal, and the water sparkling in the evening sunshine. A young couple wanders past, hand in hand and laughing with their heads together, and I feel a pang of envy that I immediately force to one side.

I look around and sigh. *Okay, lovely as this room is, it's time for me to man up to the mistake.* I grab the card and make my way out, and back to the elevator. The hotel is truly gorgeous, combining luxury with a boutique feel, and I'm not surprised that Gabe always stays here when he's in Amsterdam.

The elevator doors open and I make my way over to the reception desk, which is really just an antique, shiny walnut table only just large enough to hold the sleek console. Practical it isn't. Behind it sits a dark-haired woman dressed in the hotel uniform.

"Hello," I smile. "I've just checked in for the conference, and I think you might have made a mistake with the room that I've been given."

She looks immediately distressed, as if I've announced that

there's a dead body in my room. "Oh dear, I'm *so* sorry. Is there something wrong with the room?"

"Oh God, no," I laugh, running my hands through my hair. "It's just far too nice for me. I was expecting a standard single room, and instead I've been given a suite."

She takes my name and taps busily away on the sleek keyboard in front of her, staring intently at the monitor before shaking her head. "Oh no, Mr Mitchell, there's no mistake. Mr Foster rang up a week ago and changed the previous booking to include that suite specifically for you."

"Not for himself?" I check, my heart hammering slightly.

"No, definitely not. Mr Foster is in the Jansen Suite, where he always stays when he's with us." She smiles happily. "Can I do anything else for you? Would you like a selection of newspapers delivered in the morning, or to have breakfast in your room?"

I shake my head. "No, that's fine, thank you. I have an appointment with Lars de Vries in a few minutes to finalise the details for Mr Foster's speech, but I'll let you know if I need anything else."

I step away from the desk as she smiles her goodbye, her smile wide and white. My brain is whirring. *Why did Gabe book me in a suite?* He's never done that before. That's not to say he's a skinflint, because I always travel very well when I'm with him. He's a generous boss, unlike some of the other partners who believe that their assistants should stay in rooms at which a dog would turn its nose up. One of the Grinchy old gits had once even made his assistant stay over the other side of town from him. She'd had to travel across town every day at an early hour just to be ready for him, and he had kept her late, giving no thought to her safety in going back to her room.

However, travelling well with Gabe doesn't usually mean a suite. A thought comes to mind that maybe he's making up for the accommodation in Verbier, but I dismiss it immediately. Much as I hate it, I don't think I come into his thoughts that much, or at all.

A tingle on the back of my neck makes me turn with a sense of inevitability, and I watch as Gabe walks into the foyer. He's dressed casually in dark jeans, a garnet-red jumper and Vans, and he looks amazing with the tan still on his olive skin from the time away.

However, my attention is fixed on the man that he's with. Stunningly beautiful, he's willowy thin with dark-red hair. Dressed in tight, black jeans and a black jumper, he's clinging to Gabe's hand with his body nestled close to him, and possession stamped all over him.

From the safety of my spot behind a pillar, I watch them with a pain in my chest. I know Gabe and Fletcher aren't faithful to each other. I've had enough evidence over the years to prove that. But to see this hurts, because I know now that when he pulled back from me in Verbier, it wasn't because he *couldn't* do anything. It was because he didn't want to. He didn't want me, and all the distance since then has been his way of telling me this. Maybe he's being kind and letting me grab the hint, rather than being blunt, but my face still burns.

A wild thought comes to me that maybe he and Fletcher have discussed me. Maybe he told Fletcher I have a crush on him. I feel mortification and hurt, but also inside me a tiny ember of anger catches light, because what the fuck is wrong with me? Yes, I believe in monogamy and being faithful, but that doesn't make me a dinosaur, and it doesn't mean that I think people who do the opposite are wrong. I believe in live and let live, but maybe they think I'm provincial and naive. I know Fletcher does, so maybe Gabe does too.

I take one last, long look at the two of them standing at the desk, with Gabe's hand resting familiarly on the redhead's arse. Then I make myself turn away, grateful that they haven't seen me mooning in the corner. I'm going to go back to my fancy suite and order the most expensive and fattening items on the room service menu, and then I'm going to drink my way through the minibar, and charge it all to Gabe.

It's at this point, with the luck known only to me, that I hear my name being shouted over the foyer. I close my eyes, and open them in time to see Gabe instantly stiffen and turn his head around looking for me. I sigh and turn to see a man coming towards me. He's tall and slender, standing at about six foot. His dark hair is worn sleek to his head, and he has very blue eyes in an angular, good looking face.

"It is Mr Mitchell, isn't it?" he asks in beautifully accented English.

I force a smile, aware in the corner of my eye that Gabe is approaching, and dragging his protesting date along with him. "That's me. Are you Mr de Vries?"

"I am, but it's Lars, please." I put out my hand and he takes it, holding it a second longer than normal. I see his eyes flick down my body, before sliding back to mine as he smiles. The whole smooth move takes only seconds and impresses the fuck out of me.

I raise my eyebrow and smile politely. "It's nice to meet you. Thank you for marking out the time so we can go over the arrangements for tomorrow."

He shakes his head. "Not at all. It's a pleasure. Mr Foster is a very valued customer of the hotel, and I know that we want to see him happy."

The anger coils in me. "Do we really?" I say morosely, and he looks askance at me, before turning as Gabe walks up to us.

Up close he looks tired, with huge, dark circles under his eyes, and to my knowledgeable eye, he looks a bit ragged. It's the way he always looks when there's a problem at work, and his busy mind is working to untangle it. *Maybe I'm the problem* I think grimly. *He's probably working out how to hand me my severance package.*

"Ah, Mr Foster," Lars says politely, holding out his hand to Gabe to shake. "It's a pleasure, sir."

Gabe's date huffs slightly like a spoilt child, and I roll my eyes. Why he always goes for such high maintenance men is beyond me, as he's congenitally incapable of delivering any social niceties.

I look up in time to see that Gabe has caught my eye roll, and from the look of him he isn't happy. My thoughts shift to seeing him wrapped around the ginger, and for just a second, inevitably move to that night and his lips against mine. My spine stiffens. *Fuck him* I think defiantly.

Lars is still talking, unaware that Gabe and I are now actively glaring at each other.

"Mr de Vries was just saying how we all *live* to make you happy." My words break across the pleasantries like a gunshot.

"Some more than others," he returns snidely.

"Yes, perhaps that's because the others might have an inkling of your charming personality," I say sweetly. Lars and the redhead are now watching us, with their heads moving from side to side like they're at Wimbledon.

"Oh, really," he drawls and shifts to an upright stance, losing the redhead's hand in the process. "And which group do you find your-self in, Dylan?"

I smile with no warmth. "I'm wherever you put me, like an obedient pet. Just like all the men in your life. I jump when you say jump, just like Rover the happy, executive assistant."

"*Okay,*" Gabe says sharply, gripping my arm and dragging me past the other men. "I just need to have a word with Mr Mitchell," he tells the two men. "We'll only be a couple of seconds."

"My, my," I say snippily. "Only a couple of seconds? That must be how you manage to fit in so many men all the time." I cast a disparaging look at his groin. "Performance issues."

"What the fuck is the matter with you?" he hisses, shoving me into a corner out of sight of the others.

"There's absolutely nothing wrong with me. I'm just making sure you're happy. You know I live to do that, so tell me are you happy?"

He glares helplessly at me for a second and then leans forward, grasping my arm. "If this is about Verbier -"

Heat travels down my arm. "Why the fuck would it be about that?" I hiss, grabbing my arm free. "That meant fuck all, didn't it?"

We stare at each other for a minute, breaths coming fast in agita-tion, and just for a second, I think his gaze falls to my lips. Then his expression hardens, and he steps back. "Yes, fuck all," he says coldly.

"Excellent," I enunciate, clearly mocking him. "Now if you'll excuse me, I'll get back to the job of making sure that you have everything you need."

"I don't think even you can do that," he says hollowly. I spin back to look at him, but he's moving too, and I watch as he walks back to the other men who are looking anywhere but at each other. Grabbing the redhead's hand, he says something to Lars who smiles, before moving his man towards the elevators.

When they get there, as the man is talking animatedly to him, his head shoots up and he sees me watching. Our eyes cling for a second, until with a cold smile, he breaks eye contact, bends down, and takes the redhead's mouth in a long kiss.

Bile fills my mouth and I swallow hard, but I make sure my face is expressionless when Gabe comes up for air. Ignoring the man clutching him he immediately looks at me, and I make sure he sees me look him up and down dismissively, before moving away to where Lars is standing waiting patiently.

I give him a quick flicker of a smile. "Sorry to keep you waiting."

"Not at all. Is there something for you to sort out with Mr Foster? Anything you need to fix, because I can wait?"

I look back at the elevators. The two men have gone. "Nothing," I say hollowly. "There's nothing fixable here."

✉

The next afternoon I sit at the back of the crowd, listening to the closing lines of his speech while trying to read something on my Kindle. It's futile, because every inch of me is trained on that deep, rich voice.

Somebody slips into the seat next to me, and I close my Kindle cover, looking over to see Lars smiling at me. "It has gone well?" he asks, leaning close so that he can whisper.

I nod. "As usual."

"I was wondering ..." He pauses. "You are in Amsterdam on your own, yes?" I nod. "Well, would you like to come out with my friends and me, to grab some dinner and visit a club?"

At that point, Gabe finishes, and everyone stands up to clap enthusiastically. The two of us automatically do the same, and I think hard. Gabe will more than likely be making his own arrangements with the redhead, and the thought of sitting lonely in my room with a meal for one doesn't appeal to my pride. *Fuck him,* the new defiant me thinks. *If he needs me for anything he'll have to wait.*

Everyone sits down, and the event organiser stands up to wrap up the event. I lean close and speak into Lars's ear. "I'd love that. Thank you."

He smiles, but I become aware that someone is staring at me. Craning my head discreetly I see Gabe sitting on the podium, his silver-grey eyes looking at how close Lars is sitting to me. He has a dark frown on his face.

Lars looks up following my gaze, and gives a mock shudder. "Ooh, your boss looks very cross, like he's planning to murder someone."

"Me, probably," I say gloomily.

He smiles. "He is a tricky customer. Rather you than me." I shrug, and he leans in and hugs me. "I'll wait in the foyer for you. Is eight o'clock too early?"

I smile distractedly as I watch Gabe's hand close in a tight fist. Something is annoying him. Maybe he'd had a tough time with questions when I'd nipped to the loo. "Yes, eight o'clock is fine," I say slowly.

A few hours later, I take a look at myself in the long, antique mirror near the door. I had a nap this afternoon and then had a long, hot shower, so I feel clean and rested. I'm dressed in my dark, skinny jeans with a hunter-green v-neck t-shirt. The v is deep and shows off quite a portion of my chest, which is tanned from Verbier. I slide my feet into my stone-coloured desert boots, and then grab my parka as it's bloody freezing outside.

I'm more than ready for a meal and to go to a club. Maybe I'll even find someone and have a good, hard fuck. That's probably what the matter is with me at the moment. It's been a bit of a dry spell.

I shake my head, grab my room card, and let myself out of the room only to jerk to a stop and stare at Gabe. He's standing at my door and obviously preparing to knock.

"What are you doing here?" I ask, forgetting my anger for a second, which is probably a good idea as he's still my boss.

He runs his eyes over me, and they seem to linger on my package cupped lovingly by the tight denim of my jeans. "I was coming to get you for dinner."

"Sounds a wee bit cannibalistic. Are they not serving normal options on the menu then?" He regards me stonily. "Oh, bad luck anyway," I make myself say cheerily. "I've been asked to go out and see Amsterdam. I didn't think you'd mind."

"Why?"

"Well, because I thought that you'd found your own company," I say lamely.

"But I normally eat with you on these trips," he says stubbornly, and I hold my hands out helplessly.

"It's the boring dinner for the speakers. Be real, Gabe. You don't need me to do anything for you tonight. It's just a meal."

He shakes his head. "I don't want you to come to help me. I just thought we'd eat together like always." For a second he looks sad, which has the effect of making me angry again, because for one brief moment, I was prepared to ditch Lars and go with Gabe, anything to make him happy. *Grow a fucking backbone* I tell myself. *Man the fuck up and get on with your life.*

I make myself smile. "Well, sorry, but I've already made plans."

"Are you going out with Lars?" he interrupts, his voice tense. "He was sitting very close to you today."

I stare at him. Anyone else would say he's jealous, but he can't be. He doesn't want me and made that very clear in Verbier, but apparently he can't bear anyone to try and have a nibble. *Fuck him.*

"Yes, him and some friends." I look at my watch. "Well, I must be going. I should be meeting him about now. Have a good night, Gabe."

I leave him standing outside my room, and I can feel his eyes watch me every step of the way. It's harder than I would like to leave.

Lars's friends prove to be nice. They're artistic, and as he and I seem to be the only ones that work in the corporate world, they entertain themselves by taking the gentle piss out of us.

"I do not mind," he shouts into my ear. "I have ambitions of my own, and what I do at the moment suits me." We're sitting thigh to thigh on a small sofa in a nightclub in the Rembrandtplein area. The large table in front of us is crammed with empty glasses and bottles, and we lost his friends to the dance floor half an hour ago. Lars however, seems content to sit and chat.

"You are very good-looking," he says suddenly, trailing one long finger up my thigh to linger at my groin.

I sigh at my very uninterested crotch and smile weakly. "So are you." The irony is that he looks gorgeous, especially dressed as he is now in all black.

His finger moves, running along my zipper. "But yet I think you are still not interested. It is Mr Foster, yes?"

I look up startled. "Oh, no I -"

He interrupts me. "It is very obvious, my friend, the intensity of emotion."

I groan and throw my head back. "Shit, I have got to learn not to show my feelings on my face. My mum always says that I show what I'm feeling all over me."

He looks surprised. "Oh, Dylan, I did not mean you, although yes, I can tell how much you like him. No, I meant Mr Foster."

"*Gabe*," I explode. "Jesus, you must be joking. Arnold Schwarzenegger has more of a range of emotions than Gabe."

He smiles and shakes his head. "No joke. I saw it immediately. Mr Foster has very intense feelings for you. It is telegraphed all over his face, and when you came back to speak to me in the foyer yesterday he was watching very closely from the elevator."

"No, he wasn't. He was kissing the redhead."

He shakes his head authoritatively. "Not really. I think that was done to rile you up, and maybe push you away. I do not know. I think Mr Foster is a very confusing man and hard to read, but I know one thing ..." He looks at me. "When you hugged me to you this afternoon, he was watching, and his whole body said that he wanted to rip you away from me."

I sigh. "I wish that was true," I say sadly, something about Lars making me trust him. "But even if he felt something, we're very wrong for each other. We don't mesh."

"Sometimes that makes the best relationships." He shrugs. "Sometimes the worst." He makes a face. "Who knows which one you will be?"

I smile. "Neither of those. We're nothing." I look at him. "I like you, and I'm sorry that you've had a wasted night."

He shakes his head. "It's never wasted time when you meet a new friend. You will give me your number and we can text each other, and if you are in Amsterdam again I will take you out and show you more."

I nod, giving him my number which he taps into his phone and then gives me his. He looks up, and the smile on his face turns thoughtful as he looks at something over my shoulder. "We are friends now, yes?" I nod. "Then I apologise in advance, Dylan."

I open my mouth to ask what for, but he moves quickly, pulling me to him and fitting his mouth to mine. For a second I'm held immobile by shock, and he slides his tongue into my mouth, holding my hair in his hands. Before I can push him away, he sits back and smiles at someone behind me. "Hello Mr Foster, what a surprise to see you here."

Shock holds me rigid for a second, and then I twist in my seat to find Gabe standing there with a look that could kill on his face. He's dressed in black jeans and a long-sleeved, black shirt, which highlights the length of his body and the width of his broad shoulders. He looks angry and hot as hell, and my cock stirs when it wouldn't even twitch at Lars's kiss. *I'm fucked.*

Lars nods happily at something and stands up gracefully. "And now I will go and find my friends and dance. Dylan, I will see you again I know. Goodnight, Mr Foster."

I smile weakly at him, and Gabe completely ignores him, focusing his attention instead on glaring at me. When he's gone the silence grows, and the sound of the music swells between us. I watch Gabe's hands open and close in fists. "What are you doing here?" I shout. "Did you know I was here?"

He shakes his head, and with that sudden, swift grace that is so much a part of him, he throws himself next to me in the space that Lars has just vacated. He stares at me. "I asked the woman at the desk where Lars had gone tonight, and she told me this was his usual haunt."

"Why on earth would you *do* that?" I ask with mounting anger. "Were you fucking checking up on me, Gabe? Because I've got to be honest, you've got the whole dog in the manger situation going on with you at the moment."

He's breathing heavily, his chest rising and falling swiftly as he stares away as if thinking hard, and then I visibly see something snap in him. It must be his control, because in the next second he turns and brings my face to his. Holding my cheekbones, he looks into my eyes. "Shut the fuck up, Dylan," he says harshly, and then he kisses me.

It isn't a tentative kiss this time. Instead, it's full of heat and a harsh, driving lust, as he takes my mouth, eating at it and groaning deep in his throat. I go under immediately. He stiffens for a second when I wrap my hands around the back of his head, and it occurs to me he's expecting me to throw him off. Instead, I moan and bring him in deeper, sliding my tongue over his and into his mouth, where he meets it and suckles gently on it. One or both of us groan, and then we explode into action.

I sit up and move, and he meets me, bringing me over him until

I'm straddling his lap in this dark corner of the club. The strobe lights flash behind my eyelids, and all around us is the driving beat of Layo & Bushwacka's 'Love Story', but I pay no attention at all. My mind and body are now concentrated on his huge, hard cock, and how it feels against my own as I start to grind against him.

We kiss endlessly, lost to something I've never felt before. Previously I've always kept a part of myself back in these situations, always aware of who's around, because gay men can't afford to be unaware. Maybe it's because it's him and I feel safe, or maybe it's because I've never known such an intense desire before, where I feel like I'll die if he doesn't come inside me. Whatever it is has me fumbling at the zipper on his jeans in seconds, and he's helping me, arching his back to bring his groin nearer to me.

Then he stops and pulls back. His silver eyes have gone dark and heavy with desire, but awareness is returning.

"Not again," I groan, but he shakes his head, taking my mouth again briefly with a harsh groan before pulling back.

"Not here," he says, his voice wrecked. "I don't want you here like this. Let me take you back to the hotel. I want you in my bed."

"You're not backing out?" I ask in amazement, and he shakes his head firmly.

He grabs my narrow hips, hauling me into him, and we both moan at the feel of the other's hard cock. "I can't," he gasps urgently. "I can't stop now, Dylan. I know all the arguments I've used in the past off by heart. You work for me, and I'm not what you're looking for. But I can't stop this anymore. I need to be inside you so badly, it's all I can think about. Maybe we can fuck this feeling away."

His words penetrate my daze, and I pull back. It almost sounds as if he resents wanting me. Then he grinds up into me and groans. "Come back with me *please*, Dylan. I need to fuck you so bad."

I look down at him. I know deep inside me that this is going to end badly, but a bit of me feels it's inevitable. I run my fingertips over his wickedly arched eyebrows. "Yes."

CHAPTER NINE

To: Dylan Mitchell

From: Gabe Foster

Mr Thorpe complimented me today on having such a quirky assistant. I think quirky might have been a euphemism for scatty disorganisation.

Somehow we manage to leave the club, stopping every second to kiss and grind against each other. I'm so hard it's as if I can feel the throbbing in my blood, and for a brief, coherent second, I feel worry because I've never in my life been so desperate for someone.

Then he grabs me and pulls me down a side alley, and thrusts me against the wall, crowding in on me. I feel the harsh rasp of the brickwork against the bare skin of my back where he rucked up my shirt, and then he kisses me again, and I go under.

He sends his big, warm hands over the skin of my chest, groaning deeply as he dips and caresses the muscles of my six-pack. I let out a choked grunt as he detours and pinches my nipples hard, and the sound seems to act like accelerant on a fire. He gasps and grabs my arse, lifting me so I can curl my legs around him.

I'm six foot tall, but he lifts me as if I'm thistledown, and then lowers me until my crotch connects with his hard cock. We both moan lustily and start to grind against each other, the heat and pressure making my eyes roll back in my head.

Some men walk past the entry to the alley, and I hear shouted comments, that while in Dutch, manage to convey approval. However, it brings us back to enough of our senses to realise that we're about to fuck in an alley.

Gabe heaves out a sigh and grips my legs, lowering me gently to the ground. I go to move away, but he stuns me by grabbing me close in a tight hug, lowering his face to my neck. I shudder as I feel his panting breaths against my sensitive neck.

"Not here," he mutters and I nod, daring to wrap my arms around him. I expect him to stiffen and move away like a trapped, wild animal, but to my surprise he moves closer, nestling into my embrace with a throaty sound.

I swallow hard at the lump in my throat and run my fingers through his hair. "No, I don't think the firm's travel budget includes bail for public indecency."

He snorts out a laugh that rumbles through my body like thunder, and I can't help but grind against the hard cock prodding my stomach. "Jesus," he whispers. "It's like fucking fire." He sighs and then pulls back slightly to look in my face. His eyes are heavy-lidded, his lips full, and his hair is wild from where I've run my fingers through it. "Let's go back to the hotel," he says in a low, rough voice.

I stare at him for a second that seems to stretch into eternity, and he shifts uneasily until I hold out my hand. "Let's go."

Something that looks like deep relief crosses his face, but it's gone in a second as he grabs my hand, tugging me after him as he strides back into the street and signals an approaching taxi. I slide in as he opens the door for me, relishing the toasty warmth after the cold outside. The taxi smells of spices and dry heat, and when Gabe slides in next to me and shuts the door, it's as though we're in a dark sanctuary. He gives the driver the hotel name, and then curls his big body next to mine, his hand sliding down my thigh to clasp it in a close, warm grip.

However, some sanity has been restored to my empty brain, and I shift to stare at him. "Why now?" I ask quietly. "You said it would never happen, so what made you change your mind?"

The streetlights illuminate his expression, which shows a wry tenderness for a second. "I wondered when the interrogation would start." He laughs. "I admit I hoped it would be after I got my cock inside you, but I should have known better."

I shake my head. "You *do* know better."

"I do." There's a brief silence as if he's thinking hard, and then he sighs and shifts closer. He lifts his hand and tangles it in my hair which he seems to be fascinated with. "I just couldn't stand another minute without touching you, Dylan. You drive me mad."

"I know *that*," I say tartly. "You say it so often, it's practically written in my job description."

He huffs out a laugh. "It's more than that." He shoots me a sidelong glance. "It's always been more. I've wanted you for a very long time."

"How long?" I ask, inhaling sharply.

He shoots me a wry glance, passion and something else clinging to those clever eyes. "About thirty seconds into your interview."

"*What?*"

He shrugs. "I got hard in your interview. You were so much. So full of life, and bold and funny. I hesitated over employing you, to be honest."

"Why?"

"Because you were, and are, very distracting to me."

"So why wait all this time?"

"Because you're my assistant," he says sharply. "I thought that if I ended up fucking you, you'd leave like everyone else." I file away the *everyone else* comment for later perusal, as he keeps talking. "Then I got to know you, and I started to look forward to seeing you every day, because you made me laugh and challenged me every second you were with me." He lifts his hand and caresses my face. "No one else has ever done that, and I grew to value it. It became so precious to me that I never wanted to fuck it up with sex and then a fuck off."

I breathe in sharply. This is the real heart of the matter. "Would it have been a fuck off?"

He sighs heavily and shoots me an apologetic look. "Yes, it always is, Dylan. There are no exceptions."

Hurt flares inside me. "What about Fletcher?" I move as if to get away, but his hand shoots down to my hip and he holds me firm. Realisation dawns. "Oh my God, what *about* Fletcher? I mean, I know he's the devil's spawn, and you've shared most of London's male population between the two of you, but he's still your boyfriend."

He snorts out a laugh. "Not most of London. I haven't got the time for that."

"But you made time for a lot of men," I say sharply. "I won't be part of that with you. I don't particularly enjoy threesomes, especially not with someone I fucking hate as much as I hate Fletcher."

He stiffens. "So you've done them before?"

"Of course I have," I say tartly. "I know you persist in seeing me as Anne of Green Gables, but I'm a twenty-seven-year-old gay man. I've done loads of things."

"I don't want to hear about them," he says harshly, and then stills as if he's surprised himself. He turns to me. "I know I was with Fletcher for a while, but we were never really together in the usual sense of the word, and now it's done. I'm not with Fletcher anymore. He moved out after Verbier."

"*What?*" I yell, making the taxi driver jump and swerve slightly. "Sorry sir," I shout, aware of Gabe laughing silently. I turn back to him. "Why, and why didn't I know?"

He shrugs. "There was no need for you to know anything. It was very quick. We had a huge row over Verbier." I go to ask what the row was about but he shakes his head, and I subside as he carries on talking. "I'd had enough. There was nothing there but sex, and in the end, it wasn't even good sex."

"So you just fucked him off after a year?"

He looks at me sharply. "Don't say it like I'm a bastard. We meant nothing to each other, apart from sex and convenience. Why stay when that's no good anymore, and the other person literally bores the fuck out of you? He wasn't that bothered anyway. He never loved me, and I didn't love him. Apart from a few histrionics and plates thrown, his stuff was packed and he was out in an hour."

I consider him. "I'd like to encourage you to consider togetherness, and the warmth of shared knowledge and experiences."

"But you're not going to?" he drawls, and I shrug.

"Fuck no. I hate the tosser. If you wanted to spend a year with someone who thinks intelligent conversation is a recap of 'Hollyoaks', then on your own head be it."

He gives a shout of laughter, and tugs me into what would have been a hug with anyone else. However, as soon as my body hits his, his laughter dies and he shudders in a breath that I echo. "Jesus," he mutters, running his hands down my body and tightening his grip when he feels the shudder that I can't hide.

As if he can't help it, he lowers his head and seizes my lips in a deep kiss, tangling our tongues together before sucking gently on mine. I groan under my breath and twist to get closer, feeling like there's a direct line between my tongue and my cock.

He moans and drags his lips away, and I make an inarticulate protest that dies away to a grunt, as he lowers his mouth to lick and suck at the side of my neck. It's almost as if he has some sort of presentiment about my body, because he lingers there, sucking and mouthing at the soft skin of my neck, before biting down gently on the tendon. It sends a hot flash through my body, and I arch upwards, making a choked sound of lust as pre-come paints my briefs with hot wetness.

The click of the indicator and the slowing of the taxi drags us apart, and he shifts to sit away from me. His chest rises and falls rapidly, the sound of his breathing loud in the dark silence. "Are you sure?" he asks hoarsely. "I'm not offering anything more than this, Dylan."

I drag air into my lungs and press my hand to my throbbing cock in an attempt to relieve the pressure. He growls under his breath at my action. "I don't care," I gasp out. "I just need you inside me, Gabe. I can't wait."

"Fuck!" he mutters, breathing in sharply, before throwing some money at the driver and opening the door. "Get inside. We're going to my room," he mutters. "No more talking."

I don't remember walking through the foyer or the elevator. It's all a dark-red haze, which clears slightly as I insert his key card into the door, and then clouds again as he grabs me from behind, arms over my shoulders and his hard cock thrusting against my arse. I grunt and lean against the door, grabbing the back of his thighs and tugging at him, silently asking for more pressure.

For a second he rests against me, a groan rumbling up the chest that's pressing against my back. Then he reaches forward and opens the door. "Inside," he says in a low, hoarse voice. "I need total privacy for what I'm going to do to you."

I groan out a laugh. "Promises, promises."

"A solid-gold declaration," he says harshly and pushes me through the door.

I spin around to face him, backing up against the wall. I have a second to see the heavy-lidded face with the full lips reddened by our kisses, and then he's on me in two strides. He grabs me by the back of the neck, opening my lips with his and sending his tongue deep, and it's like being taken over by a whirlwind.

His lips are soft and full against mine, and we kiss for what seems like ages until my lips are sore and my cheeks abraded by his scruff. It feels fucking brilliant. Finally, he pushes me back and stands away, drawing in great gulps of air. I make an inarticulate sound of protest, and he shakes his head. "No, let me look at you."

For a second I'm flummoxed. This is not the way that my sexual encounters normally go. Usually, we're both hot and horny. Clothes come off, and hard fucking begins. Some of my confusion must show because a smile quirks his mouth, dying away to a smouldering look as he lowers himself to sit in the armchair by the bed.

"Take your shirt off," he says in a deep voice, and then he raises his hand as I start to strip off my t-shirt frantically. "Slowly."

I stare at him, and my brain comes slightly back into working order. *He wants a show.* I smile. *I'll give him one.* I start to raise my t-shirt an inch at a time, making sure to drag the fabric aside slightly so that he gets a flash of skin. His breathing accelerates as my chest comes into view, my nipples tightening in the cool air of the hotel room. Then, almost unconsciously, he lowers his hand to his groin to press against the hard thrust of his cock.

"Take it all off," he mutters harshly, his gaze fixed on the muscles of my abdomen. He looks up, startled when I don't move.

I make sure he's watching when I lower the t-shirt and let myself smile slowly. "Gabe, I'm fully aware that you've probably had the upper hand in all of your sexual encounters since the very first time. However, what on earth gave you the idea that *I'm* in any way compliant and biddable?"

The haze of desire in his eyes warms and turns into something else that I can't quite recognise, and then he leans back. "I'm sorry. I forgot for a second that you're incapable of taking orders."

I give a mock shudder. "Say it again, but make it your office voice." He stares at me. "You know the one. It's two parts incoherent rage, to one part bewilderment."

He gives a great guffaw of laughter. "Fuck you, Dylan." He looks puzzled for a second. "I think that might be the first time that I've laughed during sex."

"That just means it was never good sex. All good sex comes with a side order of inappropriate laughter."

He shakes his head in bewilderment. "I'll take your word for it. It's weird." He leans back in his seat. His legs are spread, and his head tipped back with his eyes challenging. "Okay, what's next, boss?"

I shudder theatrically. "I see why you like it. Just the word makes me feel all powerful."

"*Dylan*," he warns, and I shake my head, the mood changing as mercurially as it always does with us, from laughter to seriousness and back again.

"Take *your* shirt off, Gabe."

He runs his tongue over his pouting lower lip, wetting it so that it glistens enticingly. I stare hard and become aware that he's now smiling rakishly - I must have got lost in the curve of his mouth for a minute. I shake my head. "Stop trying to addle me with your fuck me lips." I look at him. "I'm going to fuck them at some point tonight."

A shudder runs through him as he reaches up, and slowly, the way it should be done, strips off his shirt button by button, until the hairy expanse of his chest comes into view. I've seen his chest so many times, but somehow knowing that it's going to be pressed against me makes it infinitely sexier than it ever was before. He strips his shirt off and throws it challengingly down in front of me.

"My turn," he drawls. "Take the shirt all the way off, Dylan, and then get those jeans off."

Holding his eyes, I throw my t-shirt onto the floor, kick my shoes off, and slowly unzip my jeans, the harsh rasp loud in the quiet room. He moves as I lower them, and I gasp as he unbuttons his own jeans and reaches in, withdrawing his cock. It glistens in the low light of the room and I groan. It's long and thick, with a prominent vein running down the underside. The head is wet and angry looking.

"Don't stop," he says harshly, and I hastily kick off my jeans, all finesse long gone. Without him asking, I remove my socks, because socks are just not sexy. Then I hesitate, my fingers playing with the edge of my snug boxer briefs. He breathes in harshly and nods, before fisting his cock in a tight grip, and beginning to pump the long length.

His eyes are blown and look almost gunmetal grey, and I hold his gaze as I slowly tug my briefs down. They catch slightly on the hard length of my dick, and I moan at the abrasive feeling. He chokes out a grunt as I lower them. "Turn around," he says thickly, and then moans when I comply. "Fuck, your arse is beautiful, Dylan." The sound of his fist moving is wet and obscene in the silence. "I can't wait to fucking stick my cock in there, and feel all that hot tightness."

I moan and my hand strays down to my own cock. It's hard as a brick, and it's a pleasure pain to touch it. "Yes," Gabe gasps. "Touch yourself." I feel warmth, and then his hands come out and he grabs my arse, pulling me nearer to him and caressing the taut globes. "Beautiful," he mutters. "Bend over."

Groaning and hoping that I know what's coming, I bend forward and push my arse against him. Then my thoughts fly away, as I feel all the nerve endings in my hole come to life, as he paints a wet stripe along my taint to my hole. When he reaches it, he pauses, flirting his tongue gently over the sensitive area.

I hastily grab my thighs to steady myself and shudder. "*God*," I groan. "Oh God, Gabe."

"Yes," he murmurs, his voice so thick I can hardly make out the words. "You taste so fucking good." Then I feel the hot muscle of his tongue flick gently over my hole, back and forth. The pleasure is almost too much, riding on the edge of unbearable, and I grunt and groan, pushing my arse shamelessly against his face until he moans and gives in. Pointing his tongue, he opens up the hole steadily, and I feel the moist slipperiness inside me. I cry out, riding the wave of pleasure just as I ride his tongue.

The room is full of the dirty sounds of wet suckling and pants and groans, and I shudder at the sharp feeling of his stubble abrading the sensitive area. Suddenly I feel familiar lightning racing down my spine, and I pull away quickly, grabbing the base of my cock to stop myself from coming.

He gives an inarticulate sound of protest, which turns to surprise as I whip around and fall to my knees. Grabbing his cock, I take a second to appreciate the sight of the warm prick which is visibly throbbing and sloppy with pre-come. I lower my head and take him down to the base in one quick movement. He shouts out incomprehensible, jumbled words as I start a heated tugging and sucking motion, tasting the tang of salt.

I feel his hands come to rest on me, fluttering like baby birds and seeming unsure of how far to push me. I've never been more thankful for my complete lack of a gag reflex, and the hours spent practising with a banana when I was a teenager. I reach up and grab his hands, pulling them down to rest on my head in silent encouragement.

He pushes his fingers into my hair and groans loud and long, as I pull off him to lick and suckle the prominent vein on his cock, tracing the length of his dick and bathing it in wetness before blowing on it. He cries out and writhes towards me in mute instruction, so I suck him back down. His hands move, one twining in my hair and exerting subtle pressure, while the other traces round my throat and presses gently to feel his dick there.

"God, so good," he groans, as I flit my tongue around the sensitive head. He's not cut, and the foreskin is retracted, showing a juicy, plump head. I know this is more sensitive than my own, protected as it usually is by the skin. I flick the tip of my tongue into his slit, and I'm rewarded with a sudden burst of salty liquid before he shouts out and pulls me off his cock.

I sit back, panting and palming my cock, staring at him. He looks utterly debauched, lying back against the chair like a king, with his wet cock glistening and me kneeling at his feet. His eyes are closed, red flags run across his cheeks and his breathing saws in and out harshly. He opens his eyes and I groan. "Bend over the bed," he says in a harsh grunt. "Arse up."

I shudder and hasten to obey, dragging a pillow down to rest under my stomach and raising my arse. I bury my hot face into the cold sheets and listen to the sound of a drawer opening. Then I hear a packet tearing and the snap of latex, followed by the click of a cap opening. I grind my face into the cold sheets as I feel wet, slick fingers touching my arsehole, and I shout out as he slides one long finger in, circling and reaching inside me, before crooking slightly.

It burns, and heat flies down my body until it feels like all the blood has pooled in my dick. I grind against the soft cotton. "More," I groan. "Give me another."

He grunts out something, and then a second finger enters, the burn making my blood spark. He works me for what seems like forever, slowly adding a third finger and scissoring until I can't stand it anymore. "Fuck me," I groan. "God, please fuck me, Gabe. I *need* you."

He lowers his head for a second, and I feel the harsh silk of his stubble against the sweat of my back. He rubs his face as if coating himself in my fluids, and I moan, the sound loud and desperate. "*Now*, Gabe."

I feel the heated length of his cock, hot and damp in its rubber covering, and for a second I worry because he's big. Then the head of his dick enters me, and all thought stops. Steadily breaching the large gateway muscle, he forces his way in, and I grasp the sheet tightly in my fists, nearly ripping the fabric. I feel an intense pressure and burn, which is just on the pleasurable side of too much. I groan and grunt out an inarticulate sound, and he stills for a minute, his body shivering against mine like a whippet.

"Alright?" he grunts, and I nod frantically. Obeying his cue, he pushes in steadily, inch by inch until he bottoms out and stills. "Wait," he says harshly, and I still, allowing my body to stretch around him.

In the silence, I become aware of the scratch of his chest hair wet with sweat against my back, the heat and heft of his balls as they press against me, and the wiriness of his pubic hair which rubs my hole. Then he moves, and the pressure and dull pain transforms into a glittering stream of pleasure, like fireworks low in my body.

"Fuck!" I shout out, and he groans.

"I've got to -" He trails off breathlessly as his hips move, pulling him back until he's nearly out of me. He croons harshly under his breath, then whips his hips, shuttling his cock back into me hard.

"Yes," I moan. "Fuck me. Do it hard." That's all the encouragement he needs as he begins a fast, deep pistoning, his cock a hot brand inside me, rubbing and stroking and making me insane.

The room fills with the sounds of wet slaps as our bodies meet and the squelch of the lube. Then I feel his hands pulling me up so I'm standing upright, listing hard against him like a drunk. The length of his cock is like a red-hot pipe in my body. He begins to rut hard against me, canting his pelvis back and forth so his cock rubs against my prostate, sending flares running through my body.

I cry out, and he groans. We're almost grappling now, his big body arched over mine, fucking me hard as one brawny arm holds me against his chest. One hand grabs me tight, digging his fingers into the skin over my ribs, while the other runs gently over my face before pushing the palm over my mouth. "Get it wet," he commands, his voice a deep wreck. I moan and lick sloppily at his palm, spit sliding down it and coating my face. A harsh, desperate sound comes from him, and he removes his hand, sliding it down my chest, caressing the slick muscles as he goes and pinching my nipples.

"*Fuck!*" I shout out as the hand lowers, and I look down to see his long fingers wrap around the bobbing, stiff length of my dick. He pumps it hard using my spit as lube, while continuing those battering thrusts in me as he gasps and moans. Then suddenly fire shoots down my spine, and I feel the familiar, insane pressure in my cock and balls.

"I'm going to come," I shout, uncaring of any other hotel guests. "Fuck, I'm going to come."

"Yes," he gasps out, his hand moving quicker. "Come for me, Dylan. Come all over my fucking hand."

My balls are high and tight, and I flush all over and turn cold as the most incredible orgasm I've ever had rushes through me. I look down, managing to keep my eyes open enough to see thick white ropes of come spurt from the slit in my cock, flooding his hand and hitting the sheets.

"God, I can smell your come," he gasps out. Then his thrusts become erratic, and he hauls me tight against him, rutting into me fiercely, until his whole body judders and I feel warmth inside me.

His body slows, until all that's left is a languid thrusting as he rides out the last gasps of his orgasm, and the occasional shudders of aftershock that hit us.

Silence falls for what feels like an aeon, and then his grip tightens. I feel him press a lingering kiss to my back, and he hums as he licks a patch of sweat away. "Tastes good," he murmurs, and incredibly I feel my cock twitch and I shudder. He gives a low hiss of pleasure, and then reaches between us, grabbing the base of his cock and the condom as he pulls out.

I wince and groan and he murmurs something, kissing my neck and ear. "Shower?" he says in my ear, and I nod, turning to face him.

We both still and stare at each other. His face is flushed and still pleasure slack, and I think he's the most relaxed that I've ever seen him. I send my gaze down his body, able to see him properly now that the haze of desire has dimmed a little.

He's truly gorgeous. His chest is wide. The hair widens across his pecs and then narrows to a long strip down his torso, before flaring out around his cock, which, although flaccid, is still an impressive sight. His arms are heavily muscled, with enticing veins running down his forearms, and his legs are muscular and long and gilded with dark hair. All of this body is covered in sleek, olive skin, making him almost glow in the lamplight.

I become aware that he's looking at me just as intensely as I've done to him, and for a second I want to cover myself, because I'm not like him. I'm muscled, but I'm slim with none of his bulk. My fingers twitch, and he must sense my feelings because he looks up and shakes his head. "You're beautiful," he mutters almost reverently. "I knew you would be, but all my imagining didn't do you justice."

"You imagined me then?" I ask, my voice hoarse from earlier.

He sends me a quick glance, smiling hesitantly. "A lot." I gasp, and his eyes sharpen as if recalling himself. "Usually it helps to envision your assistant naked. It combats the desire to throttle them."

"I think you've taken the whole seeing your audience naked in order to negate their power thing, wrong," I say tartly, and he stares hard at me, before something mysterious floods his face and he shrugs.

"Maybe. Maybe not." He reaches out his hand. "Come and shower with me, Dylan."

The bathroom is huge with a massive skylight over a claw-foot bath, but he drags me to the shower which is so big it could fit three men easily. My thoughts shift darkly to his habit of threesomes, but scatter as I feel his hands on me. He squirts shower gel into his hands, and the familiar, spicy scent of oranges rises between us, heady and warm as he washes me.

I don't think I've ever been taken care of like this before. None of my previous lovers ever took the time to learn my body like he does. Like he's imprinting it to memory. Steam billows around us, making him look mysterious and magical. I lean against his hard, warm body feeling like time is slowing, as his hands move deliberately over me, learning the contours of my body.

He leaves no area untouched, and where before I would have baulked at a lover sending wet, soapy fingers between my cheeks to remove the lube, now I just lie quiescent against him. I turn and kiss his wet shoulders, enjoying the bite of his chest hair, and he chuckles under his breath, never stopping his warm, wet caresses.

The knowledge comes to me slowly at first and with no initial fear, seemingly a part of this dreamlike shower. *I'm in love with him.* For a long second, I try out the knowledge for fit, and it does. It fits and fills all the parts of me, stretching out perfectly until I can feel it in my bones. I love this grumpy, irascible, yet sometimes tender man. How could I not? I see now that all the rage he sometimes fills me with is the flipside to this feeling, the other side of the coin.

Then the fear rushes through me, the way pain comes after a cut, because I will surely be in for a world of pain if I let this feeling flourish. How stupid am I to be in love with someone who has never, and will never, want love?

I stiffen involuntarily, which seems to bring Gabe out of his trance. He looks at me, the water streaming down his body like an aftershave ad. "Alright?" he asks, quirking one eyebrow and looking concerned.

I make myself smile. "I'm fine, Gabe."

He stares hard at me for a second, but I must convince him, because he relaxes and turns off the shower before pulling me out of the cubicle. I let him dry me with a big, heated towel, my thoughts tumbled and incoherent until he steps back. Drying himself roughly, he slings the towel over the rail and pulls me out of the bathroom. Letting my hand drop, he walks to the bed, lifting the sheets up with a groan. "God, I'm ready to sleep."

I hesitate. *Is he telling me to go? Is this the start of Gabe's after service?* I feel a cold lump in my stomach, and swallowing hard, I move to my jeans which lie in an abandoned heap on the floor. Shaking them out, I have one leg in them when he comes to life.

"Wait, what are you doing?" he asks, dropping the blankets and coming to me.

"I thought you were ready to go to sleep."

"So you thought that you'd just fuck off," he says, a trace of anger in his eyes.

"No." I hesitate. "Well, to be honest, I thought you'd want me to leave."

He shakes his head, a look of frustration crossing his face, and then he tugs at his hair which usually only happens when he's anxious. "No, I didn't mean that at all." He pauses, before saying low, "I sort of thought that you'd stay here with me for a bit."

"And sleep together?" He gives me his *what the fuck* look, and I can't help but smile. "Gabe, I'm just trying to establish parameters here. I've known you for a couple of years, and you've never given the impression of being a person who likes to snuggle."

He looks revolted. "Fuck, no. I have never done that, and have about as much desire to try it as I have to try waxing my legs. I do want you to stay for a bit though. Even the worst hook ups I've had, I've never kicked straight out of bed." He hesitates, and then says in a rush. "I never sleep all night with anyone though, Dylan. I don't like to share my bed, so the men normally go home."

I flinch at being so casually lumped in with his random hook ups, and my heart sinks a little because I love cuddling. I love touching my partner and lying wrapped up in each other. It's yet another little warning sign that points the way to the cliff edge, but when I look at him and see the hint of nervousness I sigh, because I know myself. I'm already merrily skipping to that bloody cliff, and I'm going to fall over it sometime soon.

"Okay," I say, shrugging. "I'll stay for a bit."

He tries hard, but a hint of pleasure shows on his face and he immediately guides me into the bed as if he thinks that I'll bolt at any second.

I settle gratefully into the cool sheets and watch as he lopes around the bed and slides in himself. He turns onto his side and stares at me as if taking inventory of my body and face. "What are you looking at?" I whisper, and the strangest expression crosses his face. I thought I'd seen them all over the years, but this is new. It's a little bit shy and almost awed.

"I'm looking at you," he whispers back. "You're so gorgeous, and to see you wrapped up in the sheets of my bed." He reaches over and traces my lower lip gently. "So fucking hot. Just what I dreamt of."

I can't help the jerk my body makes at his words. Unfortunately it seems to make him snap out of his tender mood, because he withdraws his hand and scrubs his face hard.

"Regrets?" I ask cautiously, and he sighs.

"For what we just did? No, I can't regret that." I relax slightly, but then immediately tense at his next words. "You're a fucking hot piece of ass, Dylan. I always knew that you would be."

Rage sears through me at his dismissive tone. "Really?" I say roughly, straightening up. "Glad I pleased you. Maybe you should leave a tip on the bedside table."

"*What?*" He sounds panicked as I move to get out of the bed, and grabs my arm to stay me. "Where are you going?"

"I am not a fucking trick, Gabe. This might be how you conduct your hook ups, calling them hot pieces of ass, but don't treat me like a twat. You may not see me as being worthy of being called your boyfriend, but I'm worth fucking more in my own eyes. So, thanks for the fuck, but I'm going back to my room."

"No, please, Dylan." His grip is strong, and against my better judgement, I let him ease me back until he hovers over me. "I'm sorry," he says desperately as I glare at him. "I'm sorry. You're right."

"I usually am," I huff, and incredibly he smiles, which is pretty fucking unfair as the sight is intense this close to him.

"Actually, you are," he says quietly. "I trust your judgement."

Seeing that I've calmed slightly, he eases to my side. "I'm sorry I called you that. You're far more than that, and you're not unworthy of being my boyfriend. I don't ever want to hear that shit again. If I was ever going to have a boyfriend, then I'd be proud to have you by my side." I shake my head, and he grabs my hand. "No, really, I'm telling you the truth. Don't I always tell you the truth?"

I nod reluctantly, and he carries on talking earnestly. "It's just that I don't *ever* want that. I don't want to be tied into a relationship. I suppose that's why Fletcher and I worked for so long; because we had absolutely no expectations of each other and made no promises. That doesn't work with everybody, and it wouldn't work with you."

Something in me dies a little at this because I know him and I can hear the conviction in his voice. "I see you, Dylan," he says suddenly. "You're gorgeous, and there's so much to you. I know you're looking for more, and you shouldn't be ashamed of that. I wish I could be the one for you." He looks sad. "Somebody will, but it'll never be me."

I stare at him, rolling onto my front to see him better. "So now what?"

He stares at me and reaches out to stroke my back, and just like that, the heat roars back as I feel his touch and catch the smell tangled in the sheets of sex and sweat and come.

His hand traces almost unconsciously down my back, and I arch into the touch like a cat, directing it down to where I want it, as he cups my arse. I moan under my breath, as the movement rubs my cock against the soft cotton, and I realise that I'm hard and throbbing and ready for him again.

"Jesus," he says, his voice so harsh it's a thread of sound. "Dylan, fuck I want you again." His hand moves almost as if against his will, and his fingers slide between my cheeks, tracing the crack down until he finds the pink hole, which is still slack and open to him. He lingers there playing his fingertips over the nerve-rich tissue, and I groan under my breath and begin to thrust against the covers, seeking relief and needing it right now.

"Fuck," he grunts, jerking to a sitting position and then rolling to straddle my thighs. Unerringly seeming to sense my weak spot, he leans down and heat instantly shoots from my neck where he suckles, to my groin. I moan and arch into him, feeling the stiff heat of his cock and the prickly heat of his balls against my legs. "I thought I'd be good with just once, but this isn't going away is it?" he says hoarsely, leaning to run his tongue down my neck.

I jerk. "Jesus, Gabe."

"What are we going to do?" he moans, beginning to thrust his body against mine, and I feel the wetness of his pre-come painting my arse. "God, I'm so fucking hard for you."

He forces himself away from me suddenly, and it seems to take all his strength as he slumps against the headboard, holding the base of his cock in a tight grip, as I cry out and hump into the mattress seeking relief. "I can't leave you alone," he finally says over the sound of our panted breaths. "I swear to God, I'm going to need to fuck you all the time if you're anywhere near me, but I can't be what you want."

I stare at him, my senses clouded with this overpowering lust that fills me again, but he's right. This isn't going anywhere, but something inside me rebels against the thought. The optimistic part of me can't comprehend that it won't be something more. "Then be what I need at the moment," I say before I even give myself time to think.

"And what's that?"

"Fuck me. Let's take it one day at a time, but what I need is for you to fuck me now."

"And what about wanting a boyfriend and a life partner?"

"You've been honest," I say softly. "I know it's not going to be you, Gabe. Maybe we can just make each other feel good while it lasts."

He looks dubious, and I can't blame him, because there is so much shit surrounding us. Our roles at work, and the fact that he makes commitment-phobes look like wedding planners, are not even the biggest problems. That belongs to the fact that I'm now sure that I'm in love with him, and hoping in the back of my mind that somehow he'll come to his senses and realise that he loves me back, like we're living in some shitty fairy tale.

But then I reach out a hand and draw it up his thigh, and it's game over. I see his complete capitulation in the groan that he gives, and the way that he comes down over me as if he can't bear to be another second without being inside me.

CHAPTER TEN

To: Gabe Foster

From: Dylan Mitchell

Due to your temper tantrum over my spilling coffee on your laptop, I am taking an early lunch. Would you like me to bring you something back? Maybe the blood of a virgin, or eye of newt?

It's scary how easy it is to fall into a sex only relationship when you're in love with that person and he doesn't know. It's easy because when he's inside me we're connected, and the only person that he's thinking about is me. Work means nothing to him at that point, and neither do other men. He's all mine, and if I feel dishonest in the fact that this is a one-sided relationship with me being the top-heavy element and him having no idea, I push it away in the heat and sweat of our times together.

For the next few weeks, we can't be in the same room and not be on each other. We have become the masters of the silent fuck at work, locking ourselves in his office and riding each other to climax, biting our hands or clothes to stop the shouts waiting to come out.

Take now for instance. I had leant over his shoulder to point out a discrepancy in a document, and he'd turned his head slightly to look at me. His eyes had darkened, and now we're lying on the floor, half under his desk. His shirt is hanging off one shoulder, the arm seam ripped where I'd fisted it, and his trousers are round his ankles. I'm stark, bollock naked apart from one black sock. We're both covered in sweat and come and breathing heavily.

"Fuck," he mutters, turning on his side to face me and running his hand down my chest, rubbing his fingers into my happy trail. I arch into his touch, my cock incredibly twitching again. "I can't bloody get enough of you. It's fucking ridiculous. I've never -"

He breaks off, and hope that's never far from me flares. "Never what?"

He shoots me an inscrutable glance. "I've never been so hot for a man. I only have to look at you, and my cock's hard as a post. I only have to smell you, feel your body, and I'm ready to come."

I roll to face him. "And that's a problem?"

His hair has flopped rather endearingly over his forehead, and I reach up to push it back tenderly. Too tenderly obviously, because he stiffens and moves away, grabbing the full, wrinkled condom from his cock and tying it expertly.

He pulls his trousers up, and rolling to his feet lithely he holds out a hand to help me up. I repress a sigh and let him heave me up, before trailing after him to his bathroom, leaning against the door as I watch him start the shower.

"You want first go?" he asks, jerking his head towards the running water.

Not going to share it then obviously? Sadness runs through me at the customary pulling away job he enacts after every fuck. Becoming aware that he's staring at me, I straighten and chill my expression. "I'll go first," I mutter, and after stripping off my one sock I edge past him into the hot spray, ignoring the hand he puts out to me.

"You okay?" he asks, surprising concern running through his quicksilver eyes for a brief second.

"I'm fine." I lather up his shower gel between my palms, smelling the fragrance of spiced oranges which is so familiar to me now. At night when I'm alone in bed I can smell it on me, as if a little bit of him is with me holding me close. Not the real thing though. He never stays the night. We get off together and then he gets off ... home. I've caught Jude's head shake of disapproval a few times too many lately.

Becoming aware of him still staring at me, I school myself. "Just thinking about the Christmas drinks, and what I'm going to have."

He smiles, relief running over his face immediately. He's a conundrum, this man. Doesn't want to hurt me, is worried about it so much, and then does it every time. "Not too much," he chuckles. "Don't forget last year and the arse picture."

I let the water pound down on my shoulders, twisting to get clean and feeling his hot gaze running down my body. "I don't think I could top that."

He groans. "Don't say topping. You'll get me hard again."

I shake my head and smirk, sending my gaze down to the bulge in his trousers. "Too late."

I leave the warmth of the spray and go to squeeze past him, but he catches me with a warm towel in his hand. I still as he rubs the soft fabric over me, and warmth flows through me for a second at the tenderness I'm sure he's unaware of exhibiting. He does this all the time, little moments of care and warmth in a sea of hot sex followed by indifference. It's what's keeping me stuck in this one-sided rela-tionship, the glimpse of what could be.

He pulls away, and kicking his trousers off he steps into the shower too, and now it's my turn to watch avidly as the water runs down his body, making him look like a soft porn video. He looks up. "I've put a spare change of clothes in the cupboard for you."

I shake my head. Gabe's a caveman sometimes, and nothing revs his engine at these times quite as much as ripping my clothes off me. I'd be a hypocrite if I complained because it turns me on so much, but the cost to my wardrobe was looking high at one point. However, deaf to my intense protests, he bought several outfits for me and stashed them in the cupboard. It seemed too much like shades of Fletcher and his kept man persona to me, but he'd ignored my protests and carried on doing it. Every time he rips my clothes off, the next day a new outfit will be hanging in what is becoming *our* cupboard. They aren't even cheap as designer labels abound, and it still makes me uncomfortable.

I move away from the door to get dressed, pulling on some skinny, grey trousers, a white shirt, red tie and grey v-neck jumper, and steadfastly ignoring the Ralph Lauren labels. Then I hesitate. "Are you coming to the party?"

He looks up and nods. "Yes. I've got to sign those documents, and then I'll be with you."

Not really, I think sourly, and the thought makes me hesitate over my next question. It's been hovering on my lips over the last few weeks as Christmas looms. I haven't voiced it because the potential for it to go wrong is high, but now I just think *fuck it, it's Christmas.*

"What are you doing for Christmas?"

He shuts the shower off, and gets out, taking the towel I hand him and rubbing it briskly over his body. I drag my gaze away from the dips and swell of his muscles glistening with water that would feel really nice under my tongue, and look up at him for an answer.

He shrugs. "Not much. I've got a lot of work to do, so I'll probably come in over the holidays when it's nice and quiet."

"Work," I say in disgust, and he grins.

"Dylan, your aptitude for business is astounding."

"Shut up," I grumble. "You can't work over Christmas. What about friends? Are you seeing them?" A thought occurs to me, and the question is out before I can help it. "Will you be going to any clubs?"

A dark look crosses his face, and something else I don't recognise. "I doubt that I'll visit any clubs." He shoots me a warning look. "Although if I wanted to, I would. You don't own me."

I jerk and he stills, staring hard at me, and that something crosses his face again before it softens slightly. "I won't do that before telling you, Dylan. I wouldn't fuck another man without you knowing."

I feel the gorge rise in my throat at the thought of him with someone else, but manage to suppress it. I agreed to this, and I've been a willing participant in it. I can't therefore whine when he doesn't say the right things.

He carries on talking quickly, as if he wants to get past the tense moment. "I won't see much of friends. Everyone's busy at Christmas."

"Even Henry?"

"Yes, Henry will be with his family." He pulls his black, pinstriped suit from the cupboard and smiles at me. "When are you off to your family?"

I stare hard at him as he pulls on his shirt and trousers and knots a gold-coloured tie, his long fingers steady and sure. "Tomorrow morning. I'll catch the morning train. Seriously, Gabe, you're going to be on your own?"

He looks bewildered. "I'm used to it." He looks at my face and groans. "Don't do that look, Dylan. I'm fine, and I actually enjoy it."

"Surely not," I say in disgust, and he laughs, his teeth white in his tanned face. "Gabe, no one should be on their own at Christmas." I pause, and the words flood out of me. "Come with me instead. Come and have Christmas with me."

"*What?*" The laughter dies out of his face, and shock replaces it. "I can't do that."

"Of course you can. My family are used to big crowds at Christmas. There are usually a couple of girlfriends and boyfriends hanging around." I falter at the look on his face that advises caution. "Not that we're boyfriends. I mean they're used to additional people and friends. They love it. There's plenty of room, and the countryside around there is beautiful. You haven't lived until you spend Christmas walking along the beach with the wind in your face."

He shakes his head, and for a brief second, warmth and a sort of sad yearning crosses his face. Then he chills and folds his arms. "It's a lovely invitation, but I couldn't." I open my mouth to protest, and he shuts me down firmly. "I like my space, Dylan. I wouldn't be good company in a family setting." He draws me close and into his arms. "Thank you though. I don't think I've ever been asked to a family Christmas before."

"Really?"

He shrugs. "I don't know why, but people seem to get a bit of a fuck off vibe from me."

I smile. "I can't understand that at all." I wrap my arms around his neck, drawing his head down to me, and moan under my breath as our lips touch. He rubs them together gently, before tangling his tongue lazily with mine. We kiss slowly and languidly, and then he astonishes me by pulling me close and lowering his head onto my shoulder.

"When are you back?" he asks almost hesitantly, as if fearing that I'll take encouragement from his words. Well, I can't help but do that very thing, because to my ears it sounds wistful.

"I know you're going to miss me," I say in a deliberately, smug voice. His head shoots up and he glares at me. "Don't worry, Gabe, you're not alone. London will be thronged with wailing men mourning my absence for a whole week, so go out and join them if you feel isolated. Don't be ashamed. They're your brethren."

"Fuck off," he laughs, and then reaches up, toying with my hair absentmindedly. "I will miss you though," he says, and although it's truculent and begrudging, my heart fills with warmth.

"Well if you do miss me, the offer's open," I say softly. "Just come. I've left the address on your desk."

He looks wildly at the desk as if it's going to threaten him in some way, and I smile sadly. He won't accept anything given to him willingly.

"Just think about it," I whisper into his ear, feeling him shudder slightly. "And just for the record, Gabe. I'll be missing you too."

=✉

Three days later, on Christmas Eve, I sit at the big table in the kitchen of my family's farmhouse. It's a beautiful day that comes very rarely in December. The sun is bright and cold, shining through the low windows and glancing off the masses of photo frames littering the Welsh dresser. They trace me and my siblings seemingly through every stage of our development and are set randomly amongst the beautiful, warm, clear colours of my mum's Poole pottery collection.

The radio is on in the background as we wait for Pop Master on Radio Two. My mum and I have been doing it for years, and even after I left home we'd still text each other, gloating and smug if we'd beaten each other. A pile of ironing is resting on the corner of the kitchen table, and on top, a small tabby cat called Katie is slumbering happily.

I stare down at the wooden surface of the table. It's older than any of us, and belonged to my dad's grandmother. It brings back so many memories of family dinners and sitting at it kicking the legs while I tried to do my homework.

If I look carefully I can find my brother's initials on one corner and the words, 'Dylan is a giant poo head'. He'd carved it when he was seven and I was five, and apparently, I'd been aggravating him. The aggravation had increased for him when my dad had found the carving, but for some reason my mum had refused to sandpaper it out and still laughs when she sees it.

A cup of tea appears in front of me, and my mum runs her hands through my hair, giving me a whiff of lilac and linseed oil. It's her smell and the scent of our childhood surrounding me. It had been there when I'd fallen and skimmed my knees, right up to the embarrassed, hot tears when my first love had supposedly broken my heart.

"Nearly time," she hums happily, looking at the ugly wall clock made by my sister. It's the only artistic thing that any of us have ever done, and my mum loves it. "Ready to get your arse handed to you with my superior music knowledge?"

"Dream big," I snark, and she gives her big, raucous laugh that makes the brown and grey curls of her hair jiggle and bounce.

She reaches into a cupboard and removes the cake tin with the picture of Charles and Diana on it. She'd loved Diana, declaring her a free spirit who'd been crushed by the oppressive palace machine, and had made me go with her to London to chuck flowers at Diana's coffin as it had passed. It had been both touching, and hideously embarrassing.

I'd tried to use the excuse of having to go to school to get out of it, but my mum had declared loudly that her children would not bow down to the oppression of the Department of Education. Luckily my dad had written a sick note, but I'd still spent the entire trip with a baseball cap on and my head low so the cameras didn't inadvertently catch me. My fears were well founded, because Jude had been suspended once for saying he had chicken pox and then being caught at a Take That concert. He'd been on the front page of The Sun gazing adoringly at Howard Donald.

She opens the tin and I groan. "Oh God, is that your apple cake?"

She smiles. "I baked it to welcome you home. It's your favourite."

"You're my favourite mum, I'm so happy," I sigh, as she cuts a large slice and puts it on a plate for me. "But make sure that you hide it from Ben. He'll eat the whole bloody lot."

She chuckles at the thought of my brother, and for a second the only sounds are our happy sighs as we munch the cake. Then she pushes her empty plate away and shoots me a keen glance. "What's on your mind, Dyl?"

I look up, catching her warm-brown eyes resting on me. "Nothing's wrong."

She shakes her head. "Yes, there is. I know the heart of you, and you've never been able to hide anything from me."

"I know that." Thinking carefully, I shrug and offer a slight titbit, in the hope she'll ignore the big picture of my life. "I hope you don't mind, but I invited a friend to stay for Christmas."

In some families that might be cause for an apocalyptic explosion, but never in mine. My mum and dad have always encouraged us to have friends, and then later boyfriends and girlfriends round to the house. My mum loves company, and the house was always full when we were growing up. We'd grown used to rubbing shoulders with people that she'd befriended, and the wannabe artists who came to her workshops, held in the barn where her studio is. Christmas and other holidays always had a few extra people added, and she'd never raised an eyebrow.

Like now, when she just smiles. "Of course it's alright. I presume it's a man."

I shake my head. "Never presume." She stares at me, and I laugh. "Yes, it's a bloke, but don't make a big deal of it, Mum. He's a friend, and he hasn't got any family."

Her gaze softens instantly. "Oh, poor man. Are they dead?"

I nod and tell her about Gabe ending up in care, and when I've finished she looks sad. "If he does come, don't say anything, Mum, because that's private. I just wanted you to know so you didn't put your foot in it." I sigh and run my finger along a rough patch in the wood, feeling it catch at my fingertips. "He won't come anyway, but I had to mention it because if you'd shown any sign of astonishment at him turning up, he'd have been back in his car like a bloody greyhound."

I look up and she's staring at me. "Not just a friend then?" she smiles.

"Yes, he's a friend," I protest. "Nothing else."

She shakes her head. "Dylan, you have never been able to fool me since you were a little boy, and you never will, because to me you're still that small boy inside."

"How do you know these things?" I groan, and she laughs.

"One sign is that your left eye twitches, but I'll tell you no more. I need to keep the rest of my secrets in my bag of tricks."

"Well, you're wrong this time," I protest roundly, and then feel the twitch in my eye. "Oh, damn it." She laughs, and I slump. "Okay, we might be seeing each other, but it's not serious and it won't ever be. He's not the type for relationships."

She looks at me steadily, and a little sadly. "He might not be, but you are, Dyl. You're a nester by nature and a born nurturer. You're my little Florence Nightingale."

"Oh God, *please* don't call me that, and especially not ever in front of Gabe."

She laughs raucously and then stills. "You're in love with him, this unexpected guest, aren't you?"

I look up, startled and horrified. "I'm not in love. I don't want to be." Her warm-brown eyes soften, and I sigh. "It's complicated."

She grabs my hand. "Dylan, love is complicated, darling. As humans, we don't seem to value or work for anything that comes too easily, but give us hard work, and we'll activate a death grip."

I look at her. "Mum, he wouldn't want that love. I don't think he'd even know what to do with it."

She sighs and looks sad. "If his childhood was deprived of love, it will be hard. He'll probably need love like no one else, and you can give that, Dylan. You're one of the most loving people that I've met, but it won't be easy. When you've gone years alone you develop a hard shell, and sometimes that shell never cracks." She squeezes my hand. "Be careful, sweetheart. This might not be an easy thing, and it might not end happily."

I look up sharply, and she stares at me and then nods. "You're not a quitter by nature. Why don't you see where it goes? But look after your heart, darling, because once it's been really broken, it never heals properly."

"It's all supposition at the moment," I say sourly. "I miss him terribly, but he's probably quite happy in London and not missing me at all."

She opens her mouth to speak, but at that moment we hear the crunching of gravel on the drive outside, indicating a car arriving. "Is that Ben?" I ask. My brother is at Edinburgh University.

Mum shakes her head. "Don't think so, love. He's not due until tonight, and he's catching a train." The oven pings and she hustles over. "Go and see who it is, Dylan, while I take this cake out."

I nod, standing up and moving along the flagstone corridor to the front door. I hear a car door slam and the crunching of footsteps before there's a sharp knock on the door. For some inexplicable reason my heart starts to race, and I quicken my steps. I fling the door open, and then gape in astonishment. "*Gabe!*"

He's standing with his hand raised to knock again. He looks utterly gorgeous, dressed in faded jeans with a blue-checked flannel shirt and a thick, navy, hooded cardigan. For a long second I stand and gape because he looks almost alien here, accustomed as I am to seeing him in an urban setting.

At his first sight of me, a huge smile had almost involuntarily spread across his face, as he took in my appearance. I'm only dressed in old jeans and a band t-shirt under an orange plaid shirt, but he stares at me with hungry eyes as if I'm wearing a tuxedo. However, as my stunned silence grows, the smile fades, and his customary, cool expression surfaces. "Hello. Earth to Dylan."

I snap out of my daze. "You came."

"Well, clearly, oh Master of the Blindingly Obvious."

I laugh out loud. "I never thought I'd be so pleased to hear you sniping."

He shifts almost awkwardly. "Why?"

"Because I missed you of course." The honesty of the statement makes it emerge with no sign of awkwardness.

For a second he looks almost bashful, but then he straightens. "Do you usually spend the holidays on the doorstep around here?"

I jerk and laugh. "Shit, I'm sorry. I'm just so fucking stunned to see you."

He stares at me. "You did invite me, didn't you?"

I nod energetically.

"Well, here I am." He looks slightly anxious. "Did you mean it, Dylan?" he asks in a low voice. "If you didn't I can -"

"Oh no you fucking don't," I hiss, grabbing his arm to stop his backwards momentum, and dragging him over the doorstep. "Come in. Of course you're welcome."

He trips as he comes through the doorway, landing against me as I automatically brace to stop him falling. As soon as our bodies touch the customary electricity races through us from me to him, like lightning being conducted. It's so strong that my body absorbs his shudder, and I groan under my breath. "Gabe," I whimper, and he jerks.

"Fuck, Dylan I missed -" He breaks off to take my mouth in a feverish kiss, but my heart soars at the broken off words. *He missed me.* He pushes his tongue into my mouth, and the familiar sweet taste of his mouth overwhelms me, and I press closer and closer, feeling the hard thrust of his cock against mine.

He grunts and grabs my arse, clutching me hard, and then breaks away from me with a muffled curse as I hear my mum shout from down the hall. "Dylan, who was at the door?"

"It's Gabe, mum," I shout out, ignoring his attempt to shush me.

"Well don't keep him out in the cold. Bring him in."

"Okay," I shout and grab him close as he tries to move away. I kiss him lustily, and then pull away to whisper in his ear, "Don't say that you're my boss." He shudders wildly at my breath in his ear and looks at me quizzically, so I nod emphatically. "Mum has some really seventies ideas about bosses exploiting the proletariat." I catch his eye and smile. "Seriously, she's one donkey jacket short of a protest march most of the time. Now come and meet her."

I grab his hand and tug him down the hallway, feeling the familiar, warm clasp of his fingers. I've felt his hands all over my body, on my dick, in my hair and between my legs sending his fingers into my body. However, somehow this warm grip feels the most intimate in the corridor of my childhood home.

I throw the door open and usher him in. He looks around, and I see the kitchen of my home through new eyes. The farmhouse is low lying to avoid the cold winds that blow across the fields from the sea. The kitchen is large and flagstoned, and over the years my mother's personality has stamped itself on the room. The cabinets are light oak, and the walls have been painted a light, clear red and echo the red and white patterned tiles which were hand painted by her.

However, his gaze snags on the huge painting that fills the wall over the kitchen table. It's one of my mum's abstract paintings of a red sky over the sea, and its reds, golds and blues echo those in the Poole pottery, and seem to catch the light streaming through the window. "Jesus, that's a Rebecca Poulson, isn't it?"

He jumps as my mum laughs and emerges from the pantry, clutching a tea towel. "I think it might be, young man. You know my work?"

He stares at her lost for words, and I enjoy the rare occasion. "I do," he finally says. "I have several of your paintings at home."

"He does, Mum. He has your tropical flowers in his lounge."

He shoots me a glance. "I do, but surprisingly you have never once mentioned that Rebecca Poulson is your mother."

I shrug and grin. "It never came up."

His gaze threatens retribution, but my mum comes towards him. "You must be Gabe. Dylan mentioned that you were coming for Christmas."

"I am," he says almost nervously. "Is that okay?" He breaks off with a gasp as she hugs him lightly. At first his arms hang loose, and then he tentatively firms his grip, staring at her as she moves back.

"Of course it's fine, but I'm afraid you'll have to get used to hugging. We're a family of huggers," she says warmly, and I feel a shaft of love towards her. My mum is awesome.

"I've noticed," he says blandly. "Dylan hasn't managed a minute for the last two years without touching some place on me."

I'm sure it's a joke, but for some reason, a vivid picture fills my mind of my hand holding his cock as I kneel at his feet in the office and direct it towards my mouth. He stares at me, his eyes darkening, and I know he's thinking of the same thing. Before it gets too heated, I clear my throat. "Well, that's us, the touchers." I pause. "Fuck. That makes us sound like one of those inappropriate, pervy cults. The sort that you'd need your safe place to think of if you're around us."

My mum lets out a peal of laughter and pushes Gabe towards the table. "Sit down, Gabe, and I'll make a coffee. Dylan, cut a slice of cake for him. After your drink, Dylan can take you upstairs and you can unpack." She smiles widely at him. "You'll be in with Dylan. As you're a friend of his, you can sleep on the pull-out bed." She winks. "Unless you're feeling *really* friendly, and then you can share his bed."

I groan and Gabe promptly chokes on the cake he's just put in his mouth, making me laugh loudly as I pat him on the back. Catching his breath, his eyes are caught by my brother's carving on the table. "Who wrote this?" he asks my mum, who laughs as she brings his coffee over.

"That was Dylan's brother, Simon. Dylan had been particularly annoying that day."

"What a wonderful idea," he murmurs. "I can really empathise with Simon. In fact, I think I might get my penknife out and carve a few things on my desk at work. Your brother must be extraordinarily clever, Dylan."

My mum guffaws. "I'll leave you to make your own mind up on that one, Gabe. He *was* the child who broke his foot karate-kicking the wall." Gabe laughs and then looks slightly alarmed as she leans forward and grabs his hand. "You work at the same place as Dylan does?" He nods. "So you must know his boss?"

He looks warily at me. "I do," he says somewhat hesitantly.

"Is he as big a bastard as Dylan says?"

"I wouldn't go that far," he says indignantly. "He's actually a brilliant bloke. Very clever and loved by all."

She shakes her head disappointedly. "That's not what Dylan says. He's always full of horror stories."

"What *does* Dylan say?" he asks, giving me a look ripe with retribution, and I groan as she leans forward and starts talking.

CHAPTER ELEVEN

To: Dylan Mitchell

From: Gabe Foster

I speak French, Spanish, German and a little Russian, but that still doesn't equip me to understand your garbled vocabulary.

An hour later we climb the narrow stairs and he huffs indignantly. "I cannot believe that you told your mother those things. I mean the story about the conference, you've wildly exaggerated that."

I turn and wink cheekily at him. "I don't think so, and don't worry I haven't told her any of the more recent stories."

Heat crosses his face. "Fuck, I wish we were on our own at this moment."

"Why?" I whisper, turning and blocking his way up. I'm a stair above him, and we're now the same height. I stare into his stormy-grey eyes. "What would you do?"

He stares at me intently, and then reaches up and runs his long fingers across my lips. "I'd put these to good use."

I shiver and then turn around. "Hold that thought."

He follows me. "What do you mean? I am *not* doing anything in your childhood home, Dylan."

"Pshaw," I shrug, getting to the top of the stairs. "My mum and dad's room is down that way in the old part of the house, overlooking the back. My brother's room is also at the back. My other brother and sister don't live at home." I grab the door handle to my room and look at him cockily. "So we're all alone, Mr Foster. Get ready to make some noise." I fling the door open with a flourish and stand back to let him go through.

He shakes his head and pauses when he's inside the room, looking around with a lively curiosity. The room is bathed in sunshine, which lays lazy stripes over the white walls and sand-coloured carpet. "Was this your room when you were little?" he asks, avid curiosity and something sad vying for prominence in his eyes.

I look around at the king-sized bed with the navy and red, hand-made quilt, and the one navy-painted wall on which is hung one of my mum's huge, six foot paintings. It shows me and my brothers playing in an old boat we'd had. She went through a stage of painting with very light colours, and the whole picture has a whitewashed, ethereal air. "It was, but they redecorated when I left home and took down all my posters of Brad Pitt."

He pouts mockingly. "Oh dear, what a tragedy."

I nod. "I know. They were from 'Troy' when he had long hair, but I really feel that his seminal work was 'Fight Club'."

He smiles. "I'm noting your use of the word seminal."

I laugh. "You were meant to."

He puts his bag down and wanders over to look out of the window, stooping slightly as the ceilings in the farmhouse are low. "I can't imagine growing up somewhere like this," he says almost wistfully, and I reach out and lay a hand on his shoulder. It's for comfort, but when he stiffens slightly I cover it by leaning over and looking out of the window.

"It was a lovely childhood. We didn't have much money when I was little, but we had each other." I trail off, horrified because that was incredibly tactless, but he smiles.

"Don't be embarrassed about having a normal childhood, Dylan. You're not rubbing my nose in it. You're always so refreshingly forthright and honest, and I like it, so don't change." He shrugs. "I actually like hearing about people's childhoods. It's nice to listen to, a bit like overhearing a really lovely secret."

He instantly looks both embarrassed and aggrieved, as if I've made him say such a whimsical thing. It's a very endearing look on him, but a sudden scratching and snuffling at the door breaks our moment and he looks up startled. I smile. "Do you like dogs?"

To my amazement, a huge smile spreads over his face. "You have dogs?"

I nod, going over to the door. "Yes, three. One's my dad's working dog, so she's out with him at the moment. The other two are house dogs." I fling open the doors, letting in the two Border Terriers who were waiting outside. They bound in with their little, cross, old man faces, and immediately make a beeline for Gabe, who I'm amazed to see is crouching on the floor to welcome them. He laughs when they reach him and stretches out his hands, stroking and petting them as the shameless attention seekers curl in on him with their tails wagging furiously.

He has the biggest smile on his face that I've ever seen. It makes his tanned features glow, and I swallow hard. I've never seen him look truly happy and engaged until now, and I feel something snap and settle in me. It's the last piece of my heart, falling for him without any input from me at all. *How could I really resist him?* I ask myself wryly. *Who could resist the damaged, beautiful man that he is?*

Unaware of my turmoil, he laughs and looks up at me. "What are their names?"

I struggle to get my mind back into gear, and then grimace. "Cersei and Jaime."

He looks puzzled. "Like the Game of Thrones characters?"

I nod slowly. "Yes."

I hope he's going to let it go, but he stares at me. "Why?"

"Er, because they're brother and sister," I say quickly, and then finish lamely, "And they like licking each other a lot."

Silence reigns for a second. Then he gives the biggest laugh I've ever heard from him. "That's fucking classic. Who thought of that?"

I smile. "My mum. I'll warn you that she also named the cat downstairs." He looks at me querying. "Katie Price, because she likes sunning herself."

"Your mum's brilliant. Do you have any other pets?"

"My dad's dog. We used to have a couple of hamsters that were called Steve and McQueen because they kept escaping. But they performed one final escape which proved fatal when they got in an old biscuit tin and couldn't get out."

He's looking at me in fascination, and it makes me unexpectedly shy. "How about a walk?" I ask brightly. "I'll show you over the farm."

"Can we take the dogs?" he asks eagerly, and I smile.

"Of course. I'll even let you pick up the dog poo."

"Thank you," he mutters.

We grab our coats from downstairs, his an elegant, navy, Burberry pea coat, mine an old, green parka of my dad's, and shouting a goodbye to my mum, we set out. I show him over the farm, letting him poke his head into sheds and barns.

He shows a keen fascination with the barn that houses my mum's studio and where she gives her workshops, but he refuses to go in, saying an artist's space is very private. I'd argue about that because my siblings and I have always run freely in and out of the studio, but I have a keen sense he's right. Apart from that he's largely silent, until we cut down onto the footpath that leads down to the village.

The footpath is lined on both sides by trees, and they lean over it, making a tunnel. The bare branches make it look like we're entering the rib cage of a huge animal. The dogs are running ahead of us, their little bums and legs bobbing up and down as they snuffle enthusiastically into hedges and grass, and he laughs in delight then looks at me.

"So, I think you'd better prepare me. Tell me who's who in your family."

I smile at him. "Well, you've met my mum. You'll meet my dad, Tom, later. He's quiet compared to my mum, but he's got a very dry sense of humour."

"Your brothers and sisters?" he asks, bending down to get the stick Cersei is holding, and throwing it for her to fetch.

"Simon's the eldest. He's in America at the moment. He runs the farm with dad, and he's studying agriculture over there as part of an exchange group. Then there's my sister, Leah. She and her husband and their two-year-old twin boys are in Thailand for Christmas. Her husband, Will, is a professor at Exeter University, and they met while at university together. She studied hospitality and worked in some of the best hotels in the world. She gave it up to come back and have kids with him, and now she runs the holiday cottages on the farm. They're doing really well and make a lot of money. The three cottages are on the edge of our land. I'll show you them later."

He nods. "Any more? It's like the fucking Waltons."

I laugh. "The Waltons, if it was set in Devon with a great deal more bad behaviour and cursing, and that's just my mum."

He laughs, and I stare surreptitiously at the stranger in front of me. There's no sign of the perfectionist boss now. He looks rumpled, his cheeks red from the cold and his eyes bright. His hair is a windswept mess, and the bright red scarf he threw on earlier compliments his olive skin. However, it's his open, almost happy expression that really marks the difference. He shoots a look at me. "I love your mum. Are you sure they don't mind me being here?"

I come to a stop and grab his arm. "I would never have asked you if they did. I would never put you in such a vulnerable position, Gabe. You must trust me on this."

He stares hard at me. His eyes are a stormy grey, and shadows from the branches overhead send light and dark over his face. "I do trust you," he says slowly. "There are very few people that I trust, but you're one of them." I really want to know who the others are, but he shakes his head. "Go on, you were telling me about the rest of your family."

I sigh at the lost moment. "Well, there's me, and lastly the baby, Ben, who's at Edinburgh University studying to be a vet. You'll meet him tonight when he gets back, and God help you."

He laughs. "So he'll come back here eventually too, I presume?"

I nod. "Lots of work around here, and he did his apprenticeship year with our local vet."

"What about you? Everyone else is home. Why not you?"

I'm startled. "I like London. I've no real desire at the moment to be back here. I like the fact that there's something going on all the time in London. There's always a museum or a gallery to go to, and I love the history that's around every corner." I look at the path ahead, and the spindly branches outlined starkly against the grey sky. Nearby, a robin sets down on a bush, its red breast almost startling in this monochrome, winter world. "I like coming back for weekends and recharging, but not all the time. What about you? Do you fancy being a weekend, country squire?"

He shakes his head. "I'm the same as you, but it is beautiful here. I can see the appeal."

By unspoken agreement, we turn back for home. When we let ourselves in, I almost trip over the large suitcase and the bin bag which is spewing what must be dirty washing everywhere. "Oh lovely," I say, kicking a pair of boxers under the telephone table.

The dogs prance ahead into the kitchen with excited whimpers, and there's a brief commotion and then a huge shout. "Dill Weed, is that you?"

I wince. "That's my brother's nickname for me," I mutter at Gabe, who has a wide grin on his face. "Use it at your peril."

Ben shouts again, and then appears at the kitchen door. I smile at him as he speeds towards me and hugs me. "Jesus Christ, Ben, have you grown again?"

He laughs and straightens to his six foot four height. His dark hair is pulled back in a bun, and he's grown a beard. "Probably," he smiles cheekily. "It's my nonstop diet of sex."

I groan. "Too much information."

"Well, Dill Weed, too many women, too little time. The Benster has to recharge sometimes."

"Did you just refer to yourself in the third person?" I ask faintly. "Because that's fairly disturbing."

Gabe laughs, and Ben turns to him. "I've just been hearing about you from my mum," he says, putting out a hand for him to shake.

"Oh dear, I hope it was complimentary."

Ben smiles. "Of course. Made better by the fact that you appreciate her art, unlike the Neanderthals she normally lives with."

I groan, used to this from my mum, and look up as the door opens and my dad's collie dog darts in. "Hi baby," I croon, bending down to give her a pat. She's cold from the air outside, and lets me cuddle her for a second.

"Is this your dad's dog?" Gabe asks. "I can't wait to hear her name."

Ben laughs. "Oh, you've heard the others. Believe me, they're the tip of the iceberg. We've had eccentric pet names for as long as I can remember."

"This one's Lizzie," I murmur, smiling up at him, and for a second his gaze seems caught on my smile. Then he focuses.

"Don't tell me. Let me guess." He stares at the dog, whose black and white patches over her eyes give her an adorably pie-eyed look. He looks at me stroking her neck, and then smiles. "Elizabeth I."

"How did you guess?"

Gabe laughs. "Because of her ruff."

"Well done." A deep voice with a Devon burr to it comes from the door, and Gabe straightens as my dad comes in. My dad is a big man. Ben gets his height and looks from him, as he stands at six foot five, with grey, flecked black hair and a grizzled beard. He looks very intimidating, but actually he's a total cliché, being a gentle giant.

Gabe turns seriously to him. "Hello, Mr Mitchell. I'm Gabe Foster. I hope I'm not intruding on your Christmas."

He gives his slow, sweet smile, and I see Gabe instantly relax for some reason. It's puzzling, because it normally takes ages for people to realise how gentle he is.

"Not at all," my dad says." Any friend of Dylan is welcome here at any time. Now Rebecca rang me to say that dinner was ready, so how about we go and eat, and you can tell me hideously embarrassing stories about Dylan?"

"That would certainly be my pleasure," drawls Gabe, and I glare at him.

"Keep them clean," I hiss at him, as Ben and my dad disappear into the kitchen.

He arches one eyebrow, looking devilish. "What on earth do you think that I'd tell him?" He lowers his voice. "How about the fact that you love it when I come on you and lick it off?"

"Fucking hell," I hiss. "Thanks for the pre-family dinner boner, you twat." He laughs, and I look at him curiously. "What made you relax so suddenly around my dad? It usually takes a while. Some of my uni mates were scared shitless of him."

He smiles almost nervously. "He has your smile."

"Sorry?"

"Ben may look like him, and you look like your mum, but you have your dad's smile. It's always made me relax."

He brushes past me towards the kitchen, and it might be the light, but I could swear he's blushing.

Dinner is a raucous affair. Huge candles decorate the table, and my dad pours red wine as if it's going out of fashion. Mum has made a big pot of beef bourguignon that smells heavenly, with shallots bobbing in the rich gravy like tiny pearls. We mop it up with homemade bread and butter from our farm. For dessert, she produces with a flourish a large custard tart, which gleams a rich, butter yellow in the candlelight.

Gabe leans back and rubs his flat stomach. "That was an absolutely fantastic meal. Thank you, Rebecca."

She raises her wine glass. "No, thank you for the wonderful heart-warming stories you've shared about my son." My dad laughs heartily, and I shoot a glare at Gabe who has overshared evilly.

My dad stretches. "Well, it's bed for me. But just one more please, Gabe."

Gabe smiles wickedly. "Once, Dylan got his tie caught in the small, portable shredder at work and actually shredded half of it before he realised. Then he was trapped because the reverse button didn't work, so he had to stay there for a couple of hours until I came back and was able to cut him out."

"Oh my God," I groan as my mum and dad and Ben let loose massive laughs like the traitors they are. "It wasn't funny," I say sourly. "It was one of my best ties, and I had a bit of a blood pressure headache afterwards."

Gabe joins in laughing, and I shoot him the finger.

My mum stands up. "Time for bed, and thank you for tonight, Gabe. As a gesture of gratitude for the years' worth of piss taking that you've given us, I'd like to leave you with one little gift in return."

"Oh, now what, Mum?" I shout.

She carries on obliviously. "Dylan came in drunk one night when he was nineteen. He'd forgotten his key and got stuck trying to come through the dog flap. He was there all night, and when we came down in the morning he was still there, drunkenly singing to himself."

Ben snorts out a huge laugh. "Oh my God, that was his 'I'm so Sad' song."

"Fucking hell you lot," I grouse as Gabe bursts out laughing, and I stand up to hug my parents. They leave us, and Ben quickly stands up.

"Thank God they've gone."

"Well, I'd agree with that," I say. "But why you?"

"I've got to wrap my presents. Is there any newspaper around?"

"You've actually bought presents? Wait, are you wrapping them in fucking newspaper?"

We stare after him, and he returns quickly with a copy of The Guardian and a small paper bag which clinks ominously. He opens it and discharges the contents cavalierly over the table. Six miniature bottles of spirits tumble out. "My God, have you been buying presents for Lilliputian alcoholics?" I ask, poking at one of the tiny bottles as Gabe laughs.

"Dude, be grateful I'm giving you first choice because it's losers weepers for whoever gets the Drambuie."

"Well, I definitely want the Jack Daniels," I announce decisively.

Ben looks enquiringly at Gabe. "How about you, Gabe? Do you want a surprise i.e. Drambuie?"

Gabe looks nonplussed. "You've got me one?"

Ben looks surprised. "Of course."

"He'll have a surprise," I say lightly. "Drambuie will be payment for all those terrible stories." I stand up. "Ready?" I ask Gabe, who stands up quickly, anticipation and something else crossing his face. *God, I want him.*

Ben waves as we leave him. I blow the candles out, but leave the fire for him. He'll bank it when he comes up. Gabe follows behind me, a dark figure at my heels, and for some reason the lightness of the evening changes, and a feeling of coiled anticipation curls between us. An invisible feeling that tugs between us as we climb the stairs.

"What time is it?" he asks, and I look abortively at my wrist.

"Fuck knows. My watch is broken."

"Still? It's been broken for weeks."

I shrug. "It was a piece of shit anyway." I look at him curiously. "Why do you ask? You've got a very expensive specimen on your wrist."

He smiles enigmatically. "Just checking." He looks at his own watch. "Well, what do you know, it's Christmas Day."

I stare at his darkened eyes and full lips, and breathe in deeply, before saying questioningly. "Merry Christmas?"

"Oh, it's going to be," he says, coming close and rubbing my bottom lip with a rough thumb. I shiver, and he smiles. "Go and shower."

I nod jerkily. "You too. I'll take the bathroom down the hall. You use the en-suite in my room."

He nods and we separate, and as I shower, paying particular attention to certain areas, I feel dark anticipation curdling in my stomach. It's only been a few days since we last fucked, but it feels like an eternity, and I need to feel him inside me like I need air to breathe.

When I come back to my room, I open the door and then gasp, before shutting it quickly and locking it. I stare at Gabe who is stark naked and sitting in the armchair by the window. His hair is still damp from his shower and his big body glistens, but my attention is caught and held by the tight grip he has on his very erect cock. His legs are spread apart, giving me a glimpse of the shadowy channel between them, and as I watch, a bead of pre-come seeps from the slit of his dick and drools over his fingers.

"God," I gasp out, feeling my cock stiffen so quickly that it actually hurts.

His eyes had been slits showing just a hint of colour, but at my gasp, he opens them fully, and they glow quicksilver in the low lamplight. "Dylan," he purrs, a debauched smile on his full lips.

"Is this my present?" I ask hoarsely, and he laughs. Still maintaining a grip on his cock, he nudges with his foot a brightly wrapped present that's lying on the floor.

I stare at him. "You have very unusual Christmas traditions, Gabe. This is the first time that I've *ever* been given a present like this. Normally, we're fully clothed with Christmas music playing."

He smiles, holding his cock loosely now with his long fingers curved over the fat head. "This is a new tradition then? Good, I like giving you new experiences."

I smirk. "I told you last week that I'd done that before."

He chuckles. "Not like I did it."

I stare at him. "No, Gabe, nobody does it like you." I'd aimed for sarcasm, but it has the unfortunate ring of truth about it, and a flicker of trepidation crosses his face. To divert a lecture on our relationship status, I book it over the room and grab the box. "Can I open it?"

He looks at me intently. "Yes, but only if you lose the towel."

I instantly drop the towel, leaving me open to his hot gaze. For a long second, I stand still as his eyes roam over me, catching and holding on my hard cock, and making a flush pass over my body. He shifts in the chair and nods bossily at the present I'm holding forgotten in my hand.

I jerk and tear open the wrapping, laughing as I realise that the paper has a pattern of tiny naked Santas holding their dicks. A smile crosses his wide mouth, before it slides into an almost predatory look as the paper falls off, revealing a long, brown box. "Open it," he whispers.

I open the box quickly, and a shudder of anticipation runs through me. Inside, in a nest of pink tissue paper is a large, black Fleshlight, its pink, internal sleeve glistening in the light. It's the arse version, and I run my fingers caressingly over the hole, shivering as I imagine my dick in there.

"Get on the bed, Dylan," he growls, and I hustle to comply, arranging myself on my back and propping my head up on a pillow so that I can see everything. I've learned to do this, because Gabe gets off on me watching.

He rises from the seat and pads towards me, his dick rock hard and sticking up from its neat nest of black curls. His olive skin is stretched tight over his long, sinewy body, and fuck Brad Pitt, because Gabe looks more like a Greek god come to life than he ever did.

He crawls up from the bottom of the bed until he's hovering at my side, leaning over my straining cock, and I can hear my panting breaths loud in the silence of the room.

"Got to get this wet first," he says hoarsely, and before I can even think, he lowers his mouth over my cock and takes me to the back of his throat. I shout out and he looks up, his mouth stretched over the angry, red head of my prick. I groan and he closes his eyes for a second, and then proceeds to suck me hard, rising and falling on my cock like an automaton.

I feel the tingle in my balls and cry out. "No, stop, Gabe."

He pops off, and wipes his chin clean of the spittle lining it. "*Already?*"

"Laugh it up. It feels like years since your office."

His expression darkens. "I know. Fuck, I know." I want to ask whether he went with anyone else, but the words won't come out, and then he shakes his head. "No one. I promised you."

I nod and then groan, as he reaches down by his leg and retrieves the slim bottle of lube that had been in the box with my Fleshlight. He squirts it into his hands and rubs them together, warming it the way he always does. Such small solicitous gestures that he makes when he thinks I don't notice.

My thoughts scatter as his long fingers wrap round my cock, and he grabs me tight in his fist. "Fuck my hand," he says hoarsely, and I groan and begin to cant my hips back and forth, pistoning into his fist and crying out as his fingers twist on the top, rubbing the sensitive spot underneath the head.

Then I cry out as his hand falls away, leaving me to fuck the air for a second of two. "Slow down," he says deeply. "I want a while to play." He reaches down and grabs my cock hard, waiting until my breathing steadies.

Then he grins wickedly and reaches over for the Fleshlight. Running a finger lightly down my wet cock he smiles as I shudder. Then I almost stop breathing as he holds my cock up straight with one hand, while the other hand positions the opening of the Fleshlight against the fleshy head. For a long second he rests it there, working it slowly and sensually against the wide, flared, mushroom head, and then looking up, he traps my gaze with his. His eyes are blown almost black, and he holds my eyes, as rocking the Fleshlight slightly he slides it down my prick.

I shout out as the slick, tight hold grips my cock. It's amazing and mind blowing, and made even more so by Gabe's expression, which almost looks feral as he watches my dick disappear into the Fleshlight.

"Oh shit!" I arch up as he pulls it smoothly back. I feel the cool air strike my cock for a second, and then the Fleshlight shuttles back down, sucking my dick into its spongy grip. "Oh God, that's so fucking good," I grit out, and Gabe moans loudly.

"You look so fucking hot," he mutters. "Look at it swallow your cock." He tears his gaze away from my prick. "I'm going to drive you out of your fucking mind."

"Nearly there," I groan, as he pulls the device up and pushes it down.

"Not yet, but you will be."

He keeps his word. He alternates long, deep, slow strokes when the Fleshlight swallows me up, with short thrusts that grind against my sensitive cock head with an insane pressure. Every time I tense to come, he backs off and lets me calm down, before starting again.

Times slows, and all I can feel is the sweat on my body and the sweet pain in my balls and cock. My muscles are so tight they feel sore, and my senses have narrowed down to the feel of my body and the touch of his hands. The sound of my moans and hoarse groans echo in the room, along with the filthy squelch of the lube and the sucking noises from the Fleshlight.

I arch into the slick grip. "Enough," I groan. "I've got to fucking come. *Please*, Gabe." My voice has a throbbing sob in it, and I hear him groan. Forcing my eyes open, I look at him and moan. Sweat coats him. His face is dark with an almost suffocating lust, and his blood-red prick throbs visibly. It's angry looking with pre-come drooling over the head. He's at my side bending over me, and I can smell the sweet, salt scent of his pre-come and sweat, and it makes my mouth water.

"Not yet," he mutters. "Not yet."

"Yes, now," I hiss, and leaning sideways I take his cock down my throat and suck hard. I'm rewarded with a spurt of come and he shouts out, trying to move away, but against his will rocking into my mouth. He's so far gone that he doesn't make any of his usual efforts to ensure that he doesn't hurt me. Instead, he rocks in hard, fucking my mouth with gasps and filthy threats.

I moan around his cock and fuck my hips up, and he jerks as if remembering what he was doing. Then he resumes his jerking motion with the Fleshlight. But now he makes no attempt to draw things out. His only concern is both of us coming, and he works my cock relentlessly with the device. Then he reaches down, and after caressing my balls he sends a finger down, coating it in the lube slicking between my thighs, before pushing it into my hole.

I moan a garbled sound around his cock, as he pushes the Fleshlight down, and it's for the last time. He crooks his finger inside me massaging my prostate, and it's game over. Sparks shoot down my spine and I feel the come broiling in the base of my cock, before the insane pressure breaks, and I shoot seemingly endlessly, emptying myself into the plastic arse.

As the last spurt leaves me, Gabe pulls himself from my slack mouth and spins to face me. He's frantic and lust drunk. "Now. I've got to -" he gasps, shuttling his hand over his cock.

"On me," I moan and he nods frantically, before throwing his head back and calling out hoarsely. I spare a quick thank you that nobody sleeps nearby, but then he jerks and spurts over me, ropes of hot cream hitting my chest and neck and lips. I lick my lips, moaning at the taste, and he comes down over me kissing me deeply. He slicks his fingers in the cream and coats my lips with it, so we share his come as we kiss with spunk-slick lips.

Silence descends and I fall into it with abandon, aware only of the sweaty, hot body holding me tight, and the slowing of our breaths.

After a while he moves, and I tighten my hold on him. "No," I chide, and he chuckles.

"I'm just going to get a wet cloth." I let him go, hearing the door open and close, and then he's back, gently removing the Fleshlight and wiping me down. "I'll clean that tomorrow," he mutters and I nod, enjoying the warm brush of the cloth on me. He flings it down by the side of the bed, but when he doesn't come back I force my eyes open, to find him hovering by the bed looking uncharacteristically uncertain.

"Gabe?"

"Where should I sleep?" he asks, and I groan and sit up quickly.

"God, I'm sorry. I forgot you don't like to share a bed. Do you want me to get the pull-out? It won't take a second."

He shakes his head quickly, running his hands nervously through his hair as I stare at him, unsure what's happening. "Would you ... could I sleep with you maybe?" The words come out in a rush, and completely unlike his normal fluid and smooth diction, but I feel them bang and batter against my heart.

"Of course you can," I say tenderly, and he shoots me a warning glance. However, when I pull back the duvet to let him in, he moves quickly and eagerly, sliding in and nestling against me. I try to hold myself a little apart, aware that he isn't used to sharing a bed, but I give in when he nestles against my skin and gives a throaty sound of happiness. Ignoring his startled gasp, I open my arms and drag him close. He stiffens, but almost immediately capitulates and rests his head on my shoulder.

I hold him tight, aware when his breaths slacken into the deep, even sounds of sleep, and I can kiss his head and inhale his scent without him protesting. I don't let go. I feel the need to grab a tight hold on him because, like water, he's going to slip through my fingers and flow away sometime soon. I can sense it.

CHAPTER TWELVE

To: Gabe Foster

From: Dylan Mitchell

I do hope that you're not viewing the hotel room mix-up at the conference, as payback for you calling me a cretin in front of Clara from Acquisitions. It's just that I'm such a scatter-brained minx I can't manage to hold a thought in my tiny brain for very long.

I come awake the next morning slowly. I'm toasty warm in bed, which is rare for me as I always hover on the cold side. I stretch, and when my leg slides against a warm, muscled, hairy leg, my eyes flutter open. Instantly memories flood back of the fucking hot events of last night, and my cock involuntarily stiffens. Then my eyes fall on Gabe, and I smile.

He'd moved away from me last night, being a bit standoffish even in sleep, but now he's curled around me like ivy. One leg is flung over me as if keeping me prisoner, and his head is lying on my shoulder. His hair is a dark mess, the silky strands glowing red in places where the sun touches it. His mouth is pouting adorably, and his morning stubble is a dark shadow on his jaw, making him look like a pirate. An irresistible impulse seizes me, and almost before I realise that I'm going to do it, I blow on his face.

His nose twitches like a rabbit then evens out as he slides back into sleep. Waiting a second, I do it again, manfully suppressing the fit of giggles waiting to seize me. Slowly his eyes flicker so I blow again, but it's too much and his eyes open wide. He looks confused for a second, and I tense, waiting to hear what comes from his mouth. Then he looks up at me, a bemused smile on his face. "Did you just blow on me, Dylan?"

I laugh out loud, cuddling closer to him. "I did."

"Why, for fuck's sake?" His words are harsh, but a smile plays on those full lips.

"You looked so peaceful."

"So you decided to blow on me like a bloody serial killer?"

I'm diverted. "Is that what serial killers do? I thought they just stuck to murder and dismemberment."

He can't hide the quirk of his mouth. "No, first they torture their victims by staring at them while they sleep, and then they blow on them."

"How did you know I was -" I break off and he looks smug.

"Of course you were staring at me. Who wouldn't?"

I shake my head mockingly. "I really feel we need to work on your confidence level, Gabe. It's *so* low. You have so much to offer. Just believe in yourself."

He stretches lazily, the duvet slipping to reveal his wide, tanned shoulders and hair-roughened chest, and then he presses against me. "I do have a lot to offer, Dylan. Thank you for reminding me."

I groan involuntarily at the feel of his hard cock. "Yes, you really do."

"Dylan," he says throatily and rolls onto me forcing me to my back. Then he hovers over me, examining my face as intently as if he's revising for an exam. "You're so fucking gorgeous," he mutters.

"That's you, not me."

He shakes his head, something passing over his face that I can't decipher. "No, it's you, inside and out." He lowers his hips, and we both moan as our stiff cocks press against each other. "How did I manage to keep my hands off you?" he mutters, and it's as if he's talking to himself. "It was so much work to keep away from you."

"Well, all I can say is well done for putting your hands on me now." I reach up and coil my arms around his neck, drawing him further down onto my body. He groans under his breath and thrusts his hands under me to cup my arse and bring me into him, starting to rub and slide against me. I laugh. "I heartily approve of where you're putting them now."

He chuckles, but just as he's lowering his mouth to take mine, there's a loud bang on the door. "Dylan, it's ten o'clock. Breakfast's ready, and Mum wants to know if you're going to the beach."

We both jerk and fall apart, and Gabe groans, reaching down and fisting his cock tight at the base. I smile at him, running my tongue lecherously over my lips, but he shoots me a look of disapproval, before pulling the sheet over himself like a prim, maiden aunt. I laugh out loud and then shout, "Yeah, we'll be down in a minute." I look over at Gabe as Ben's heavy footsteps fade away. "Sorry, do you want to go to the beach? It's something I always do, but we don't have to do it if you don't want to. We'll stay here."

"Can we take the dogs on the beach?" he asks cautiously, and when I nod, he grins. "Of course I want to go." He bounds out of bed, and I groan. "What?" he asks.

I jiggle my hard cock at him. "You're leaving me like this, honestly?"

He shakes his head disapprovingly. "Cersei and Jaime need a walk."

"And Dylan needs you to give him a wank."

He snorts and moves towards the door, grabbing a towel and stepping into a pair of blue-checked pyjama trousers. "Dylan needs to be patient and do as he's told."

"Yeah, that's not going to work. I challenge you to name a time that it ever did," I shout, hearing his deep, hoarse chuckle as he walks down the corridor to the bathroom, leaving me the en-suite.

Fifteen minutes later, we clatter down the stairs and into the kitchen. Gabe is dressed in jeans, a checked shirt and a grey, round-necked jumper and smells gorgeous, while I'm in dark jeans and a cream Henley.

I look around the kitchen appreciatively. The fire in the hearth is roaring, fairy lights glisten in their haphazardly strung lines over the cabinets, and Christmas music is playing merrily on the radio.

My dad and Ben are already there eating. Ben is still in his pyjamas, and my dad is fully dressed with Lizzie sitting expectantly next to him. Cersei and Jaime jump up straightaway from their beds in the corner and come prancing over to Gabe, bypassing me completely. "Traitors," I mutter and Gabe laughs, crouching down to pet them.

"They just know quality," he murmurs, and I shake my head.

My mum turns from the cooker. Her wild hair is caught back by a red and green bandanna with a holly pattern. She's wearing jeans and an old jumper of my dad's. "Morning boys," she smiles. "Merry Christmas."

"Merry Christmas," Gabe murmurs, as I pad over to draw her into a hug.

"Sit down and I'll do your breakfast. Full English alright, Gabe?"

"Sounds wonderful." He smiles widely at her, before taking a seat next to my dad at the table which is loaded down with plates and cups. "Have you been out this morning?" he asks my dad, who smiles at him.

"Yes, the farm waits for no man. The cows don't know that it's Christmas."

"Maybe if you played them Christmas music they might embrace the festive season more," Ben says around a mouthful of bacon.

"Or maybe you could sing them your very own special milking song," I say slyly, and then flinch as he punches me lightly in the side.

Gabe stares at him. "Milking song?"

My dad laughs. "Yes, that was priceless. Thank you, Dylan, for reminding me of it."

I smirk at Ben. "You're welcome. It's his turn today."

My dad turns to Gabe. "The children all had to do jobs around the farm when they were young, and Dylan and Ben had to milk the cows. Ben had a little song to help the cows."

"What was it, Ben?" I ask sweetly, and Gabe snorts. My dad grins at him, as Ben mutters something under his breath. "I'm sorry I didn't catch that, Ben," I say.

He looks up, and says reluctantly and quickly. "Oh, we do love our cows. We love our cows more than those ugly, old sows. They give us lots of love and milk and cream, and on apple pie it tastes like a creamy dream."

Gabe bursts out laughing, and I can't help but stare at his gorgeous face, so full of life and laughter. Becoming aware of someone looking at me, I turn and catch my dad's eye. I flush, but he shakes his head and then gives me a deliberate nod of approval. I stare at him nonplussed. My dad keeps his opinions to himself, and in the past has rarely expressed a judgement on my old boyfriends. Becoming aware that Ben has moved on to tell Gabe some of the ruder versions that we made up as we got older, I laugh.

"Fucking cows. Pain in the arse."

"So you all worked on the farm together?" Gabe asks. "That's really nice." His voice is even as normal, but he can't quite keep the note of wistfulness out of it, and I see my mum looking at him, her face warm and soft.

"Well, if you're here long enough you'll be press ganged in too.

Tom is nothing but Musketeerish about the farm." He looks up in query as she leans over him, putting a heaped plate of food in front of him, before hugging his shoulders and stepping back. "All for one and one for all."

He looks startled at her touch, but there's something warm and yearning in his eyes that makes me swallow hard. "I think that's really good," he says softly, and then shifts awkwardly as he realises everyone's eyes are on him.

Feeling intensely protective of him, I reach out and clap him on the shoulder. "You won't be saying that if you have to clean the cottages."

Ben makes a sound of disgust. "Fuck, no. Do you remember that hen party last year? I actually threw up in my mouth. It was nearly enough to put me off women for life."

"Nearly?" I query, and he laughs.

"I'm not called fucking Pimp Master Ben for nothing."

"You're not called Pimp Master Ben at all," I say faintly, and Gabe laughs out loud.

We all fall on our food, talking happily and discussing horror stories of past guests, including the woman who was mortally afraid of cows.

An hour later after we've cleaned up the kitchen, my mum chases us out. "Off you go," she says brightly. "Blow some cobwebs away on the beach and walk these dogs. They're driving me mad under my feet."

I throw on an old, navy sweater and grab my parka, before looking at Ben who's still in his pyjama trousers and a baggy old t-shirt. "Aren't you coming?"

He shudders. "Fuck no, it's cold out there. I'm going back to bed."

I shake my head disapprovingly.

"Are you sure that you don't want some help, Rebecca?" Gabe asks, taking the coat that my mum passes to him but not putting it on. "I can stay if you want."

She smiles at him warmly. "Bless you, no. I like my kitchen to myself. I'll potter and get dinner on, and then it'll be ready when you get back."

"And after that, presents?" Ben asks eagerly, looking like he's six again.

"Yes, we wouldn't want to miss your presents," I say sourly, and then dodge his punch neatly.

Twenty minutes later we park in an empty car park, and Gabe steps out of the car breathing in deeply. It's freezing, and the wind carries the strong, briny smell that I associate most with home. "I love that smell," he says, smiling at me as I come around the side of the car to him.

I quickly pull on a blue beanie, and watch him do the same with a grey one. It suits him, drawing attention to those clever eyes and high cheekbones.

"Have you been to Devon before?" I ask, as he opens the car door and lets the two dogs out. We become occupied with clipping their leads on, so it takes a few minutes to get an answer.

"A couple of times with Henry on uni holidays. His grandparents lived in Ottery St Mary."

"You're really close to him, aren't you?" I ask as we walk out of the car park. We find the sandy path and start picking our way along it.

"I suppose so," he says thoughtfully. "He's my closest friend but _"

"What?" I ask carefully.

"I don't think I'm really close to anyone, but he's one of the closest, I suppose."

"Who are the others?"

He shoots me a quizzical look but doesn't answer as we reach the top of the dunes where the pale grass billows in the wind. We stand there silently for a minute looking down to where the empty beach is spread out before us, a wide swathe of sand that looks almost leached of colour today. The sky is a cold, grey colour, and the wind hits us suddenly.

"Jesus," he laughs, the power of it making even him sway slightly. "It's *wild*."

I laugh out loud and shout into the wind, "I fucking love it." He laughs as the dogs echo my wildness and jump around us, barking and tying our legs together in a mad jumble of leads, before he grabs them gently and sorts them out. We unclip them, and they race down to the bottom barking happily. We follow at a slower pace, and when we reach the bottom, we set off walking briskly, the wind blowing our coats back and hitting us in the face.

Gabe looks at me curiously. "You really like it like this, don't you?"

I nod, shooting him a smile. "Yeah. Growing up here we used to come to the beach in all weathers, but this was my favourite. The others weren't so keen, apart from my sister Leah, who loved it too. When we were older and wanted time away, we used to come here and walk and talk."

"Are you closest to her, do you think?"

I consider it and then nod. "Probably. She knows most of my secrets, and I know hers. She was the first person I told that I was gay. I miss her now that she's married and living down here. She lived with me and Jude before she met Will."

He smiles. "I'm trying to imagine two of you and Jude. How did that go?"

"It was trouble," I say judiciously, and he throws his head back laughing.

I stare at him, incapable of saying anything more. He's so utterly beautiful like this, free and unencumbered by any responsibilities, laughing and warm. I feel an insane urge to draw him into my arms, and I fist my hands in the pockets of my coat to stop myself. I can just imagine his reaction if I did that. It doesn't exactly fit the parameters of whatever we are. Sadness and longing strike a pang in me, but I manage to paste a smile on my face by the time that he turns back to me.

By mutual accord, we fall silent and walk across the sands

companionably. The wind blows and buffets us and the sea echoes it, boiling and frothing onto the sands in a fury. The dogs dart here and there, occasionally bounding at the sea and barking furiously as if warning it not to misbehave. They find driftwood and bring it to Gabe, solemnly dropping it at his feet and waiting while he examines it and throws it for them.

"They've adopted you," I say, as he straightens up.

He smiles. "I love dogs."

"Why don't you -" I hesitate, and he smiles.

"Ask me, Dylan. It's not like you to be reticent." He laughs. "I swore the day that you stopped asking me personal questions I'd hold a party, but I find myself curiously edgy when you actually do it."

I nudge him playfully and then look sideways at him. "How come you don't have a dog if you like them?"

He shrugs awkwardly. "I work such long hours it wouldn't be fair, because they need a lot of looking after." The answer is reasonable on the surface, but it sounds almost pat, and I feel a wave of disappointment. *He's not going to confide in me. He doesn't trust me enough.*

Something of what I'm feeling must show because he stops, the wind blowing his black hair around his face, his eyes glowing silver in the stark light. "That's not the whole truth actually. When I was eight one of my foster carers had a dog, a little pug called Arthur. I loved him a lot. He was just so happy. He didn't want anything except your company. When I got back from school he was always just so fucking happy to see me. I hadn't had that for -"

He breaks off and looks at me self-consciously before starting walking again, and I jog to keep up. He carries on talking. "He loved bacon. The foster woman in that home was nice enough, but she was very insistent that we eat everything that she gave us, and she could get quite nasty if we didn't. That was easy enough for me, mostly because I was a growing boy and always hungry, but she used to make bacon with the fat on and I couldn't eat it. It made me gag. My mother used to cut it off, but I'd learnt by that point in my life not to ask for things." Incredibly he laughs. "Arthur was a godsend. He used to wait under the table, and I'd slip the fat to him while she wasn't looking." He pauses and smiles. "Actually, looking back that's probably why he was so glad to see me all the time."

"Not true," I murmur. "Dogs are very perceptive. What happened to Arthur?"

He shakes his head. "I don't know. He'll be dead by now, but I was moved from there after a few months, and it was onto the next home."

I want so desperately to hug him at this moment, my heart and belly hurting at the thought of a vulnerable little boy being too scared to tell someone that he didn't like fat on his bacon.

"I'm sorry," I say softly, and he shakes his head.

"It doesn't matter." He looks contemplative, and his next words come as if he's thinking aloud. "I think that's really why I don't want a dog. You get so attached to them, and I can't bear to lose anyone else." He breaks off and gives a startled *ouf,* as I give in and tackle hug him, dragging him into my arms and hugging him tight.

"Dylan, for Christ's sake, what has got into you?" he tries to say in a grumpy voice, but it sounds almost like an actor putting on a character, and suddenly he gives in and hugs me back, holding me tightly.

"Gabe," I say softly, and he raises his head, and as if to stop me talking he seals his mouth over mine, kissing me softly. We kiss for ages on the deserted beach, buffeted by winds but holding tight to each other, and I can't feel the cold. All I can feel is him.

=✉

Christmas dinner is raucous and alcohol fuelled. Crackers bang and we read out corny old jokes, laughing as if they're new. Gabe and my mum sit talking enthusiastically about art, and I can tell she's loving having someone who understands her work.

We eat a turkey reared on a neighbouring farm with homegrown vegetables that Gabe swears he can taste the difference from supermarket ones. My dad serves wine from his wine cellar, telling Gabe that he might have come home to run the farm, but he was dammed if he was going to drink scrumpy cider like his father had.

Gabe sips the wine and makes an appreciative noise, which is alarmingly close to the noise he makes when he fucks into me, and I shift awkwardly. "This is gorgeous. You said you came home. Were you living away?"

My dad nods. "I was in London at university doing a finance degree. I was going to be an investment banker. That's where I met Rebecca."

My mum laughs. "I was doing my art degree when I met him in a pub. He was going out with a girl I knew. We hit it off, and before I knew it, he'd dumped her and asked me out."

"Fast worker," Gabe smiles. "So how did you end up here?"

My dad shrugs. "My father took ill and later died. There was only me, so I came home."

"But you wanted to do something else?" Gabe asks softly, and my dad smiles.

"Family first, Gabe. It's the way I was brought up, and I couldn't change that. In the end, I didn't want to." He looks around the room, memories soft on his face. "Sometimes we think that a certain path in life is the way we have to go. We see other routes, but we avoid them because we're so insistent they're not for us, that we might get lost or hurt. Then sometimes fate sets in, and someone takes your hand or waves you over. You step off your chosen path, and find that although this one is new and scary, somehow your feet know the way to navigate it. You might even find that it leads you the way that you were always meant to go."

There's a short silence as we all stare at him. I'm not sure what he's saying, but I am sure he's not just talking about his coming home, and it's meant for Gabe in some way.

Gabe stares at him, thoughts slipping across his face too quickly for me to read, and then he looks at my dad and nods, before turning to my mum. "And what did you think to the change?"

My mum smiles and looks at my dad lovingly. "It was too late for me by then. I loved Tom, so I came with him."

"And left your art career?"

She laughs and grips his arm lightly. "My career was something that happened around my real hopes and dreams, which were tied up with having this family and growing old with Tom. We didn't have much money then, but we were all together. The art career and the success are just icing. I love it, and it feeds my soul, but my kids and Tom are enough. They always will be."

Ben breaks the moment. "Fucking hell, this is way too touchy feely for me. Let's open the presents."

We make tea and wander into the lounge. It's a big room with a view over the hills to the sea. Our old, insanely comfortable sofas are still here, and the room is lit with the glow of the lights on the Christmas tree. This is weighed down with decorations, some of which are older than we are, and others made by us when we were children.

Mu mum hands around a plate of homemade mince pies, and we munch happily as we open presents. Gabe goes out of the room for a minute, and when he comes back he has an armful of brightly wrapped gifts which he hands out. I watch as my family opens them and look astounded.

He's bought my dad a case of wine which from my dad's expression is expensive stuff. My dad looks up at him, his eyes bright. "Gabe, you really shouldn't have, but I'm definitely not going to complain."

My mum opens the envelope inside her parcel and exclaims loudly, before coming over and drawing him into a tight hug. "Oh my God, a weekend in Venice in time for the carnival. How did you know that I've always wanted to go there?"

Gabe smiles, looking pleased and awkward at the same time. "I didn't, but it's a fantastic time to be in Venice. I hope you can get away from the farm okay."

"We will," she says firmly, looking at my dad who laughs.

"I'll do as I'm told, Gabe, like always. Thank you, son, that's so thoughtful."

Gabe flushes red and sits back down, accepting a fist bump and an awed thank you from Ben who is looking at the brand-new Play Station in its shiny box.

"It's nothing compared to what you've given me this holiday," Gabe says in a soft voice. "Thank you so much for letting me join your holidays." He reaches for the last present which is a small box, and hands it to me. "This is for you, Dylan."

"I thought you gave me my present last night," I say without thinking, and then reach out and kick my brother when he makes a retching noise.

Gabe smiles, and I think only I see the wolfish side to it. "No, this is my real present."

"But I didn't get you anything," I protest. "You said we weren't doing that."

He shakes his head, a smile flitting over his mouth that's surprisingly tender. "I changed my mind. You already give me enough." He gestures to the present impatiently. "Open it then."

I tear off the wrapping, and then still in surprise. "Gabe, what the hell?"

"Fucking hell," Ben whistles. "That's an Omega Seamaster watch, Dyl. They cost a fortune."

"I hope you like it," Gabe says. "Because I had it engraved."

I extract the watch from its velvet home with shaking fingers and turn it round, only to burst into laughter. On it is engraved the words, *'Hopefully this will rectify your appalling timekeeping'*. I burst out laughing. "That is so fucking you," I hoot. "I love it." I hug him tight, feeling the warmth of his body and inhaling the scent of spiced oranges. "Thank you," I whisper into his ear, and he shudders and puts me away.

Mu mum and dad look at each other and stand up. "Be back in a minute," she says, and they leave the room. Ben busies himself throwing the wrapping paper on the fire, but not before checking it carefully. We'd learnt to do that when my sister once inadvertently chucked two hundred pounds on the fire.

"Thank you," I whisper, snuggling up to him daringly, and he draws me close for once.

"I know you've needed one since that piece of crap broke."

I smile. "That's what you were doing last night when you asked me the time."

He smiles bashfully. "Do you like it?" he asks almost awkwardly, and I slide it onto my wrist and admire it.

"I absolutely love it, Gabe, but it's too much."

He shakes his head. "No, it isn't. You give me a lot."

"This is just a few days at Christmas."

"Not the holidays." I open my mouth to ask what, but I'm interrupted by my mum and dad dragging in a huge rectangular object covered by a dust cloth.

"What's that?" Ben asks, turning away from his mini bonfire.

"This is Gabe's present," my mum says brightly, and Gabe gets to his feet.

"Oh my God, you shouldn't have got me anything, Rebecca. I didn't expect anything."

"I don't think you expect much at any time, Gabe," my mum says softly. "I hope that changes in the future."

My dad smiles and balances the object against the wall. "Well, tear the cloth off, lad. Put Dylan out of his misery."

I sniff. "I can't imagine what you're implying, Dad. I'm just sitting here minding my own business like normal."

My dad laughs, but Gabe walks over and grabs hold of the cloth, before pulling it gently and almost reverently away. The cloth falls away, and he gasps loudly. "Oh, this is too much."

It's one of my mum's paintings, a bold and very dramatic rendering of the moor under a stormy sky. The colours are dark and wild with blacks and greys and muted greens, but from one of the wild clouds a shaft of gold is coming down and illuminating a pool of water to iridescence.

My mum comes to stand next to him. "I didn't know what to do with this," she says softly. "And then I met you, and I realised that it was yours." He jerks and looks at her, and she nods. "I think it's a bit like you, Gabe, and I'm hoping very much that you get your own break in the clouds."

"I can't accept this," he says hoarsely. "It's too much."

She smiles. "You can and you will. You're a friend of Dylan's now, and a friend of ours too. Our door will always be open to you, regardless of whether you bring Dylan or not."

"Actually, we'd prefer you to *not* bring Dylan," Ben says though a mouthful of mince pie, breaking the moment expertly, and giving Gabe a second to regain his composure and hug my mum and dad. I shoot Ben a grateful look, and he smiles kindly back.

=✉

Later that night I come awake suddenly. Not sure why, I lie still, listening. The wind is roaring around the eaves. It's wild sounding, but it's not what woke me up. I've been hearing that sound since I was little, and it's almost like a lullaby.

Then I become aware that Gabe isn't wrapped around me, and I'm cold. I turn my head and frown, because he's lying huddled against the far side of the bed, facing away from me. As I watch, he gives a deep groan and rolls to his back, his face screwed up and his body glistening with sweat in the moonlight.

"Gabe," I whisper, and put out my hand thinking he's sick. However, at that point he arches his neck and rolls again, and gives out a hoarse moan which must be what woke me up. Realising that he's having a bad dream I reach out, but just as I touch him he sits bolt upright and shouts out, "No, no, no." I sit up hurriedly, hovering on my knees in front of him as he stares with unseeing eyes.

"Gabe," I say hoarsely. "Sweetheart, you were dreaming. It's okay." The endearment slips out unknowingly, but I don't care. He blinks like a startled owl. "Baby, it's me. It's Dylan. It's okay. Everything's okay. It was just a dream."

His eyes clear of the dream, and something desolate and despairing runs over his face, and I can't help but reach out. I pull him close, holding his sweat soaked body against me and offering comfort. Whatever he needs, he can have from me.

For a second he holds himself rigid, and I prepare for the emergence of his gruff persona. It happens every time he feels vulnerable, but this time it doesn't. This time he folds almost like an accordion and lets me have all of his weight. I grab him with a firmer grip, coiling one hand around his back to hold him tight. The other hand I run through his hair, stroking and whispering nonsensical words of comfort.

We stay there for what seems like aeons, but then he raises his head. "Dylan," he whispers.

"I'm here."

"Dylan, I -" He chokes off his words, and then the next ones come in a rush, as if they've been waiting behind his wall of resolve, ready to flood out when he removes a few bricks. "Dylan, I need you."

Instantly, my body floods with heat. Adrenaline and something stronger coursing through me and readying my body for him. "Anything," I whisper. "You can have anything."

"I want it all," he mutters, and pushes me down onto the bed, following after me and stretching his hot, hard body over mine.

This time is different. I know it instantly, and so does he. There's a new tenderness in the fingers that run over my face and body that has never been there before. That he's never *let* be there before. I also know that I'll pay for this as soon as it's finished. Maybe that's why the whole encounter assumes a dreamlike feel, a sequence of mental snapshots that I'll store away when he goes back into emotional hibernation.

My senses reel. I feel the heat of his lips as he kisses me, the moist warmth of his mouth, and the tensile strength of his tongue as it tangles with mine. I feel the tremble of his hands, as he runs them over my body as if memorizing me. I absorb the way he sends his fingers, wet with lube, between my cheeks as he readies me, but he lingers over the act, turning it into an act of devotion rather than just simple preparation. I see myself arching into him as he eases into me, and I hear the heated whispers of praise that fall from his lips.

He tells me how my body feels to him, how the act is different with me. I feel the slow, languid thrusts grow fevered. I see the fire in his eyes, and feel the tremor that runs through his body as he thrusts harder, lost to passion and need. I throw my head back as I come, and I feel the warmth as he comes into the condom inside me. I remember that for a brief second, he looks into my eyes and I let him see everything, and later I remember the touch of wetness against my cheek as he rests his face against mine.

I hold him closer, and memory fades as the darkness drags me under.

Payment comes sooner than I expect, as I wake up the next morning to an empty bed. Hearing movement, I force my bleary eyes open and jerk as I see Gabe. He's fully dressed and moving around the bedroom, picking clothes up and pushing them frantically into his bag.

I swallow hard. I can feel a wave of pain inside me, but I push it away. I can't show it to him. Not yet. He'll guess my feelings and pull away, and I know I'm close now. I knew last night that he'd fight it, but apparently, he's opted for the simple tack of flight instead.

"Going somewhere?" I ask, and he jerks to a stop, halting his silent, frantic packing.

"Dylan," he says, and then nothing else comes out.

I raise my eyebrow. "You were expecting someone else?"

"No. I, no -" He thrusts his hand through his hair, and when I see the tremor, I'm overwhelmed with the need to protect him. I think it's always been there, and I can't see it ever vanishing.

"Is there an emergency at work?" I make myself say.

Relief and something else that looks like regret crosses his face before he recovers. "Yes, I have to go back. I'm sorry."

I shrug. "Don't be sorry. You can't help it, can you?"

He shoots me an uncertain look. "No, but you stay here and enjoy your holiday." He attempts a smile. "You can take an extra few days off. Come back after New Year."

Pain lodges in my ribs, but I refrain from flinching. *He doesn't want me with him for New Year's Eve.* I'd had visions of being with him on that night, doing the countdown and being the man on his arm when he looked the new year in the face, but I let them slide away. It's not time yet.

"That sounds good," I say calmly. "Thank you."

He hesitates and then nods jerkily, disappearing out of the door and then returning with his shaving kit. He forces it into his bag, and then zips it up with a final sound. I look around the room. It's as if he's never been here.

I slide out of the bed, grabbing my jeans and a hoody and pulling them on. "What are you doing?" he asks, a touch of panic in his voice, and I make sure he sees me roll my eyes.

"I'm seeing you out, Gabe. Is that okay, or should I just wave a handkerchief faintly from the window?"

"Twat." He smiles, but it's a faint facsimile of his normal grump and sarcasm.

He follows me out of the bedroom and down the stairs, and we stop as my mum appears from the kitchen. "You're up early, boys. Ready for breakfast?" Then she sees his bag. Understanding runs through her eyes, and she shoots me a quick, commiserating glance that he misses.

"I'm so sorry, Rebecca, but there's been a work emergency and I've got to go back. Thank you so much for the last couple of days." He stops, and when he speaks again it lacks the usual polish and sounds almost raw. "It's really been the best Christmas I've ever had."

She smiles and pulls him into a hug, kissing the side of his face. "Oh, you're very welcome, sweetheart. Don't be a stranger."

He pulls back almost reluctantly. "I'll arrange to have the painting shipped to me if that's okay."

She nods, and I lean against the wall. "I'll do it, Gabe. Don't worry about it."

He hesitates. "Are you sure?"

I smile. "It's my job."

He flinches slightly, and then rallies quickly. "I'll just put my bag in the car and go and find Tom to say goodbye. Will you say goodbye to Ben for me?"

I nod. "I will."

I watch him open the door and move towards the car, and then see my dad emerge from the cowshed and walk towards him, Lizzie trotting at his side like a shadow as normal. The two men talk, and my mum turns to me.

"Are you okay?" she whispers.

I shrug, fighting down the feelings that are threatening to emerge in all their ugly glory. "I'm fine."

She slings her arm over my shoulder. "Maybe sleeping with your boss was a reckless thing to do."

I jerk and stare at her. "*What*? You knew?"

She laughs. "Of course I did. I'm your mother, Dylan. I don't have to be Mystic Meg to realise that the Gabe you've gone on about for two years, the bastard, is also the man who you're in love with."

I stiffen. "I'm not -" I break off as she gives me a sidelong glare. "Okay, I *am* in love with him, but I can't let him know, Mum. He'd run for the hills."

She stares at Gabe as he talks quietly to my dad. "If I was a sane woman, Dylan, I would be telling you to get out now. That he has heartbreak written over every gorgeous inch of him, and that he'll never love you back."

I stare at her. "But you're not sane. We all know that."

She smiles. "Exactly. Dylan, that man needs love like no one I've ever met before. It's like he's starved himself of any meaningful connection." She sighs. "He reminds me of Fagin."

I jerk. "Do you mean the scraggy, old dog that used to sniff around for scraps? *That's* who my boyfriend reminds you of."

She laughs. "It's actually a good comparison. Fagin had been beaten and neglected all his life. No one knew who he belonged to, and although people tried to help him, he wouldn't have it. He'd appear at your door and let you feed him, and sometimes he'd even let you pet him. When you did, he'd lean against you for a while as if he couldn't understand what a good touch should feel like, and you'd feel so powerful and happy. But you've got to remember that when he'd done that, he would always move away and be on his way."

"Okay, lesson learnt. I'll remember it," I say, but she shakes her head.

"Gabe might be worth all this handling, Dylan. I happen to think that he is, and I'm crossing my fingers for you because the two of you could really be something together. I think he cares, but that's not what I want you to get from that story."

"What then?"

"Fagin would bite if you got too close. Gabe's like that, Dylan, so you need to be careful, because if you corner him, he could hurt you badly."

CHAPTER THIRTEEN

To: Dylan Mitchell

From: Gabe Foster

When I was a small boy, I liked to eat soil. My mother worried, but she needn't have been concerned. Unbeknown to both of us, I was actually just preparing myself to drink your coffee.

I remember her words later on when things begin to change between us.

I didn't notice at first, but looking back, I can see that from the time we came back from Devon, he started to change. At first the distance I felt between us I put down to actual distance, as he'd been asked to go to Bath to help our sister office with a case that had proved difficult. For the first couple of weekends, he came back and rang me every night, cajoling me into epic rounds of phone sex.

But now as the case drags on, the calls have started to come further apart, and he offers feeble excuses for not travelling back at the weekends, saying that he's too busy. However, he never asks me to go to him, and I draw what I know is the correct assumption – he's getting ready to dump me. That moment in bed when he'd clung to me and looked into my eyes, he'd seen things that I didn't want him to see. He'd needed me, and it had set the clock ticking on our relationship.

I recognise it for what it is, because who hasn't had this happen to them? However, the time it had happened to me before, I'd never really cared. This time I do, because I've never been so in love with one person, never felt that my happiness is so tied up in one surly, bad-tempered idiot. It hurts to know that fate has given me the perfect person for me to love, but has failed to make it reciprocal.

Still, it's hard for me to believe this is happening, despite all my mental preparations. However, the first time I ring his hotel room and hear the voice of another man in the background, then I know it's for real, and I have to begin the process of distancing myself for my own wellbeing, because God, this fucking hurts.

I lower my phone slowly to my lap and stare into space. I don't know how long I space out for, but when I look up Jude is standing in front of me with a worried look on his face. "What happened?" he demands.

I sigh and attempt a smile. "There was someone with him."

"*What?*" he explodes. "No, surely not. I know he's a twat, but I've seen him with you." He shudders. "Jesus, I've *heard* it with my own ears."

I try to smile, but to my shame, I feel my lip tremble and seeing it, he comes down next to me. "No, Dylan, don't babe. Please don't cry over him."

I firm my lips and take a shuddering breath. "I won't," I say hoarsely. "But God, Jude, this hurts so much."

"He's a fucking bastard," Jude hisses, and I shake my head.

"It's not his fault. He was always so honest that this was just sex, and that we'd do it until we didn't want to anymore. I guess he's just reached that point ahead of me. This is my fault. I'm so naïve, Jude, because I just hoped that he'd see me and realise that we're actually pretty perfect together. It's not his fault that I'm not the one for him."

"A blow-up doll is obviously the one for him," he says poisonously. "I'm sorry, Dylan, but I think the man's a fucking wanker. Anyone with eyes could look at you and know that you do not have *just sex* written over you."

"Or perhaps I'm being stupid," I mutter, and he tightens his hold on me.

"Listen to me - you are not stupid. Someday someone is going to come along and take one look at you and see exactly what a fucking prize he's getting, and they will fucking settle down with you so quickly that your head will whirl. And you know what?" I look at him. "I'm going to enjoy watching Gabe's face when it happens, because that man has deep feelings for you, Dylan. He just seems so emotionally stunted that he'll never do anything about it." He strokes my hair affectionately. "You're worth more than this arrangement. Please think about that."

I do think about it. I think about it as January waltzes out in blustery winds and ice-cold showers, and Gabe stops calling. The first week of February comes and goes, and one day I walk into the office and stop dead.

Gabe turns to me. "Good morning," he says almost nervously, his eyes running feverishly over me. He looks gorgeous in a gunmetal-blue suit with a brilliant white shirt, and turquoise, spotted tie, but he seems to crackle with nervous energy, like a fallen power line.

"I wasn't expecting you," I say, proud to hear how cool my voice is, and covering my agitation by hanging up my coat and dumping my bag at my desk. *Decorum* I tell myself, and remember Jude's words of a few weeks ago.

I walk over to the kitchenette to start coffee, aware with every fibre of my being that he's shadowing my footsteps. I stop dead in the doorway and stare in disbelief. "You started the coffee?" I say faintly.

He rubs his hand down his face in embarrassment. "I thought we'd cut out the middleman, and just proceed to the drinkable coffee," he says as if trying to coax a laugh out of me over our old coffee joke, but for the life of me I can't summon a smile, and his face falls.

For a second I want to take back my coldness because even now I can't bear to see him sad, but then I remind myself of the weeks of silence and the man's voice in his room, and when I speak my voice is like ice, and he winces. "Did the case finish okay?"

"Yes, we won, which is a miracle. I mean I knew we'd win, but the others didn't, and it was such a shit storm." He's almost babbling, but I make myself nod and get my tablet from my bag.

"That's good," I say in a distracted voice while pulling up his diary. "Well, as you're back I'll make appointments for Mr Simpkins and Mr Bridges. They've been asking, but I hadn't heard from you, so I didn't know when to slot them in."

To my horror I hear my voice waver, and so does he. "Dylan," he says hoarsely, reaching out to lay a hand on my arm, and then staring as I back up so sharply I bang my elbow on the desk.

"No," I say sharply. "That's fine. It's as it should be. Now I'll pour you a coffee, and we can go over the arrangements for the week." I move away busying myself with papers and pens, as he hovers at the door watching me intently as if I'm some sort of mystery to him.

He wrings his hands together, the ultimate sign of nervousness in him. "Dylan please, I have to talk to you. I'm sorry. I -"

"Well, hello, Gabe," comes the booming voice of Michael, one of the senior partners, from the door, and I jerk my attention to him immediately. Gabe is slower, but he turns his look from me to him as Michael carries on talking. "Good job on the Stoughton case. I've had exceptionally good reports, so well done. Lunch today?"

"I don't know about lunch," I hear him say, shooting me a look

from the corner of his eye, but I look up immediately from my blind
perusal of his diary.

"Yes, you're free, Mr Foster," I say coolly.

"But -" he starts, and Michael interrupts.

"Excellent. Now come with me, because James wants a blow-by-
blow account of your month." He stops to laugh coarsely. "Not too
much detail though, man. I saw the young man you were hanging
around with when I came down there, and I don't think James's heart
will stand a retell of everything, or *everyone* you got up to."

My hands tighten into claws on my tablet, and I hear the intake
of my breath as if from a distance.

In the background, I can hear Gabe telling Michael in a hoarse
voice that he'll follow him in a minute, but I've already edged past
them and am moving down the corridor to the men's bathroom. Once
inside, I pace tightly in the small space for a second, wringing my
hands at the intense pain. I knew he'd had someone, but to have it
confirmed makes my stomach and chest hurt so badly.

I bend over breathing heavily, and then run the water until it's
freezing and splash my face until I gasp. I'm drying my hands and
face with a paper towel when the door bursts open behind me and
crashes into the wall.

"Dylan," he gasps. "*Please.*"

"No," I say sharply. "You know, Mr Foster, I think I feel ill. I'm
going home now if that's okay with you?"

"No, please," he says. "I have to tell you -"

"You don't have to do *anything* for me," I interrupt coldly, and
some part of me is impressed by how detached I sound. "We're
nothing to each other. Why would you explain fucking another man
to someone who's just a hook up anyway? You never promised me
anything after all."

He flinches, and puts a hand out as if to touch me. "Yes, but I
know that you feel something. I know it's hurting you."

"Oh, fuck you," I shout, losing my temper like a snapped elastic
band, grabbing his hand and pushing it away from me. "You don't

fucking get to do this, you patronising wanker. You've spent all these weeks reinforcing how detached you are from me. Never calling or texting unless you want phone sex. Fuck telling me anything about your day. As long as we both come, that's all that matters to you. Even when you were here and we had sex, afterwards it was like fucking clockwork. I must tell poor Dylan not to expect too much from me. I must let him know he's just another convenient hole. Poor, poor, naïve Dylan. Well, I got the fucking message when I heard that other man in your room that night." He makes a beseeching gesture, but I push my face into his. "Fuck this, Gabe. Fuck you."

Ignoring his whispered plea, I shoot out of the bathroom, glad that there's a breakfast meeting on this floor so no one is around to see my hurried exit from the building. He doesn't follow me.

=✉

The frenzied knocking comes at my door earlier than I expect, and I sigh because I know I have to speak to him. For a second I wish Jude was here, but I don't need a third party getting involved. It's messy enough already.

I walk over and removing the chain, I crack open the door but have to stand back quickly as he comes in like a whirlwind. "Please let me talk," he says hoarsely. "I just need to tell you that I didn't sleep with him."

"Who was he?"

"A paralegal at the company. He was assigned to help me."

I try for a smile, but it must look more like a grimace. "Is that a euphemism? Another office romance, eh? You're really racking them up at the moment, Gabe." A tremor runs across his face, and I immediately hold up my hand. "Sorry, wrong word choice. I know you're practically allergic to the word *romance*. Let me try again, another office fuck friend."

"I need you to know that I didn't fuck him," he says with a dogged determination that confuses and hurts me at the same time. I want to believe him so much, but the force of that need frightens me.

I shake my head, suddenly so tired of feeling like this. "You don't need to do this, Gabe. It doesn't matter."

"It fucking does," he shouts suddenly, looking almost astonished at his volume. "It *does* matter," he finishes more quietly. "I'm not going to lie to you. I *can't* lie to you. I didn't do anything."

"But you could have," I say tersely, and he shrugs, looking uncomfortable.

"I could have, but I chose not to."

"Why?" I ask baldly.

He looks puzzled. "Because I'm with you." My heart rises so fast from my boots that I almost get whiplash, but then, unfortunately, he carries on. "I mean it wouldn't be fair. When I do it, I'll tell you first. I won't keep secrets."

I feel vomit rise and burn my throat. So simple, like he's doing poor, simple Dylan a favour and explaining the rules. Like it's inevitable that he *will* fuck someone else.

"Why do you look sad?" he asks, coming closer. "I hate that. Please don't be sad, Dylan. I'm sorry I didn't ring you, but it was so busy and I don't know -"

He trails off, and almost reluctantly I say, "What?"

He shrugs almost awkwardly. "I missed you, Dylan, and every time I rang you and heard your voice it got worse, so in the end, it was simpler not to ring."

I hate myself that I feel a sad joy at that admission, because to me it means something else. It means that he didn't care enough to make sure that he wasn't hurting me when he cut himself off. He had felt something, and he'd immediately acted to shut it down.

But still those hopes batter against their cage. He was feeling something for me, more than he'd wanted. *Surely that's a good sign? Maybe if I just hang in, he'll realise what all this means.* And underpinning all of this is the usual dark hunger for him, which weakens my resolve with the desire to feel him against me. I know the chances are high that we're ending. *Would it be so wrong just to have one last memory of him?*

He senses my wavering of course, and moves closer, drawing me into his arms, and my heart notices the deep sigh that he gives at feeling me against him. "Baby," he says deeply. "Please forgive me. Tell me it's okay."

I shake my head and instead pull his lips to mine, wanting to divert him because he knows we're ending too. This is just the death knell.

The same bright passion springs up between us and he growls, dragging me to my room and throwing me on the bed, but for the first time ever between us, it's just sex. My mind has distanced itself from him, and he knows it. I sense that in the tightness of his grip and the desperate way he fucks me as if trying to make me remember. The problem is that I can't forget.

✉

The next week passes slowly, and I drift through it like some sort of robot, programed to follow his urges and needs, but at a distance, as if I lack the heart anymore to feel. At first, he appears almost desperate to get that back, but then he seems to grow angrier. However, for some unknown reason, I still try to make it work.

I honestly can't say where my head is at this point. The only joy I get is from the sex and the knowledge that he isn't with anyone else, but I know that doesn't mean he's really ever with me. Over that week we drift into different roles, switching as our moods dictate. I'm alternatively conciliatory and distant, and he's either angry or uneasy.

Then Valentine's Day happens, and I drop my guard without even knowing. Maybe it's the fact that he's been tender this morning. Lying in bed with us wrapped together, it seems like he's making love to me as he stares into my eyes and slowly thrusts inside me, pulling back every time we get close, until we're dripping with sweat and when I come it's like the sweetest pain. He lies there afterwards hugging me to him, and it just happens. I let him back in, and when I smile at him fully for a second, he looks like it hurts him.

"You seem happy," he says hoarsely.

"Well, it is Valentine's Day," I say lightly, and sigh when I see his face tighten. *Of course he wouldn't celebrate the festival of love.* "And it's Saturday." I squeeze his arse to move so that I can go and clean up. He'd stopped doing that after Devon, as if it was too intimate. A pain hits my heart, and I can see him watching me intently.

"We should do something," he says swiftly, and I sigh and shake my head.

"Don't be silly. There's no need to do that for me. That's not we're about."

He looks angry for a second, and then folds his arms stubbornly, his olive skin glowing against my mint-green sheets. "Come on, let's do something different." He looks up. "Let's go out for a meal."

"Gabe, Valentine's Day is for lovers, for people who love each other, not fuck buddies." A flinch runs through him, and I stare at him. "Are you okay?"

"Yes," he says stiffly. "I want to do this." He pauses. "I know it's been different lately, that you're hurting."

I shake my head. "It is as you said it would be, Gabe. I was being a naïve idiot, holding out for some wonderful relationship where we love each other."

"And you're wiser now?" he asks hoarsely, holding himself tightly, almost as if he's hurt.

I make myself shrug carelessly. "We both know where this thing between us is going."

"Good," he says harshly. "Saves us having a long conversation about it then." He flings the covers back and dresses quickly, shoving his legs into his jeans as if he can't wait to get out of here. As he gets to the door, he throws back over his shoulder. "Be ready at eight. I'll pick you up."

But he doesn't come. At eight o'clock I look up from my position at the window, where I'm poised like a sad twat waiting to see him.

Nine o'clock comes and goes, and I watch couples hand in hand going into the Italian restaurant opposite my flat, which is decorated with pink balloons and hearts. By ten o'clock I know that he isn't coming, and I give a shuddering sigh, trying to keep the tears at bay. Anger freezes them away, a hard, burning anger that I'm here yet again at his mercy.

I move over to the kitchen to find the duty-free whisky that Jude brought back, moving stiffly after sitting in the chair for so long. I pour myself a drink and look down at my outfit of a black suit with skinny trousers and a white shirt. I shrug and ditch the jacket and loosen my black tie, before taking a hefty slug of the whisky and making myself cough.

Four large glasses later and I feel no pain, as I sit in the darkened flat listening to Alison Moyet sing about heartbreak and loss.

The knock at the door makes me gasp and spill my drink. "Shit," I slur, licking whisky from my fingers. The knocking comes again. "I'm coming," I holler, and then stand stock still as I open my door and find Gabe standing there with another man.

"What the fuck?" I say slowly.

"Sweetheart," he exclaims loudly, coming close and trying to kiss me. I shove him away, wrinkling my nose at the smell of alcohol that's coming off him in waves. I notice his outfit of jeans, Converse and a blue and white raglan t-shirt, and feel anger stir. *He never, really meant to go out.*

"What's the matter?" he slurs. He turns to the other man. "I'm sorry. How rude of me. This is Ollie. Ollie, this is the missus."

"Fuck off," I jerk out. "You're drunk."

"I am," he says delightedly. "I am drunk because aren't we celebrating the festival of love, my dearest. Better known as the day you kick me to the curb because I can't be what you want."

"I thought we were going out for a meal?" I stare at the other man's hand on Gabe's arm, drifting languorously up and down like seaweed.

"Oh, so did I, but then I had a much better idea." Gabe says hoarsely, his eyes glittering.

"Did you find it at the bottom of a bottle?" I reply slowly, and he laughs delightedly.

"So pert, my darling. Isn't he adorable?" he says, turning swiftly to Ollie, who looks me up and down smoothly before smiling and nodding. Gabe turns back to me, swaying slightly at the sudden movement. "We're going out dancing tonight." I shake my head, and his eyes drift down my body. "Since you've gone to so much effort for me, I thought we'd celebrate, and I can give you my gift."

"What gift?" I ask slowly, unable to keep up with this jittery mess.

Gabe laughs harshly and turns to Ollie. "Ah, the missuses. Every single one of them has always liked the presents."

Ollie laughs and my temper snaps. "Fuck off," I say angrily. "You're a fucking twat, Gabe."

I step back, but he shoves his foot in the door to stop me shutting it. "But you haven't unwrapped your present yet."

"You haven't got me a -" I stop, a horrifying idea forming in my head, and Gabe grins, standing back with a sneer fixed firmly on his face. He makes jazz hands and flourishes them around Ollie.

"Here he is, my dearest. Here's your present. Isn't he pretty?"

He twists the man's face to his, and to my horror he bends to kiss him. He sends his tongue languorously over Ollie's, before reeling back, barely stopping himself from backing into the wall. "He's delicious, darling. Only the best for you."

I stare at him feeling anger course through me, obliterating everything like napalm and leaving only the strongest desire to hurt this man who is hurting me so much. "This is what you want," I say coldly. "A threesome to finish it?"

For a second I think that I see a wild pain flare in his eyes, but I must be mistaken because the next minute he's leering at me. "That's why we're so perfect, Dylan. You *always* give me what I want."

"I'm doing that now," I say, ice cold and referencing more than he is, because I'm finishing us. It's what he obviously wants. I throw open the door. "But why waste money on a club, Gabe? There's a bed in here, and you're lucky, I haven't even changed the sheets yet."

I reach out and grab Ollie's hand and drag him into the flat, staring at Gabe the whole time. "Let's do it," I snap, and for a second, apprehension flares in his eyes, but I ignore him as I tug Ollie onwards.

"This is a bit of a dump," he sneers, looking around with a disgusted expression on his face.

"Well don't worry, sweetheart, you won't be here long," I return, stripping off my shirt and tie, and pushing him towards the open door of my bedroom.

"Wow," he whistles, reaching over to drag his fingers down my chest. "You didn't tell me how fucking gorgeous he was. You're a lucky bastard, Gabe."

Gabe hovers behind us, watching as Ollie touches me, running his fingers down my six-pack and dipping down to trace the v of my pelvic muscles. "Lucky?" he asks hoarsely.

"Yes, darling," I drawl, taking Ollie's shirt and jerking it apart in one swift move so that buttons fly everywhere. Ignoring his deep moan, I draw him to me so that our chests touch and I can see Gabe's face over Ollie's shoulder. "Gabe *is* the lucky one. He manages to go through life with a smile. No pesky emotions and feelings for Gabe. He doesn't have them," I whisper loudly into Ollie's ear, making him shudder and moan.

"Is this what you want?" I ask Gabe coldly, as he falls back against the wall, looking clumsy and tortured. "Are you watching me play with my present?"

He swallows hard as I reach down and graze my hand over Ollie's hard dick, never breaking our eye contact. He breaks in the end, looking away with a groan that doesn't sound pleasured. Instead, he sounds almost pained, like he's hurting inside, and it drains my anger suddenly and completely.

"Wait," I say, and then gasp as Ollie surges up and takes my mouth with a throaty groan, but with my anger gone this is wrong, *so* wrong. His hands feel hot on my body, and I have a second to wonder when I'd got so cold. I lift my hands to push him away, but his warm body is suddenly gone. It isn't until I open my eyes and see him on the floor with Gabe standing over him, that I realise Gabe has pulled him off me.

"Enough," Gabe shouts. "Don't you fucking touch him, Ollie."

Ollie looks up at him from his position on the floor. "You're so fucking *weird* at the moment, Gabe. I don't know what the fuck is going on with you, but this has not exactly been my idea of a fun session. I'm going." He huffs and stands up, leaving the room quickly. The front door slamming sounds like a klaxon in the stone-cold silence of my bedroom.

"Dylan," Gabe says hoarsely. Then there's a click as he switches the lamp on. I flinch at the brightness, and put my hand up to shield my face, before shivering.

"You're cold," he whispers, and he reaches down and grabs the comforter from the bottom of the bed and wraps it around me, no sign of drunkenness about him now.

I pull it closer, needing the comfort. Idly I wonder if that's how it got its name, but I sigh instead of asking Gabe, who knows acres of trivia. "Some Valentine's Day," I say sadly, as the corrosive anger vanishes, leaving behind only a bone-deep coldness and sadness.

"I'm sorry," he says hoarsely. "I'm so fucking sorry, Dylan. I don't know what I was thinking."

"It doesn't matter." My voice is hollow, and he flinches, but I want to end this with the truth now because that might make me feel cleaner about what happened tonight. "I can't do this anymore," I say softly, and he jerks, visible tremors running through him.

"No, don't say it." His voice is hoarse, and when I look up, his eyes are full of tears.

"Oh, Gabe," I say sadly, reaching up to touch his face. "I have to, sweetheart." He closes his eyes at my touch, leaning into it the way that a plant does to the sun. I take a deep breath. "I love you," I say clearly, and his eyes fly open and I swallow hard at the look of blind panic there.

"No," he says frantically. "Oh, don't do that, Dylan. Don't love me."

My heart breaks because here we finally are at the end, and there is no going back from him rejecting my love. "But I do, and you knew that, Gabe. That's what tonight was about after all wasn't it? You wanted to let me know my place beyond all doubt."

For a second I think I see confusion cross his face, but it's quickly replaced by agitation. "Push it away," he says urgently. "We can still be together. We'll just have to try harder, and pick a better partner next time."

I push his hand away, stung out of my calm. "*That's* how you treat my telling you that I love you. You tell me to try harder to sleep with someone else." I shake my head. "A long time ago, I'd have dreamed of you telling me you loved me too and begging me to try, but I know better now." I take a deep breath. "I know that I can't do this with you anymore, Gabe. I'm worth more than being a fuck toy for someone who hasn't got the balls to try for more."

He flinches back as if I've struck him, but I can't regret my words because they're true.

Anger fills his face. "So that's what your love comes down to," he says furiously, standing up and pacing away from me. "It's a trap, Dylan. You love me, but only if I do what you want. Well, fuck you. I will never be, or do, what you want."

"But if I'd done as *you* wanted tonight, I'd be fucking another man," I say gently and watch as he actually gags at the thought. "I'm sorry, Gabe. I love you, which means I can't be with someone whose reaction to knowing that his partner cares for him, is to bring another man into their bed as a Valentine present. I'm worth more. I want to matter, and not be treated as if I'm an old dildo that gets tossed in the drawer when the battery goes. I want to be there for someone. I want to grow old with someone. I want to die knowing that I loved with all my heart, and to the best of my ability."

"And I'm not fucking worthy of that?" he spits, anger riding him with flushed cheeks and shaking hands. "Well fuck you, Dylan. Fuck you and your stupid, provincial ideals of a cottage in the country and matching dogs. You go out and get your fucking country squire. I'll be out enjoying myself, and I can promise you one thing." He leans closer. "I won't think of you again."

Then he's gone, with the slam of the door the only sound to echo the fact that my heart is broken.

I lay back on the bed, wrapping myself in the duvet until all I can smell is his and my scents mingled together, and I weep because he's never coming back, and although it *was* the right thing to do I've broken my own heart in the execution of it.

CHAPTER FOURTEEN

To: Gabe Foster

From: Dylan Mitchell

Forrest Gump said that life is like a box of chocolates. If it was, today would be like one of those nougats that take out your filling. Oh, by the way, your boyfriend is waiting in my office when you've finished your meeting.

One Month Later

I right click on my document, and a second later the whirring sound tells me it's printing. I reach over and slide the sheets into a folder, and then, gathering the other paperwork from the corner of my desk, I stand up and knock on my boss's door. Hearing her shout to come in, I pop my head around the door.

"I've got the contracts you asked for, and the printout of the book from your slush pile that we were talking about."

My new boss, Morna, looks up over the top of her horn-rimmed glasses. She's a tiny, middle-aged woman, who, with her steel-grey bob and short stature could be mistaken for a grandma. However, if anyone treated her like that they'd be in for a world of pain, as she's a formidable woman. She'd been at the forefront of women in publishing and is now a very renowned senior editor with a famous publishing house. Sharp tongued and fierce on behalf of her clients, she apparently had a habit of going through staff like a wild fire, or so the temp agency had told me.

However, I had worked in the front line of grumpy bosses with Gabe, and to our surprise, we'd found that we meshed extremely well. After I'd been with her for only a couple of days, she'd asked me to work for her full time, and it had been a surprise to find that I actually enjoyed the work. It was varied and interesting to be doing something that I didn't know like the back of my hand, and lately, she'd even taken to asking my opinion about work that she'd received from new authors and prospective clients. I'd dived into this, and this week she had made a comment about training me to be an editorial assistant.

She smiles at me. "Thank you, darling. You're so good, Dylan."

"I know," I say calmly, making her snort with laughter. Then she propels her chair back after retrieving a packet of cigarettes and a lighter.

"You're going to get busted one day," I warn, as she moves over to the window. "Health and Safety will string you up for violating the clean air agreement."

"I didn't agree to the clean air agreement, so I will not be held to ransom for someone else's stupid ideas. I'm too busy and too old to run up and downstairs every time I need a cigarette."

I suppress a smile because there are shades of Gabe here. She pulls the contracts to her, and begins to sign them. "Aren't you going to check the corrections?" I ask, surprised.

She shoots a grin at me, with her cigarette clenched between her teeth like Clint Eastwood. "No need, darling, I've been watching your work, and you are meticulous to a fault. I trust you." She pauses and shoots me a keen glance. "Makes me wonder what that old boss of yours was thinking about to let you go."

I flinch slightly, covering it with a cough, but not well enough as her beady eyes analyse me.

"Hmm, I suspect there's a big story there, and I should know, I've made a career out of big stories." She waves her hand, dropping ash all over her desk. "You'll tell me in the end I hope. I fancy myself a fairly good listener for those people I like." She looks at me. "You're one of them by the way."

I'm absurdly touched. "Thank you. I like you too."

She shakes her head and gives a cackle. "You're one of the few, darling, apart from my clients." She shoots a look at me. "Go and get off home now, sweetie. You look tired."

I am tired. I haven't slept well since Gabe walked out of my life, and I know my face reflects the fact.

I move towards the door. "If you're sure?"

"I am. Another thing I'm sure about is the old quote about getting over your man by getting under another one."

I laugh incredulously. It feels wrong to get love advice from someone who looks like she should be knitting, but in truth, she's incredibly ribald with no sense of barriers.

She smiles at me. "I'm not joking, Dylan. If this person you're breaking your heart over isn't coming back, there is no point in walling yourself up in a monastery. Get out there again, because with the benefit of my long years I know there will always be another one along if you missed the last one."

"He wasn't a bus." I shake my head at her, and she cackles again. Waving goodbye, I shut her door and stroll back to my desk, gathering my bag and switching off my monitor. I hear a noise, and looking up, I hold back a sigh.

Richard is also an editor, but Morna detests him. He's lean and dark-haired, sporty and very pretty, and made no secret of his interest in me the other night at a book launch. He comes across as very self-possessed, which I think could pass very quickly into self-absorption.

"You done for the day?" he asks happily, and I nod. "Fancy going for a drink?"

"Oh, Richard, I'm sorry, but I don't think -"

"Come on," he cajoles. "One drink, and I promise to spill all the gossip from this place."

I consider him for a long second. It's been a month, and Gabe has made no effort to get in touch with me. My things had been packed and delivered from the office without a note, and that was it. Not a lot to say for two years and a lot of love. I have no doubt that he's moved on. In fact, I'm sure that after losing his temper on that night, he'd raced right off and fucked someone else. He'd been angry enough.

Which beggars the question: why have I put myself in isolation? Jude had demanded to know that last night, and I'd had no answer. Perhaps this is the start of getting back to me again, and God knows I like to make friends where I work.

I smile at him. "Maybe one drink, and you promise all the gossip?"

He looks astonished for a second, making me wonder how stand-offish I appear at the moment. "Oh, absolutely," he says quickly. "All the dirty stuff."

I throw my messenger bag over my body. "Lead on then."

He takes me to a small wine bar near work where the walls are exposed brick. Old advertising pictures hang everywhere, and the rough wood tables have hurricane lanterns on them, giving the room a warm glow. I look around while I sit down at a table. It's filled with mainly business men in suits relaxing after a hard day, mixed with a spattering of the fashion crowd as a large magazine has its headquarters nearby.

When Richard asks me what I want to drink I order a Budweiser, then watch as he wrinkles his nose. "Really? Bit studenty for you, isn't it? Okay then."

I stare at him. *In what universe is Budweiser a student drink?* I pause. Maybe it is. Maybe Jude and I are *those* types of students - the eternal ones. Should we be holding dinner parties and sipping sherry? I snort as I imagine us in smoking jackets, sipping from tiny glasses with our little fingers held up, and saying things like 'chin chin old boy'.

Pulling out my phone while I wait for Richard, I check my messages and see one from Jude.

JUDE: WHERE THE FUCK ARE YOU?

I stare at it and shrug, before typing quickly.

ME: HAVING A DRINK WITH A COLLEAGUE FROM WORK. WHY ARE YOU SO CONCERNED, MOTHER? HAVE I OVERSHOT MY CURFEW?

A second later my phone beeps.

JUDE: IF I WAS YOUR MOTHER I WOULD SPANK YOU.

I snort and tap quickly.

ME: IF YOU WERE YOUR DAD, I'D LET YOU.

I chuckle thinking of his reply, and the phone beeps obediently.

JUDE: FFS. THAT'S DISGUSTING. ANYWAY, NEVER MIND THAT. I NEED YOU HOME ASAP.
ME: THIS ISN'T THE SAME SITUATION AS WHEN YOU HAD BILLY

THE MODEL ROUND THE OTHER DAY IS IT, BECAUSE I'VE ONLY
JUST DE-BLEACHED MY EYEBALLS.
JUDE: NO, IT ISN'T. BLOODY BILLY. ONE WATCH OF FIFTY
SHADES AND HE THINKS HE'S THE MASTER OF BDSM. I KNEW HE
WOULDN'T BE ABLE TO GET THAT KNOT UNTIED.
ME: IT PUZZLES ME WHY HE COULDN'T JUST USE A PAIR OF SCIS-
SORS, RATHER THAN CONTRIBUTE TO MY FUTURE THERAPIST'S
WORKLOAD.
JUDE: IF HE'D USED SCISSORS I COULD HAVE FALLEN AND HURT
MYSELF. ANYWAY, STOP CHANGING THE SUBJECT. PLEASE COME
HOME ASAP.
ME: WHY?
JUDE: BECAUSE I SAID SO.

I stare at my phone, but there are no more messages. *Hmm.* I'm
interrupted in my thoughts by Richard, who comes back from the bar
carrying a bottle of red wine. "Sorry, they didn't have Budweiser, so I
thought we could share this instead."

As if red wine is a substitute for Budweiser I think sourly. I'm
already starting to form the opinion that dear old Richard is a bit of a
prick. Then I tell myself off. He's not Gabe. No one ever will be, but I
should move on. Everybody keeps telling me to go on dates. This is
me, putting my toe in the water, so I should cut him some slack.

Well, I do cut him some slack. I cut him enough slack to suspend
Nellie the Elephant from the Eiffel Tower, and it still doesn't work.
Richard is an opinionated wanker. He spends the entire two hours
talking about himself and his views on the world, which are slightly
fascist in tone.

I listen politely, trying to drink the wine as quickly as I can to get
this over with, but unfortunately, this has the effect of him buying
another bottle while I'm in the loo.

By the time we leave the wine bar, I'm fairly unsteady, and we're
holding onto each other like we're walking in a hurricane. "Where
now?" he asks happily. "Shall we eat?"

At this point, my phone beeps, reminding me of Jude and the emergency I've forgotten for two hours. "I'm really sorry, but I've got to go home. My flatmate keeps messaging me, asking me to go home."

"Oh, great, I'll come back with you."

"Oh, no, I don't think -"

"Nonsense, it's a good idea. I can come back to yours and meet your flatmate. Is he as pretty as you?" he slurs.

I feel quite drunk by now, and in no mind to stand around arguing. "Prettier," I say firmly, briefly trying to remember what a good friend Jude is, before shrugging and throwing him under the bus. "He's a model. An *underwear* model," I add deliberately. "And he'll absolutely adore you."

I throw out my arm for a taxi, and as I slide into the cab, he follows closely behind like I'm the pied piper of underwear models. I shrug. Jude can deal with him. I'm too drunk.

I stare out of the window at London rushing by as he talks in a monotone about how wonderful he is. I wonder what Gabe is doing at the moment, but I shy away from the thought of what, or who, he's probably doing. However, like sticking my tongue on a loose tooth, I keep coming back to that thought and growing more morose. When will I be over him? *Will* I ever be over him?

We fall out of the taxi when we reach my apartment, and bypassing the elevator which is broken again, I point Richard to the stairs. He huffs and shakes his head, starting to talk about health and safety and landlord laws, but after five floors he can't talk anymore apart from panting. I mentally fist bump the elevator.

He follows me down the corridor. "Fucking hell, what a bloody dump," he exclaims.

"Oh, Richard, you sweet talking devil." Once again it goes over his head. The man literally has no sarcasm detector.

He comes up close to me. "I am quite silver tongued thank you, Dylan. Wait until it's in your arse and you'll find out." I put my key in the lock, but to my astonishment he pushes me into the door, leaning hard on me so that I can feel the outline of his cock against my arse. "Let's skip dinner, Dylan, and stay in."

I shrug him off crossly. *Cheeky, fucking wanker. The only company I want tonight is my dildo and some porn, where I can turn the sound off the way I wish I could do to you.* I swallow hard as his face goes slack with astonishment. "Oh shit, I said that out loud didn't I?"

He nods. His face is flushed, which is probably more to do with my mentioning a dildo in polite company than any offence. He doesn't seem to register at all that I've just called him a cheeky wanker. "Fuck, Dylan, you're so fucking beautiful. I noticed you as soon as you started working for Morna, but I didn't see any point in getting to know you because the rancid old bitch chases every assistant off. Then you stayed, and I figured I'd get first go."

"First go!" I splutter and then jerk. "Morna's not a rancid old bitch. What a fucking rude thing to say."

I twist the key, but as the door starts to open Richard presses forcibly against me again. Too forcibly for someone who has just drunk a bottle of wine on an empty stomach. As if in slow motion we fall through the door, landing with a colossal thud on the hall carpet.

"Oh, fuck," I groan as Richard's full weight lands on me, and then for a few seconds, we lie there as if too surprised to move. Then, unfortunately, Richard regains the power of speech.

"This is much more like it," he exclaims. "Let's just fuck here, Dylan. Maybe get that pretty flatmate involved. I haven't had a threesome in ages, and you said your flatmate would fancy me." He nuzzles my neck, licking a very wet stripe along my jaw. It's like being mauled by a golden retriever.

"Richard," I begin, but we're interrupted by a rage filled voice.

"What in the ever-loving *fuck* is going on here?"

I jerk my head up so quickly I crash the back of my skull into Richard's jaw, putting a stop to the licking, but giving me an instant headache.

"Fuck," I mutter as sparks dance across my vision. I look up and shake my head in stupefaction. "Am I seeing things?" I ask no one and squeeze my eyes shut. However, when I open them, Gabe is still standing over us, with Jude hovering behind him.

I stare hungrily at him. He's thinner than when I last saw him, and looks absolutely terrible. I've never seen Gabe look bad before, apart from the time that he was ill, but he does now. He's wearing dark jeans and a blue and white striped shirt, but the jeans hang from his hips, and the shirt looks too big. His face is pale, and he has massive black circles under his eyes. For a brief second, I feel the most incredible sense of gladness at seeing him. Then concern floods through me.

"Gabe, you look terrible," I say, but at that instant, his whole expression changes, becoming utterly rage-filled as Richard groans against me.

I try to push Richard off me, but oblivious to our company he starts to grind against me. "Richard," I hiss, but before I can say more he's torn off me, and I gape at the sight of Gabe with his hand around Richard's throat, pushing him into the wall.

"Gabe, what the hell are you doing? Put Richard down," I shout, and then remember a few salient facts. "Gabe, I have to work with him. Don't hurt him."

Gabe turns a snarling face to me. "It didn't take you fucking long, Dylan. You've moved your schedule along. I waited two years. What's it taken this bastard, a week? You've obviously lowered your fucking standards."

I struggle to my feet. "Now wait a fucking minute, you utter twat. What gives you the right to lecture me on my sexual partners? You've got no fucking right."

Shafts of pain cross his face and still my words before the blinding anger comes back and fills his face. "I just want to know -" He stutters to a stop as if he can't say the words, but unfortunately he finds them. "I want to know if you're fucking this idiot?"

"Now wait a minute," Richard mutters, and squirms.

"Shut up!" Gabe and I shout in unison, and for a second I see *him* in his eyes again, before the rage-filled twat comes back.

"Is this what you want? Is he giving you the nice, boring sex that you really wanted?" He shakes Richard like a rat. "Are you settling down now, getting a dog and adopting two-point-four children? Is he better than me? Is he going to give you that life you tried to trick me into?" I gasp, and he shakes his head. "You're worse than a fucking whore, Dylan. At least I got a bill for them. Instead, you're a fucking liar."

"Oh, I don't think -" Jude begins, but when we turn murderous faces to him he shuts up, but not before muttering, "And don't think that we won't be having words later about pimping friends out, Dylan."

I ignore him. "Oh, I see the problem now," I say sweetly, turning back to Gabe with my rage going ice cold. "It's that *you* didn't pick this one for me." He flinches, and I laugh. "How dare you mock the things I want. You, who couldn't hold a relationship down, even with cable ties."

"Dylan -" Jude warns, but I'm on a roll.

"Of course he's fucking better than you. Because he wants a real relationship with me." I'm conveniently ignoring the fact that I've only just met Richard, and would rather form a relationship with Charles Manson. Richard looks startled and mutters something about just wanting a threesome, but I tune him out, my rage filling me like I'm the Incredible Hulk. "He could be a complete idiot but I'd still want him, because he's not *you*. Too fucking scared to do anything apart from fuck men who are little more than toys. You should have kept that Fleshlight, Gabe. You'd have more of a relationship with that and your fist than you would with a human being. Why the fuck would I want to be with you, when I can't trust you with me? I should be able to trust the man in my life to have my best interests at heart, but you don't. You only think about *your* needs, because you're so fucking selfish."

I come to a stop panting, and suddenly it's as if all the rage I've felt against him drains away. I'm suddenly aware of the utter stillness of the hallway, and the way his face has gone the colour of milk. I think about what I just said, and shame and regret fills me. *How could I throw that at him?*

"Gabe," I say hoarsely, but he shakes his head, and moving like an old man, he releases Richard who promptly loses his balance and slides down the wall. Gabe shoves his hair back, and I dimly notice that his hands are shaking. "I'm sorry," I try again.

"No, I'm sorry," he says in a dead voice. "I'm sorry for everything. I wanted to see you so badly, but I had no right to throw that fit. I don't own you, don't have any rights over you, and I don't know what I was thinking." He looks at Richard who is struggling up with his mouth open to say something, and a tiny ember of rage kindles again. It's enough to have Richard sitting back down again quickly. But then Gabe blinks, and all that's left is a fathomless loneliness before he shutters even that.

"I'm glad I came," he says suddenly. "I had to see you, and now that I know you're alright I'll leave you alone. You won't have to see me again." He looks up at me, and says almost formally, "I'm so sorry for the way this ended. I should never have started it with you. It was never my intention to hurt you, and it was all so pointless because I've done the very thing that I was most frightened of anyway."

"What were you frightened of?" I ask, but he shakes his head and moves to the door. Suddenly the knowledge sweeps through me that this is it. Somehow I'd always known we weren't quite done, but now I know with certainty that after this day I will never see him again. I'll never be in the same room, I'll never hear his grumpy wit and see his badly hidden smiles. I'll never smell his scent of spiced oranges, or feel the sturdy warmth of his body that offered me safety and warmth, but only as an illusion. The knowledge sears me, and I feel a pain as if someone is trying to cauterize a killing wound.

"Gabe," I say entreatingly, but he opens the door and goes through.

On the threshold he turns back and I feel a sudden hope which is killed instantly at his dead expression. "I wish you a good life, Dylan. I hope you find that someone who'll appreciate you the way you should be appreciated. Someone who will look after you and make you happy the way you deserve. I hope that someone knows what a gift he's been given. Someone warm and loving and loyal." He looks hard at me, as if memorising my face. "I'm so sorry for everything. Be happy, and I hope at some point you can remember me fondly. I won't forget you."

The door closes, and like a puppet that's lost his string, I slide down to the ground. "Shit," I murmur through a throat clogged with tears. "*Shit.*"

"That about sums it up," Jude says calmly, coming to sit next to me and drawing me into a tight hug.

Richard struggles to sit up. "Dylan, is this the flatmate you mentioned? He's very pretty."

"*Shut up!*" we both shout at him, and he subsides, muttering. For a second I can almost see my new career going down the drain, but then I remember that Morna hates him.

Jude shakes his head sadly. "I really thought you were going to get back together. He's just spent two hours talking non-stop about you. He went on and on about every little thing you ever did. It was blindingly obvious how much he missed you."

"Why the hell didn't you tell me he was here? I wasn't doing anything with this prick."

Richard says *hey* indignantly, but we ignore him.

"I did," he says patiently. "Check your texts."

I fumble for my phone and swipe the screen, and there, clearly, is his message.

JUDE: GABE'S HERE. GET BACK NOW!

I'd heard the beep and forgotten to check the message. "Too late," I whisper, and his arms tighten.

"You might be right, Dylan."

CHAPTER FIFTEEN

To: Dylan Mitchell

From: Gabe Foster

There isn't enough Tippex in the world to deal with the errors in this document.

One Month Later

The firm knock on the door startles me from my position under my desk where I'm fiddling with the printer wires. I jerk and bang my head hard. "Shit, bollocks, fuck!" I mutter, and then still and raise my head apprehensively, wondering who's at the door that might have heard that.

I'm greeted with a deep, masculine chuckle, and for a second I worry that it might be Richard, but then I remember he's avoided me since that night like I have leprosy. I relax as I see Henry standing at the door.

"Thank God it's you," I mutter as I stand up and smile contentedly when the printer whirrs back into action.

He looks instantly interested, his hazel eyes gleaming. "I'll admit that many men have said that before, but not usually in an office situation. Why?"

I shake my head and tsk disapprovingly. "Because I can't let bad language loose like that here."

"Dylan, I've heard you use bad language many times before."

I shrug. "Well, Gabe didn't mind ..." I trail off.

He smiles. "I've heard him use it a fair few times as well, most noticeably when you spilt tomato juice down his light-grey Armani suit."

"It looked like he'd been shot," I say fondly, remembering the tantrum. Then the subject matter sinks in, and I stiffen. "Why are you here?" He starts, and I grimace. "I'm sorry, that was a bit abrupt. Why are you in the building?" I smile. "Selling your life story?"

He laughs. "Too many litigious stories there I'm afraid for any publisher to be comfortable." He pauses. "No, actually I stopped by to see if you fancied grabbing lunch with me?"

I stare at him and he shifts. "Why?"

He smiles and makes a helpless gesture. "Can't an old friend take another old friend out for lunch?"

"They certainly can," I say levelly. "And if we were actually friends that would make perfect sense."

He looks slightly hurt. "Aren't we friends then, Dylan?"

I sigh. "You're Gabe's friend, Henry, and I was just his assistant."

"Not just his assistant," he says sharply. "Unless they've changed the job description for that particular career while I haven't been looking." He smiles wolfishly. "I may become much more involved with hiring new staff if that's the case. So many men, so little time."

"Well, I'm afraid Gabe would be shit out of luck," I say coldly.

"He's fucked most of London. There can't be that many left to employ."

He stares hard at me, and for a second I think he's going to give me a cutting reply. He is Gabe's best friend, so I'd expect nothing less, no matter how much I like him. But then he relaxes and holds his hands up pleadingly. "Just one lunch, Dylan. That's all I'm asking for."

"Why?"

"I need to talk to you," he replies, clearly unwilling to say more, and I shrug.

"Okay, one lunch."

Half an hour later I stir in my chair at the wine bar he's brought me to. It's in the basement of the offices of a big firm of lawyers and is consequently very busy. I shoot a quick, surreptitious look around to check that Gabe isn't lurking. I've got a feeling that he often used to meet Henry here.

"He's not here, and he's not coming." Henry's voice breaks into my perusal of the room.

I turn back to him. "I thought you were going to try some sort of silly stunt to get us to talk," I admit, lifting up my glass of wine and taking a deep gulp.

He shakes his head. "I admit I considered it, but I like it here. I've no wish to get thrown out when the furniture starts flying around."

My head shoots up. "That would *never* happen."

He shrugs, looking at me intently. "Anything's possible with you two. When there are deep feelings involved, anything is possible, including property damage."

I set my glass down sharply. "There aren't deep feelings, Henry. Don't be ridiculous."

He leans forward challengingly. "Really? Don't bullshit me, Dylan, because I've been in the same room as you two many times. It's like there's an invisible string connecting you and him. You even think alike. Sometimes the tension was that strong I needed to leave. I've never seen any two people who were more meant to be together."

I gape at him, unable to see where all this is coming from. "You sound like you've been reading Mills and Boon."

He shakes his head looking almost disappointed in me, and I feel a sudden, brief sense of shame for denying what we had. I sigh. "Okay, you obviously know that there was something, but when it's as one-sided as our relationship was, it can't last. It's like running a car without fuel. Eventually, it grinds to a halt."

"But it wasn't one-sided," he says, leaning forward in agitation. "I wish you could see how he really feels about you. It's so clear if you'd only look. If you'd only take the time."

"I *did* take the time, and it was extremely clear how he felt." I'm stung because I thought he'd come to commiserate, not criticise. "It was clear when he told me that I was good for a clandestine fuck, but nothing else. It was *abundantly* clear when he tried to make me shag another fuck buddy of his so that I could get my pesky feelings out of the way."

"Shit." He sits back and runs his hands over his hair, the dark-red strands glinting in the light. "That's not the full picture. I just wish you could -" He breaks off in agitation. "It's such a fucking mess, Dylan."

"It's not a fucking mess," I say clearly. "It *was* a fucking mess, and now it's *over*."

"Really, because you don't look so good, and my best friend looks like death warmed up."

Against my will that goddamned, fucking concern springs up in me. I wish it would just fucking die, but it won't, and against my will, I ask, "Is he ill? He didn't look well the last time I saw him."

A flicker of relief crosses his face, almost too quick for me to catch it. "Yes, I heard about that in all of its gory detail. Not his finest hour."

"Not mine either," I mutter. I look up. "Is he ill, Henry? Tell me now."

"He's not good," he says in a low voice. "He misses you."

I shake my head and lean back, agitated. "*Why?* Why the fuck does he miss me, because he *had* me, Henry. He had all of me right in his hand, but he opened his fingers and threw me away. So why the fuck should he miss me, and why the fuck should I even be bothered?"

"Because you don't know the full story," he bursts out passionately and loudly, making nearby tables look up at us before they go back to their conversations. Lowering his voice, he leans towards me. "Listen, I'm going to take a risk and tell you something." He looks torn. "I'm breaking a confidence here. A confidence I was very honoured to get, because Gabe doesn't tell anyone anything about himself that might make him vulnerable."

I shift uneasily, torn between wanting desperately to know anything that might explain the enigma of Gabe Foster, but equally worried about the fact that it's private. Concern wins out. "Don't tell me anything if it's private. You're the only real friend that Gabe has. I'd hate for you to lose each other over this. He needs you."

He smiles, a real, gentle smile that reaches and warms his eyes. "Now I know I should tell you, because you really care for him and see him, so I know it's safe with you."

"Is it about his time in care? Because he's already told me about that."

He looks surprised, his mouth gaping open for a second. "Fuck, he never tells anyone about that." I feel a loose tendril of warmth around my heart, and squash it quickly. Henry stares at me. "Did he tell you why he was in care, Dylan?"

I shrug. "He told me his mum and dad died, and his grandmother was too infirm to care for him. Was it something like a car accident?"

He looks sad. "I wish. That would have been better for Gabe." He shakes his head, and seems to gain resolve. "His dad killed his mum, Dylan."

Shock slams into me and my hand jerks, knocking into my glass and making it wobble alarmingly. Henry catches it and sets it right, staring down at the glass and tracing its stem absentmindedly.

"He was a very powerful financier, made a lot of money. They had it all. An apartment in the city, a villa in Italy, and a beautiful house in the country. That was their main home, and Gabe's mum stayed at home with him. Apparently, they were happy for a while and wanted Gabe to have a childhood away from the city. Then the recession happened, and his dad lost a lot of money. There were accusations of insider trading, and he started to drink. Apparently, he'd always drunk heavily because the city has those sort of machismo traditions, but it became an addiction. Steadily, he started to grow paranoid, and they began to argue a lot. He'd accuse her of being unfaithful to him, telling her he knew that she was planning to leave him and take Gabe. He accused her of sleeping with old work colleagues, even the bloody local landlord, and no matter what she said, it got worse."

"Gabe witnessed all this?"

"Some of it. He witnessed a lot of the major arguments. The rest of it he found out from reading court documents when he was emancipated from care."

"What happened then?" I whisper.

He winces. "Apparently, he'd been drinking for two days straight, and she'd finally had enough. She packed a bag for Gabe and herself and was going to take him away. They actually managed to leave, but Gabe had left his teddy bear behind. He was only a little boy, and he was attached to it and cried, so his mum went back. She made him stay at the gate, but I'm afraid that when he heard the shots, he ran straight back into the house."

My mouth dries and my stomach heaves. "Did he see anything?"

He takes a deep, almost desperate gulp of his wine. "They were both dead when he got there. His dad had shot her as soon as she walked in the house, then turned the gun on himself. The neighbours heard the bangs and called the police. The police found Gabe sitting by his mum's body."

"Oh my God, he never said anything," I whisper.

He shakes his head. "Don't take it personally. He doesn't talk about it at all. The only reason I know is because we shared rooms at uni and he had a few nightmares. We were already friends by then, and he felt close enough to tell me. He was shaken that night, enough to need a friend." He smiles sadly. "It was the last time we spoke about it. He never mentioned it again and acts like I don't know, but I can't forget it and I wanted you to know, Dylan, because it's the reason for everything. He doesn't trust love, and he doesn't want it, because to him, it's death."

I think back to that night on the farm, when he'd woken from a bad dream and made love to me so furiously. It was the start of him drawing away, and looking back, it had probably been brought on by being with my family. I wince. That happy family setting must have been like grinding salt into a cut for Gabe, who'd never had it himself.

For a brief second, I'm filled with this absolute resolve to go to him, to find him and soothe him. But then I remember the awful things we flung at each other the last time. So many horrible things had been said, and he was so final at the end. He doesn't need soothing anyway. He lives a strong, inviolate life now, threatened by nobody and keeping his feelings locked away like a miser with gold. I can't help him if he doesn't want that help. He had the chance to confide in me in Devon, and instead ran away. Why the hell would he need me turning up out of the blue now?

Henry, being the good lawyer that he is, reads my feelings immediately and slumps. "It hasn't changed anything, has it?" he says dejectedly. I put my hand on his and shake my head sadly.

"No, I'm sorry, but it can't change anything, Henry. Thank you so much for telling me. It explains a lot, and in some ways, it makes the way that we parted easier to deal with. But at the end of the day, the only person that can change anything is him. I could go to him now and demand something from him, knowing that he might need it, but you know him, Henry, he wouldn't take it. He'd close up tight like a clam, and probably say something poisonous to send me away. We said enough poisonous things the last time we saw each other. It was pretty clear that it was fully over for him." I sigh. "And my heart can't take that again."

He sighs sadly and sits back. "I know you're right, Dylan. He didn't mean anything that he said. He was just so angry." He holds up a hand as I start to protest. "I know he had no right to be angry, and I know you weren't doing anything and so does he. Maybe he needs to heal himself first, and then maybe, just maybe, he'll come round. If he does, will you see him?"

"You have no right to ask that," I say firmly, shooting him a smile to make sure he knows I'm not angry with him. How could I be, when all he wants is for his friend to be happy?

However, I'm not convinced he's right in that I'm the missing piece in Gabe's life, the one thing he's been searching for. I think of the time apart with no phone calls or messages. Gabe doesn't seem to be looking that hard at the moment.

=✉

That afternoon, I walk out of work and groan. "Not you as well. Is the universe actually *trying* to fuck up my day?"

Jude looks up from where he's leaning against one of the pillars outside the building, and grins. "Well, good afternoon to you as well, my little snuggle buns. I thought I'd brighten up your day by walking home with you."

"Why?"

"Such a suspicious boy, and what did you mean not me too? Who else have you seen?"

His tone is far too innocent for me to believe after all these years. "Fuck you, Jude." I shake my head. "You rang Henry, didn't you?"

He looks on the verge of arguing, but then shrugs gracefully and gives me one of his wide smiles. It doesn't work on me, but a woman passing by collides with a post while staring at him. "Well?" I say dangerously.

"I didn't exactly ring him per se." I stop and raise my eyebrow. "Okay, I might have run into him at Vibe last night. And we might have had a long chat about the stupidity of our mutual friends."

I feel weary and off-balance after my conversation with Henry, like my life is out of whack. The trouble is that I know what I need to right it, and I can't ever have that, and I feel this sudden, deep anger towards Gabe. It's totally unjustified because I can't blame him for being the way he is, not when I know what he went through. Thinking of that doesn't stop the feeling of rage inside me, but it cools enough for me to push it away and remember what he was like on Valentine's Day. I need to remember that to strengthen my resolve.

I shake my head at Jude and start walking again. "I'm not stupid, but I definitely would be if I went back to him and got involved in that situation again. I'd be stupid if I ever told him I loved him again, only to have him reacting like I'd got fucking herpes."

A woman walking past us gasps, and Jude turns to smile to her. "He hasn't by the way," he shouts, and then catches me by the arm and stops my forward momentum. "Look, I know he hurt you and behaved like a complete twat."

"Yes, he did," I interrupt, "And I'm puzzled as to why it suddenly seems like you're advocating for him."

He shakes his head indignantly. "I'm not advocating for him, Dylan." He pauses. "Look, what he did was really shitty, but you didn't talk to him last time." I open my mouth, but he holds up his hand to stay me. "Shouting and yelling at each other isn't talking." He shrugs. "I know I said some harsh things about him when you split up, but I was wrong about him."

"Why?"

"I thought he was using you and I hated him for that, for not seeing what he had. I saw it as him taking what he wanted without any care, and still being ready to move on at the next opportunity." He bites his lips thoughtfully. "Now, I don't think anything about your relationship was carefree for him. I think it went against every-thing he stood for, but he still did it."

"Why?"

He shoots a sharp glance at me. "I think he was in love with you, Dylan. The man who spent two hours telling me funny stories about you, and wanting to know whether you were okay, isn't the prick he appeared to be. He cares a lot about you, and he's hurting. I could see that, and after talking to Henry last night, I know it's true." His voice gentles. "He misses you, Dylan."

I scoff. "He misses me organising his life for him. He can get another piece of ass anywhere." A pain hits me in my heart. "He's probably dick deep in half of London by now."

"He isn't," he interrupts. "Henry said that he doesn't go clubbing anymore. All he does is work or sit at home. His concentration is for shit, and he does nothing apart from bang on about you." His voice softens. "All I'm saying is that the man you want, the one you're in love with, he cares about you and he's miserable without you. Isn't that everything you ever wanted?"

I stare blindly at the hordes of commuters, not really seeing them. "I did want that, Jude. I'd have given anything for him to care about me, but that was before he tried to pimp me out for a threesome."

"He couldn't go through with it though, could he?"

"I *know* that," I say patiently, "But it was his first reaction when he thought I was starting to care for him." I laugh humourlessly. "Most men would give chocolates or flowers, he just wanted to give me another dick to play with."

"Henry said he's tortured by what he did."

"But he still did it though, didn't he?" I say simply and then sigh. "I've seen him in his previous relationships, and they were all like this with the men kept at a distance. I don't want that." I pause, and then say sharply, "I also don't want to talk about this anymore please."

He sighs and nods, and we join the crowds of people flocking down into the underbelly of the underground. "I fucking hate rush hour," I say sourly over my shoulder to him, as we go down the stone steps.

He shrugs, grinning at me. "For your next go round why don't you try for a nice daddy? Get yourself treated well."

I open my mouth to chat shit back at him, but at that point I feel a sharp blow hit my back and feel myself pushed forward. I reach out an arm to the rail to try and stop my fall, but my weight carries me forward, and the next few seconds are a whirl of blurred impressions and pain as I bump down the stone steps. I land on the floor in a flurry of arms and legs and feel a gut-wrenching pain. Then my head bangs hard into the stone floor, sending spangles across my vision, so I close my eyes automatically.

I must have blacked out, because when I open my eyes it's to find Jude and an old lady bending over me with concern written all over their faces. "What happened?" I say groggily.

"Oh, thank goodness," the old lady gasps, and Jude puts out a hand to stop me lifting my head.

"No, stay there for a second, mate. You had a bad fall and knocked yourself out. Lie still."

"What happened?"

"I'm so sorry," the old lady flutters. "It was all my fault. I missed a step and fell onto you."

That must have been the weight that hit me. "Are you alright?" I murmur groggily, turning my head slightly and then cursing at the immediate, slamming pain. "Fucking hell that hurts. Sorry," I immediately apologise to the lady.

"No need to be sorry," she says sweetly. "My husband was in the Navy. I've heard more bad language than you've had hot dinners. Anyway, this is all my fault, and in answer to your question I'm absolutely fine." She smiles. "You sort of cushioned my landing, sweetheart, so thank you."

"It was my pleasure," I say. Ignoring the pain in my head and body that's now making itself felt, I look around. I'm lying on the floor at the foot of the steps, and as per usual, nothing is stopping the London commuters. They surge past us, stepping around me, and a couple of times over me. It reminds me of a nature programme I'd watched once, showing a colony of army ants on the march and ravaging everything in their way. I suppose at least the rude commuters aren't eating me. "Okay," I groan. "I need to move."

Ignoring Jude's protests, I hold out my arm, and he grabs me, hoisting me up to a sitting position. My head throbs sickeningly, but red-hot, blinding pain shoots down my leg, and I gasp out a curse. "Shit, stop." He hovers worriedly. "Okay, I don't think I'm moving. I think I've broken my leg."

"Are you sure?"

"It's the same pain as when I broke my arm when we were fifteen."

He gets out his phone. "I'm going up top to phone for an ambulance." I start to protest at the embarrassment, but he shakes his head. "Dylan, we can't move you. You'll need strapping up and some painkillers before they can even try. So I suggest that unless you want to just lie here, being stepped over by complete strangers until you claim your pension, or get a medal from the London Underground, you let me ring the ambulance."

I gasp. "Oh shit, work. I'm supposed to be back there at eight tonight for a book launch. Can you ring Morna for me?" I feel in my pocket for my phone, which luckily has survived the fall. "Her number's in there."

He takes the phone, and stares down at me for a long second. Something is working behind his eyes that looks very much like calculation, but before I can say anything, he simply nods and is gone, leaving me with the old lady for company.

The next few hours are a whirl of activity and embarrassment, as everyone on the Jubilee Line is treated to the sight of my getting gas and air, before being strapped to a trolley and lifted out. The activity stops however as soon as we get to the hospital. It's extremely busy, so Jude and I settle down for a long wait in our cubicle.

We've been sitting there for an hour when I sigh. "That was so embarrassing." He nods and grins happily, so I shoot him a sour look before continuing. "I can't believe London Underground were so huffy about me resting my broken body on their floor. You'd think I was staging a sit in." I shudder. "And all those people *staring*."

He snorts. "Never mind, you'll have forgotten it soon."

"I highly doubt that," I say sourly. "I saw you filming me while I was screaming like a little girl." I look at him beadily. "That'd better not end up on Facebook, Jude." He shakes his head, diverting the subject, so I know it's already on there. "How many comments?" I sigh.

"Two hundred and forty so far," he says happily. "They're not all horrid either."

"I bet there are more trolls on there than in 'Lord of the Rings'," I say gloomily, and then look closely at him. "Are you okay?"

"Yes, why?"

"You're jigging about like you're waiting for something." A thought strikes me. "What have you done?" I demand, leaning up on my elbow. "I know you, Jude, and you've got a guilty look on your face. I know you've -"

I'm interrupted by the sudden sound of a commotion outside. "What on earth is that -" I start to say, but the voice rises, and I gasp as I recognise who that voice belongs to. "Oh my *God*," I whisper. "You didn't ring him. Tell me you didn't ring him."

He sniffs and says primly, "Well I *could* tell you that, but let's face it I'd be lying, and you know what they said about lying at Sunday School."

"This is not bloody funny -" I cut off because the commotion is getting nearer.

I can hear a woman's voice saying, "Sir, I am going to call security if you don't stop. You cannot come back here unless you are with a patient."

"I *am* with a patient," he says in a very loud voice. "I just need to find him first."

"Sir, I did tell you about patient confidentiality."

"And I told you it's fine if you want to abide by that, but I do not choose to do so. So instead I am going through this casualty ward, opening every curtain until I find him."

"Oh my God," I groan. "Go and get him, before he pisses the staff off so much they put my leg on the wrong way round."

He gives me a startled look. "I'm not sure that you should have any more of those painkillers, Dylan."

"*Jude!*" I warn, and he throws his hands up.

"Okay, I'll go."

He goes to the curtain, but before he can open it, it swishes back so forcefully that the rods nearly come off the wall, and Gabe's face appears.

"Oh my God," he gasps. "Baby, are you okay?"

He's dressed in a navy blue pinstriped suit, with his tie at half-mast as if he's been tugging at it. Sweat is beading on his forehead, and he half falls into the cubicle, followed by a very ticked off nurse who looks at me. "Are you okay with this man being here?"

"Of course?" I say nervously, and she huffs and draws the curtain closed with a sharp jerk.

"Great," I groan. "That's put us back another couple of hours."

He doesn't answer me, instead, coming towards me. He astonishes me by running his hands gently through my hair, before bending over and nestling his face into my neck and giving a great sigh. Before I know it, my arms have come up to encircle him and pull him close.

I'm dimly aware of Jude leaving, but my attention is drawn, as it likely always will be, to the man in my arms. "Gabe," I say, but he shakes his head, rubbing his face into my neck and gifting me with his warm, spicy scent. I inhale it greedily. It feels like aeons since I've been near him like this.

We stay silent for long minutes as I stroke his hair, and then I become aware of him trembling slightly, a shudder running finely through his body.

"Gabe?" I ask, pulling lightly at his hair. "Gabe, are you okay?"

He sighs and raises his head, and I gasp as I get my first real look at him. He looks awful, with dark circles under his eyes, and a pasty white complexion. "Gabe, what is it?"

He shakes his head, coming down to sit carefully on the side of the bed, and running his hands tenderly and lightly down my face. "I was so worried," he says hoarsely. "God, it was awful."

"What was?"

"Jude rang me, and all he could say was that you'd had an accident on the Underground, and were waiting to be taken to hospital. I walked out of a meeting, didn't say anything. They're probably still there waiting." He rubs his eyes, and I see to my astonishment that his hands are shaking. "I had so many fucking gruesome images flash through my head, and I didn't know how you were. I didn't know if you were -"

He shudders to a stop, and I reach for him, all anger gone in that second in the desire to soothe him. Seeming to sense my mood, he immediately shifts nearer. "I'm okay, Gabe, I promise."

"But what happened?"

We're interrupted by the curtain sliding open, and Jude edging back into the cubicle. "Sorry. I'd have stayed out there, but the nursing staff were all glaring at me, so it was a tad uncomfortable." He hands a cup of coffee to Gabe and puts one on the side table for me.

"Oh God," I sigh, but Gabe waves his hand.

"It'll be fine. I'll call someone and we'll get you seen privately." He looks around and shudders. "My God, don't touch anything, Dylan. You might catch one of those flesh-eating bugs."

I sigh and say patiently, "I would have to have an open flesh wound to catch one of those."

He looks me over anxiously, running his hand lightly down my side. To my embarrassment a visible shudder runs through me, making Jude smirk, but Gabe looks worried. "Where does it hurt?" he asks anxiously.

"It's my head and my leg," I sigh, closing my eyes as my headache comes back with a vengeance.

"Lie down," he says hoarsely. "I'll call and get you seen."

I open my eyes and grab his hand, making him immediately still, and his eyes close as if he's in pain. "I am not going private, Gabe," I say firmly. "I'm staying with the NHS. It was fought for by my ancestors, and we need to support it."

"Your ancestors were farmers," he says smoothly. "They were

likely digging up turnips, so we will do what *my* ancestors did instead, which is pay for good service and complain when we don't get it."

Jude snorts, but I glare at them both. "Listen to me very carefully, and think hard about what happens if you go over my head to do something for me that you think is right. What is my normal reaction?"

Gabe slumps slightly. "Not favourable?"

"No, to put it mildly. Now, you need to go out there, apologise, and lay on the charm."

He nods obediently. "Okay."

"Pretend they're customers who are paying by the hour," I suggest.

He shakes his head at me. "You make me sound like a fucking hooker." He takes a sip of his coffee and shudders as if he's been tasered. "Jesus, that is foul." He snatches mine and Jude's cups away and slings them dramatically into the bin.

"Hey!" I protest.

"You're not drinking that," he says firmly. "We'll get you something decent, like a nice latte or something."

I sigh. "Good luck finding that here. Now go and make nice."

He grins a piratical grin at me. "I'll charm them so well, they won't know what's hit them." And then he's gone, the curtain swishing closed behind him.

Jude looks at me and sniggers. "He's adorably high-handed where you're concerned, isn't he?"

My eyes slide closed. "With anyone."

"No," he says thoughtfully. "Only you. He really can't be bothered with anyone else, unless they're connected to you. You're all he sees."

I would have liked to argue, but I feel very funny and my head hurts badly, so I let myself drift off to sleep.

I come awake I don't know how much later, to find Jude asleep in his chair and Gabe talking into his phone. "Okay, Alistair, you've got the correct coffee order, and could you call in and pick something up for us to eat? Stop at Harpers. Dylan loves their flatbread sandwiches. He'll have a chicken salad and hummus on rosemary bread, and get Jude and I whatever they've got left." He pauses. "In fact, just get a load of sandwiches. There are a lot of people waiting here with relatives who can't leave them. You've got my credit card haven't you, so use that." He pauses as if listening and then nods, making me smile because he often does that on the phone, forgetting that the other person can't see him. He starts talking again. "He's fine, Alistair. Thank you for asking. We're just waiting to see the specialist. Please make sure that you sign me out of the office for the next week. If anyone questions it, tell them it's personal leave. I'll ring Magnus myself." He clicks the button to end the call, and then sighs and runs his hand down his face, and I frown because he looks weary.

"Was that your new assistant, and please tell me that he's not running all over London getting coffee?" I ask sleepily, and he jerks and turns to me.

"Of course he is. I can't leave you, and yes that's Alistair."

"Ah, my replacement." He winces. "You're a lot nicer to him than you were to me."

"I don't spend my whole time lusting after him, and then making myself be distant the way I did with you," he says absentmindedly and comes forward to push his hand gently into my hair. "How are you feeling, sweetheart? You look so tired."

For a brief second, I let myself arch into his touch, and avoid mentioning his endearment. I'm injured so it shouldn't count. "So do you, and what do you mean about being attracted? I irritated you for years."

He shakes his head, his face gentling and making me stare at him. "Never. You've never irritated me. You've challenged me and made me laugh, but irritation is far too bland an emotion to fit the range of the ones I have for you."

I stare at him, but before I can answer, the curtain is pulled back, and a weary-looking doctor walks in, making Jude wake up with a snort.

"Ah, Mr Mitchell," he says. "How are you?"

"My head still hurts," I say slowly. "But the painkillers the nurse gave me have taken the edge off."

"Well, you've got yourself a concussion." He takes out a slim penlight and shines it into my eyes.

"What does that mean?" Gabe asks anxiously.

The doctor smiles. "There's no need to be worried. Dylan shook his brain about a bit, so he'll have a bad headache for a couple of days. Our main concern is your leg, Dylan. There's a break in the lower part of your tibia. We're going to put a temporary cast on it, as the leg will normally swell a bit. In a week, the orthopaedic doctor will need to see you again to properly assess the damage, and most likely at that point, we'll put a proper cast on it."

I groan. "How long for?"

"About six to eight weeks normally," the doctor says, grinning sympathetically.

"Well, that'll make the Underground fun."

"You won't be on the Underground," Gabe says firmly. "I'll put a car and driver at your service."

"You can't do *that*." I'm scandalised. "What a waste of money."

He grins, all teeth and attitude. "My money, so my waste don't you think?"

I shake my head and regret it, as the pain clangs brightly.

The doctor looks at me kindly. "You're going to have a very nasty headache tonight, and maybe for the next couple of days. You're also going to need somebody to stay with you, as you'll need to be woken several times in the night to ensure you're fine. I'll give you some painkillers, but they'll be generic over the counter meds because you can't take anything stronger with a concussion. Now, have you got anyone to stay with you, because if you haven't, we'll have to keep you in?"

"He's coming home with me," Gabe says decisively.

"I am bloody not." I turn wildly to Jude. "Jude can stay with me. He's at home."

Jude shoots a quick look at Gabe that he thinks I don't see. "No, can do," he says casually. "I'm at an industry party tonight, and Paul already told me that my presence is obligatory."

My splutter at the traitor is cut short when he bends down and gives me a big hug. "Well, now that I know you're okay, and as Gabe's here, I'm going to head off." He seizes my chin and kisses my cheek. "Love you, babe."

"Love you too." I smile and accept his hug. "Sorry for such a long afternoon, and thanks for being here."

"No, thank you," he says seriously. "It's rare nowadays to see you acting as an OAP stunt mattress, but I don't think you're very good at it so maybe stick to the day job."

Gabe smiles and shakes hands with him, and then they hug briefly. I narrow my eyes. *When did they get so close?* For a second I feel almost jealous, then tell myself off heartily. I must be feeling worse than I thought because neither Gabe nor Jude would ever do that to me.

The doctor who had been standing patiently watching us like we were on the set of EastEnders, stirs. "Are we settled?" he asks gently. "Are you going home with this gentleman?"

"He is," Gabe says firmly.

"Okay then, Dylan. We'll get this temporary cast on, and then you can go home."

"Not my home," I correct him slowly, feeling the urge to close my eyes again.

Gabe says something, but my eyes are too heavy to open.

CHAPTER SIXTEEN

To: Gabe Foster

From: Dylan Mitchell

If you were thinking of calling a whole staff meeting, try looking in the stationery cupboard for the missing people. They retired there an hour ago, while you were chastising me over the mail mix-up.

I come awake drifting slowly. It's dark and quiet in the room and has the feel of the very early hours of the morning. I lie quietly for a few minutes analysing how I feel, and to my relief, I feel a lot better. My headache has largely gone, and although my leg is still sore, it's settled into a faint throbbing.

I suddenly become aware that I'm not in my room and for a second, my mind whirls but then the events of the last two days come back to me, and I relax. Gabe and I had left the hospital after I'd had my leg casted and he'd filled my prescription for painkillers. He'd wheeled me painstakingly out of the place and loaded me into a waiting car, then brought me back to his house.

At first, I'd tensed up, but he'd sent me such an intense, pleading look that I'd given in, even when he helped me into his bed. I think I might have rebelled at that point, until my sore body felt the blissful cotton sheets and the thick mattress and I'd relented. He'd tucked me in as tenderly as if I was a child, and I'd slept for most of that day and the next, waking only to drink whatever he gave me, and to take the proffered painkillers. My headache had been so intense that I'd struggled to even keep down water.

He'd obeyed the instructions given to him by the hospital religiously, waking me every few hours to ask questions. He'd taken it very seriously, and didn't even crack a smile when I'd said falteringly, "Is that you, Grandma? Shall I go to the bright light?" I'd had to stop him picking up the phone and calling the hospital after that, and had been soundly told off.

For a while I lie there with my mind drifting, enjoying the relief from the terrible headache. Finally, my thoughts of Gabe bring me to wonder where he is, and I turn my head slowly, which is when I see him. He's sitting slumped in a chair by the window, staring into space and dressed only in a pair of pyjama shorts. The moonlight is full on him, leaching the colour from his skin and highlighting his sharp cheekbones, wide chest and the dips and swells of his muscles.

I lie there for a long time, watching him and marvelling at his stillness. It's so rare to see him still, and I wonder what thoughts are filling his head tonight. Then I see the trailing wire from his earphones and realise that he's listening to something on his phone. It can't be work, because I've never seen him do anything work wise and not be upright and energised.

Tonight, he looks almost like he's dreaming, and suddenly my heart is filled with so much love and affection flooding through it, like an icy puddle cracking in the thaw. I hadn't overthought his actions over the last couple of days. I had been in too much pain to think very much about anything, but now I try to analyse what I feel, and the simple answer is – love. It's as inevitable as Christmas following Bonfire Night that I will keep loving him.

As if he senses my thoughts, he suddenly looks over to check on me, and jerks as he sees that my eyes are open. He stands up quickly, and I swallow hard at the sight of all his muscles moving in the moonlight. He strides over to me quickly and rests his fingertips gently against my forehead. He doesn't seem to take my temperature, just lingers there as if he needs to touch me.

"How are you feeling?" he asks softly. "Any pain?"

I move and stretch. "I feel a lot better," I say in a low voice. "The headache's gone."

He gives a relieved sigh. "That's good." He pauses before bursting out. "Jesus, baby, you worried me. You were so quiet and still for the last two days."

"I'm fine now. I think I just needed to sleep it all off." He shivers slightly in the cool air of the bedroom, and I move over. "Gabe, it's cold, and you're not wearing a top." I pull the duvet down. "Come on, get in." He hesitates, a look of hope almost painful on his face for a second before he shivers again. "Now, I said. Come on."

He nods and slides gracefully into the bed, pulling the covers over us and encasing me in the warm, soft, sweet-smelling cave. To my surprise, he doesn't move to get closer, but instead just lies on his side, facing me and looking at me steadily. I shift onto my side wincing slightly, and he puts out a hand in mute protest but then lets it fall onto the mattress where it lies palm up, looking somehow vulnerable.

Before I realise what I'm going to do, I reach over and slide my fingers through his. For a second he's totally still as if in surprise, and then his fingers move, clutching mine in a death grip.

"I can't believe you're here," he says hoarsely. "I've dreamt it so many times."

"What were you listening to?" I interrupt, suddenly needing to know.

He blinks, and then a wry smile tilts his lips. "A song," he murmurs.

"What song?"

"One that makes me think of you." He pauses, and then adds almost shyly, "Do you want to hear it?"

I nod slowly, and he reaches over to the bedside table and captures his phone. He turns back instantly onto his side facing me, but closer this time so I can smell the sweet, minty scent of his breath. He looks at his phone and taps something on it. Then he reaches up and slots one of the earbuds into my ear while taking the other one for himself. "Ready?" he asks, and I nod. Still looking at me, he taps his phone, and I blink as the recognisable opening chords spill out.

"That's Peter Gabriel, isn't it?" I ask. "'In Your Eyes'?"

He nods solemnly. "This is the song that makes me think of you." I open my mouth, but he shakes his head. "Just listen to it."

So I do. I listen to Peter Gabriel singing about being lost and empty and running to someone who really knows and fills him up, and suddenly tears fill my eyes. He reaches out and tenderly rubs them away, before anchoring his hand in the hair on the back of my neck. It lingers there as he stares into my eyes while we listen to the music, and it's almost unbearably intimate.

When the song comes to an end, I stir. "I don't know what to say," I admit, and he smiles almost tenderly.

"That's a new development." He seems to fill with a resolve. "Luckily, I finally *do* know what to say. I did so much wrong when you were with me. Instead of enjoying what we had and binding you close to me, I pushed you away so fucking hard because I was frightened."

"I know," I say quietly. "I know about your mum and dad, Gabe."

He stills and then smiles. "Henry, I suppose?" I nod, and he sighs. "I should have told you. I should have let you in, but I couldn't, and by the time I realised that I needed to try, it was too late, and you were walking away." He pauses and swallows hard. "I want you to know that I didn't go to anyone else on Valentine's Day." I feel almost weak with relief because that had been at the back of my mind since that night. "I went to a hotel instead and paced the floor all night. I was so stupid to bring Ollie to you. All I could think was that I just wanted you to hurry up and fucking leave me, because it was going to happen anyway."

I jerk, and when it looks like I'm going to turn away, he grabs my chin and makes me look at him.

"That decision was the worst decision of my life. I was so fucking stupid to do what I did." His voice goes hoarse. "I knew immediately that it was wrong, but something in me just kept forcing it along, and then I saw his hands on you and I couldn't bear it. I've been with a lot of men, Dylan, and I've seen them with other men and felt nothing, but that night – fuck. I wanted to kill him for touching what was mine." He laughs mirthlessly. "It was a fucking awful time to realise what I felt, and you were right to leave me."

I breathe in sharply, and he smiles. "You were right to leave me, because I needed to take a long look at myself. I know now that you're somehow everything I never knew I needed. You're funny and clever and irreverent. You don't let me get away with anything, and you stand up to me. You're kind and generous and warm, and when I see you, something fills up in my chest, and it feels so good. But then you leave, and it's lonely again, and I'm so fucking tired of being alone and too afraid to try."

He sits up slightly and lays his hand on my chest over my heart as if making a vow, and I hold my breath. "The truth is that I will always need you more than you need me. It's also the truth that I'm not a good bet for someone as vital and young as you. I'm bad tempered, a perfectionist who is too serious, and too used to being on my own. You could go out tomorrow and find someone better for you, but the truth is that no one will ever need you like I do." He pauses and then says firmly. "No one will ever love you like I do."

I gasp, but he carries on talking almost frantically. "I want you forever, Dylan, but not to share. You were right in what you said before, that you couldn't trust yourself with me. It hurt like a motherfucker, but I've had months to think about this, and what I needed to do to change. I swear to you that you can trust me now because I know what you mean to me. You're the most valuable thing in the world to me, and I promise I'll keep your heart safe. At the end of the day, I might have had all the fancy education, but you have always been the more astute out of the two of us."

His words come to a stop, and for a second there is utter silence, and then he swallows hard. "Do you ... do you think that you can forgive me and start again, Dylan, because this is it? I don't have any more clever words."

I reach out immediately and stick my hand over his mouth, stopping that clever, ceaseless tongue. "I don't need any more words, Gabe. I love you too, and of course I forgive you. I want everything with you."

His wide, grey eyes seem to glisten silver for a second, then he pulls my hand away from his face and leans over to gently kiss me. "God, l love you," he says softly against my lips. "I've never loved anyone before." He pauses. "Sometimes it's not exactly pleasurable."

I laugh. "I know, but you have to have that to come out stronger."

For a second we stare at each other, and then, as if synchronised, we both lean in and our lips meet. The power of feeling his lips against mine after so long sends a jolt through me, and he groans and grabs me close. We kiss for ages with slick lips and deep sighs, and then I pull back. "Gabe," I gasp. "I don't need you to be gentle."

"But you're hurt."

"I *was* hurt. I feel loads better, and a few aches and pains are not going to stop me getting you inside me again. God, Gabe," I groan. "My cock hurts way more than my fucking leg."

He gives a breathless laugh, and then he's on me, and all the long months of separation explode, and suddenly we're on fire. We bite and lick, then suckle the bites better. Our lips cling and twist, shared spit wet on them. I suckle his tongue, feeling his panting breaths hit my cheek, and he suddenly pulls back panting. His cheekbones are red and his lips full, and he gives me a salacious smile that makes my cock throb.

"I've had an idea of what we can do that won't hurt your leg." I go to protest, but he shakes his head. "Shut up. Do you trust me?"

I look deep into his warm grey eyes, and almost as if answering a different question, I tentatively nod. "I'm starting to, Gabe."

He gives a shuddering sigh, and his body relaxes slightly, as if he's been keeping himself tightly wound. Then he gives me a bold, buccaneer type of smile. "You will do, I know it."

He shifts back and then slides down the bed, giving me a glittering smile that contains a wild tenderness inside it. "I want you to be very still."

"Why, what are you –?" I break off with a choked grunt as he lifts my stiff prick up and swallows it down in one smooth motion, which is far too practised, I think darkly. Then he swallows, and the head of my cock is enveloped in a heavenly tugging motion, and my thoughts scatter like sand in the wind.

"Fuck!" I shout out, and he chuckles around me, making me mutter inarticulate words. He lifts off me and taps the head against his tongue a few times, making me cry out and arch towards that clever mouth, but he moves teasingly back.

"Dylan, I think I've finally found a way to shut your clever mouth up."

I raise my head, panting. "You love my clever mouth."

I expect a sarcastic remark back, but instead, I get a warm smile that brightens and warms his eyes like the sun coming out. "I do," he says softly. "I love your sharp mind and even sharper tongue. Don't ever change."

I open my mouth to say I don't know what, but then he bends purposefully and nuzzles into my crotch, inhaling deeply and lazily licking the base of my cock like a large lion.

I jerk. "God, you teasing bastard, do it." He smiles at me, and then sends his tongue fluttering over the sensitive frenulum, before encasing the head in his mouth and starting a heated suckling.

"Gah," I shout out. "Don't stop."

He hums happily and begins to deep throat me with a passion and dedication I've only ever seen him apply to work before. Within what feels like seconds I can feel a tingling in my spine, and I flush hot and cold. "Stop," I cry out, grabbing his head and pulling him off my cock.

He raises up and then lowers himself over me, his mouth swollen and red and his eyes heavy-lidded. His hair flops all over the place from where my hands have been. "You alright?" he asks, his voice hoarse. "Is your leg okay?"

"God, yes," I mutter, and he relaxes instantly. "Just too much. It's been so long for me, I was going to come." He stares at me for a long second that seems to stretch. Then he bends his head, focusing on his fingers which have started an absent caressing of my chest. He seems unable to meet my eyes, and I frown. "Gabe?"

"How long?" he asks in a low voice, and when I make a sound of surprise his head shoots up. "I won't be angry if you've been with anyone else," he says hurriedly. "I mean, it's my fault we were apart, and if you were with anyone else then I've only got myself to blame, and -"

I put my hand over his mouth. "There's been no one," I say clearly, and his face clears of worry, a huge smile breaking over his serious expression.

"Seriously? Not even the idiot who was with you that night?" I shake my head firmly, and laugh as he seizes me in a hard embrace. "Thank God," he mutters. "I have absolutely no right to that feeling because of what I tried to make you do, but the thought of anyone else touching you and being inside you makes me feel so angry. I can't share you, Dylan."

I hug him tight and rest my face against the black silk of his hair. "You have every right to that feeling. I won't be with anyone else, Gabe. You're it for me, and I don't cheat. It's not in me." I pause, and then say firmly, "I hope it's the same for you, because I don't share either, particularly not my lover."

"It's absolutely the same," he mutters into my neck, his breaths striking warm against the sensitive skin and making me shudder. He looks up at me. "I didn't go with anyone else either."

Something in me relaxes instantly. A tight feeling in my body that has been with me since I left him now unwinds and leaves me loose with happiness. "I love you," I say firmly, and he smiles, those mercurial grey eyes that were always so cold before, but are now full of a warmth and happiness that is palpable.

"I love you too sweetheart, so much." He lifts his head to kiss me, and suddenly the heat flares back into life, like a fire when smouldering coals are nudged. "God," he whispers, thrusting his cock against my thigh, the pressure and heat like a brand. "I want you so much."

"Yes," I whisper harshly. "Need you, Gabe. Need you now, baby."

He wrenches himself away, fumbling in the bedside table for supplies. He comes back to me and kneels to the side of me, spilling the lube bottle and a cascade of condom packets onto the sheets.

I look at them and raise an eyebrow. "Ambitious?"

He smirks. "Realistic. I'm so fucking horny, the only times you're leaving this bed are for food and an occasional shower."

"Occasional, eh? You like me smelling of you, then?"

He shudders, a dark look crossing his face. "Fuck, yes. I want the scent of my skin and my come all over you. I'm warning you, Dylan. I've discovered that I'm a very possessive man."

I shiver theatrically. "Super." Then I pause and grab his hand as he reaches for the condom packet. "Do we need those if it's going to be just us?"

He goes stock still, his face inscrutable. "You'd let me bareback?"

I stare hard at him. "I've been tested recently, and I'm healthy. How about you?"

He nods. "A couple of weeks ago as part of my annual fitness check-up, and it was all clear. I've never gone without a condom before, but you've got to be very sure, Dylan. That suggests a level of confidence and trust in someone, and you know my background. I was always safe, but I was never picky. I've been with too many men, so don't suggest this if it's just to make me feel better." I grab the condom from his hand and throw it cavalierly across the bedroom, and his lips quirk as he follows its trajectory. "Is that your answer?"

I nod. "I trust you in this, Gabe. You're a very honest man, sometimes brutally honest. You never promised any of those men anything, and you were always honest with me, so I do trust you. I trust that you love me, and won't do anything to jeopardise that trust."

He bends over me and takes my mouth in a heated kiss, thrusting his tongue against mine and moaning into my mouth. I grab his head, holding him against me, and arch upwards in an attempt to feel his body against mine. He pulls away and I groan. "Please, Gabe, I need to feel you. I can't wait to have you bare inside me." I shudder deeply. "I can't wait to feel your come slipping out of me."

I watch as a full-body shiver passes over him, but then a smile crosses his lips. "You'll have to wait a bit longer, Dylan." I struggle up on my elbows, ignoring his outstretched hands as he tries to still me so I don't jerk my leg. "Careful," he murmurs, and I glare.

"Fuck that shit. You had better not be backing out of this, Gabriel Foster, because I need you to fuck me right now. I -"

I break off and shout out in surprise, as his hand wet with lube grabs my cock and slicks it up with firm strokes. "What are you doing?" I manage to get out, before collapsing back onto my back and arching into his warm, tight grip.

He looks at me, all laughter gone now. "I never said that we weren't fucking. I just said that *you'll* have to wait to feel my bare cock. I'm going to feel yours instead."

For a second I'm struck dumb. "Are you sure? I thought you didn't bottom."

He stares at me intently, his clever hand still stroking me, making it hard for me to think beyond the tight grip. "I don't usually. I did it once when I was seventeen, and the experience was so decidedly painful and awkward, it was enough to make me reconsider doing it again. I have to really trust someone to let them fuck me, and I never trusted any of the men that ran through my life."

He shrugs and releases my cock, before throwing his leg gracefully over my prone body and hovering over me. "I trust you though with everything, and I want you to make love to me." He looks down my body. "Besides, this position will be the best to not hurt your leg, so you're going to let me do all the work, and you're going to lie still while I use your body."

I groan out a laugh. "I'm fully prepared to be a sex object. Please use me as you see fit, Master."

He groans. "Two years of full-time employment, and *now* you give me my rightful title."

"Jackass. That's your rightful title," I sigh, and then groan as he reaches behind himself. "Fuck, Gabe, are you stretching yourself?"

He gasps and nods, and I snap my fingers to get his attention. "Turn around and let me do that. It's my job to get you ready."

He stills and then nods, turning around so that his arse faces me with his mouth hovering near my hard cock. It's a vulnerable position to be in, particularly for someone as unrepentantly alpha as Gabe, so I stroke my hand down the long, sleek expanse of his back until he relaxes.

I stare at his high, tight arse, and lick my lips. "Jesus, this is beautiful." He pants out a breath and throws his head back with a wild, startled groan as I raise my head and lick over the tiny, pink hole. I pull my head back. "Fuck, that's a sexy hole." I grab his arse cheeks, spreading them, and then start to lick him in earnest. He arches his back frantically and starts to rut against my mouth almost unconsciously. I pull away for a second. "That's it, baby. Fuck my mouth. Sit on my face, and fuck yourself with my tongue."

He shouts out and complies, grunting as I stiffen my tongue and push it into him, tasting the dark, earthy taste of him. This is something that I haven't done that much before, judging it too intimate for the short-term relationships I was in, but now I love it. I love tasting him and driving him wild, and he is wild now, lifting and swivelling his hips lewdly, and pushing demandingly back against my face.

I pull back slightly and spit into his hole, watching the liquid glisten. Then, before he can say anything, I insert one finger, twisting it gently and working him. He looks back, and his face is almost debauched, slack and blind to everything but pleasure.

"More," he gasps out, and I pull out and reach my hand up to his mouth. He grabs my fingers and sucks fiercely on them, sending a shaft of heat to my cock. I pull back, and gently push them in one by one, scissoring them so that his hole slackens, and I feel the muscle inside loosen its tight clasp. I crook them slightly when I feel the spongy knot inside him, and he cries out, his body going rigid like he's been shot.

"Oh fuck, Dylan, now," he shouts out, and I groan.

"Turn around, love. I need to see your face."

He raises himself and turns to face me, crouching over me with all his wonderful body on display. His sleek and powerful torso is wet with sweat, and his cock rises from the dark pubic curls, angry and red looking with pre-come puddling down the sides.

He reaches back and grabs my cock, positioning it against his hole, and I feel the first heated touch, like a little mouth suckling at me. "Go easy," I pant out, sounding like I've been running for miles. "We'll go at your pace."

He stares hard at me, his eyes intent on me, the silver deep and dark like gunmetal as he pushes back. I groan as I feel the furnace like heat inside him. "Shit," I moan. "It's so hot in there. I had no idea how much the condom held back."

He grunts, throwing his head back, a wince of pain crossing his face as he bites his lip hard. "Easy, sweetheart," I croon. "You're doing so well. Go slowly, and the burn will go. Just go easy."

He shakes his head, and ever impatient, he thrusts himself down on my shaft in one long, sharp push, and I shout out as I feel my cock encased in a hot, tight dampness. He stills panting, and I run my hands up his thighs comfortingly. "Are you okay?"

He opens his eyes, a fire burning in them. "Fuck. That feels good."

"Not too painful?"

He shakes his head. "At first, but now it's a burn and a stretch, and fuck, even that feels good. Now I just feel -" He wriggles experimentally, and then groans. "Now I feel so full. Jesus, Dylan, it feels amazing." Then still holding my gaze he starts to move, lifting up and lowering back down, slowly at first, and then picking up speed until he's slamming down onto me.

The headboard bangs against the wall, but all my attention is on him, as he writhes on me, canting his hips lewdly so that his stiff cock thrusts back and forward as if he's fucking the air. The air fills with whimpers and groans, and the scent of sex rises around us as I stare at him, eating him up with my eyes. All that power and strength in his body. It's like fucking a thundercloud.

I thrust up into him and he gives a sharp cry, but opens his eyes immediately, looking worried. "Watch your leg," he gasps harshly, sweat running down his face.

"Never mind my fucking leg," I whisper, my eyes half-closed. "Concentrate on coming, because I'm not far off." I start a series of thrusts upward as he bounces on my cock and shouts out, his eyes closing and his hands rising to fist his hair. He undulates on me, and I feel everything bare inside a man for the first time since I started having sex. The walls of his passage are tight and hot like a fist, enclosing my dick in hot dampness. I angle my hips, and he arches back as I hit his prostate.

"Fuck, yes," he shouts. "Right fucking *there*. Don't stop."

I grunt, rubbing over that spot repeatedly, and reach up to grab his cock. He cocks his hips, riding me furiously and pushing his cock into my grip.

"Fuck," he shouts. "Dylan, yes."

Creamy ropes of come shoot out of his cock, painting my chest and neck and filling the air with the sharp smell. His passage tightens around me so hard it's a pleasure pain, and lightning shoots through me, racing to my balls which tighten. Then I'm shooting, coming endlessly into his hot depths, feeling it bathe my cock.

We collapse down onto the damp sheets, senseless for a long time. Then he snuggles into me, instantly taking my mouth and kissing me frantically. He traces his fingers over my face like a blind man. "I love you," he gasps.

"I love you too." I pull him into a tight embrace, as we both hold on through the tiny aftershocks.

After a while, he gives an experimental wriggle as my slack cock slips from him. "Fuck, I like that," he whispers.

"What?"

He takes my hand, guiding it over the curve of his arse cheeks and under, until I feel the wetness slicking his hole and his inner thighs.

"That's so sexy," I murmur, and he smiles.

"I know. I could get addicted to that. Can't wait until it's my come in you."

I shiver and he laughs, before lifting gingerly off me and leaving the bed. The bathroom light gleams and I hear water running. When he comes out, he's carrying a damp towel and proceeds to wash me tenderly, lifting my spent dick gently and wiping it clean. Incredibly it stirs, and he looks up with a grin. "Forget it, hot stuff. I need a fucking sleep."

"Okay, old man." I laugh as he snaps me with the towel. He wipes himself casually and throws it back into the bathroom, before sliding into bed, snapping off the light, and drawing me to him. He snuggles in and gives a small sound of happiness that catches me in the back of my throat.

"I haven't slept properly," he whispers into the darkness. "Not since I lost you."

"I know. The bed was too empty without you. But we're together now."

"Yes, forever," he says sleepily, and I smile as he drifts off to sleep holding me tightly. I nestle further into him, feeling his warm scent wrap around me. I feel like I'm finally home.

Gabe was right. I *could* go out and find someone else who on paper would be a perfect match, but the absolute truth is that I won't. I can't, because he's it for me, and I love him deeply and fiercely. I don't want to be without this tall, stern man with such a tender, hidden heart. He might have all the faults that he listed, and many, *many* more that I can think of, but he makes me feel more alive and real than I've ever felt before. He challenges me and believes in me, and he makes me want to be the best person that I can be ... for him.

No one will ever need me like him. To him I'm necessary, and I like that. I feel now that I can start to trust him, and I'll hopefully never lose that. Life doesn't come with any guarantees, but at the end of the day, the one fact I know for sure is that we're both incredibly stubborn men who will refuse to give in.

I remember that day in Verbier when he'd nestled against me, and I'd made him look up into the sky, sharing that moment together as the snow cascaded down around us. Realisation hits me that this is how life will be with him – dizzy, unpredictable and sometimes a bit off-balance, but always safe and just simply more enjoyable with him. I smile. I can certainly live with that.

EPILOGUE

To: Dylan Mitchell

From: Gabe Foster

You look tired today. Perhaps you should ask that hot boyfriend of yours to give you an early night ... alone. Who am I kidding, that's never going to happen. I love you.

Eight Months Later
Gabe

I'm late. In fairness, it isn't my fault. I have never been grocery shopping, let alone Christmas grocery shopping, so I didn't know that I needed to book out the whole of December in order to find a parking space at Sainsbury's. Having found one, I throw my coat on and half walk, half jog through the car park, dodging the hordes of people who all seem to be moving along at the same speed as someone from 'The Walking Dead'.

By the time I get to the entrance, I'm overly warm and feeling cross and agitated, but that all eases the second that I see him. I pause, and ignoring a couple who are cursing after nearly walking into me, I stand and watch him. He's wearing jeans and a thick, navy sweater with a long, striped scarf wrapped around his neck that makes him look like Doctor Who. His messenger bag is slung over his body, and he has a ridiculous, woolly pompom hat on. He's staring at his phone with a warm smile on those mobile lips as he types something.

I stare at that smile for a while. He always smiles at everyone, being one of the sunniest and most gregarious men that I've ever known. However, he has a special one that seems to be only for me, and I hoard the sight of it like a miser with gold, because it's happy and so full of love. It doesn't surprise me when my phone chirps, and I pick it up, grinning as I read the message.

DYLAN: WHERE THE FUCK ARE YOU? MUCH AS IT PAINS ME TO ADMIT THAT YOU WERE RIGHT, I'M THINKING THAT THIS WAS A MISTAKE. LET'S DO WHAT YOU SAID, AND GET AN ONLINE DELIVERY AND SPEND THE AFTERNOON IN BED. IT'S LIKE HELL IN THERE.

I laugh, and he looks up, that smile brightening and widening as I walk towards him. "But this was your fucking bright idea, so take the pain," I call out.

"Twat," he says affectionately, grabbing my arms and drawing me closer. He shoots a quick glance around, and then reaches up and rubs his lips gently over mine. When he goes to pull back, I grab his head and pull off that fucking, ridiculous hat.

"*What?*" he laughs. "You really don't like that hat?"

I stick it in the pocket of my coat. "Nope, it hides that gorgeous hair."

He runs his hand through it. It's longer now and has a sight quiff, which always seems to be on the verge of collapsing. With that and the rough beard that he's grown, he's even more gorgeous than when I first met him. However, I like him best when he's naked in bed, and at that thought, I huff indignantly. "Do you realise that we could be in bed now, all naked and sweaty?" I look up as the electronic doors open, sending out a pulse of hot air. "Rather than just sweaty."

He shakes his head, moving back. "Thanks for that, you bastard," he mutters. "I cannot have a hard-on in Sainsbury's. It's just not done."

"It is in our family." I smile widely at seeing his face soften, but it's the truth. He is my family. He's everything to me.

He reaches out and grabs my hand, squeezing it gently. Then resolution fills his body and he claps his hands determinedly. "Okay, let's do this. Can you get a trolley?"

I look over and see the ranks of trolleys sitting to the right of the door, and make to go and get one.

"Wait," he says, sticking his hand in his pocket and getting out a handful of change. "You'll need a pound."

"Why?"

"For the trolley."

"You mean I have to pay for the *trolley*. That's outrageous."

He bursts out laughing. "No, it's a deposit to make sure that they get the trolley back. You'll get the pound back when you return the trolley."

"I am going to be spending an obscene amount of money in this shop. As far as I'm concerned they should throw in the fucking trolley as a bonus."

He shakes his head and makes shooing motions with his hands. "Go and get the trolley. I *knew* I should have listened to Jude."

I look back at him. "Why, what did he say?"

"He said taking you to a supermarket was like taking Prince Philip to Laser Quest."

I shake my head, sticking my coin in the fiddly little slot, and pulling forcibly until the whole row of trolleys shake. Eventually, the fucking thing comes loose, and I turn back to find him laughing at me. "What?"

He smiles. "Nothing. Come on and let's get this done."

"And when we're done we can go home and go to bed, and you'll let me do that thing," I say solemnly. "You promised."

He flushes and looks around, before stepping close. "Baby, if you do this food shop, you have carte blanche for the week."

I swallow hard, already thinking of all the depraved things I want to do to that fantastic body. "What are you waiting for?" I say briskly. "Let's go shopping."

His laughter follows me into the supermarket.

Unfortunately, for the next hour, I do nothing but follow *him* around. He darts here and there, grabbing things and throwing them into the trolley, then crossing things off a list that has more items on it than a spoilt kid's Christmas list. I'd followed him gamely at first, but now I'm just slumped over my trolley, staring into space, which is reminiscent of the last time he'd taken me to a garden centre.

I look around and notice a display of Christmas lights. I whistle, and he looks up. "Want to get some more Christmas decorations for the house? Surely there must be a spare inch that hasn't been covered by fairy lights yet."

He shakes his head and raises his middle finger at me. "Stop taking the piss. I love Christmas."

I scoff. "Our house looks like Christmas threw up in it."

"You love it," he smirks and wanders off down another aisle after giving me an absentminded kiss. I traipse along after him like a puppy, but I'm smiling because I do love it. I was taking the piss out of him, but it's a recognisable fact that the man does love the holiday season. He started playing Christmas music on December 1st, and it shows no let up so far. However, our house looks gorgeous.

I'd never bothered with Christmas before, but now I come home to a massive tree in the lounge, all glittering lights and silver and white decorations. White fairy lights are twined around the bannisters, and the house smells of mince pies and spices. I can't wait to get home, and he'd laughed the other night when he came home late to find me in the lounge with all the lights out, sitting in the glow of the fairy lights.

What I love most, however, is the ability to say *our* house. He'd resisted moving in at first, and for a few months we had dated, enjoying going out to eat and trips out to the theatre and the cinema, or just meeting friends at my local pub. I'd never been in there before, but now the landlord knew my name, thanks to my man's ability to attract friends anywhere.

I'd taken him away for weekends to New York and Rome, but gradually the nights we spent apart had started to grate. I found that I couldn't sleep without his warmth next to me. When he'd confessed the same, we made our minds up, and he moved in with me the next day. He'd immediately set about giving me a home for the first time in my life.

I'd always loved my house as it had been a link to the last of my family, but although it was beautifully decorated and furnished to my tastes, it had always been a bit of a shell. Lovely to look at, but empty. Now, it's full. Full of laughter when it's just us or when friends come over, because they do that all the time now. Dylan made himself at home in my kitchen, and I'd found to my surprise what a homebody he is. He loves cooking and having people over to sit for hours, drinking and eating and talking, and so I discovered a love of it too.

The house had gradually absorbed his presence, and got brighter for it the way that I do. Bright cushions appeared, as did new pots in the kitchen and herbs on the windowsill. Photos of us and family and friends are now everywhere, filling the previously empty spaces. We shopped for artwork together on rainy weekends away, and the house became his as well.

I'd wondered what it would be like to share my space, because I'd been so protective of it after years in care, but it's amazing. It's like having my best friend with me all the time. Sure, we argue and shout, and Dylan has proved to be quite the door slammer. Sometimes needing space I'll retire to my study, or he'll go out running, but we're getting better at knowing when we need our space and giving it to each other.

I had known he was a game changer the instant that I'd seen him, when I made the woman from HR cancel the rest of the interviews. I'd been fascinated from that first moment, and then he'd come to work for me and scared me shitless. His humour, his brain, the way everyone gravitated to him, even the way that he knew all the shit going on around us. It all attracted me to the point of madness, so I instantly put up barriers. I became the cliché of the dickhead boss who lusts after his young employee.

I'd wanted him for so long, but despite my efforts, we got closer, and that was torture too, because then I knew when he was seeing people. I could stand next to him and smell the scent of his apple shampoo, and be close enough to touch, but never allow myself, and know that someone else had that freedom. It was like the Greek myth of King Phineus who could never eat the banquet laid before him every day. Every time he met someone I would torture myself with the idea that this would be the one, and then sag with relief when it wasn't.

I'd thought I knew what I was doing when I reached for him and changed my rules, that I was in charge, but to be honest, I had no control over anything. I had simply looked up in that club that night and seen his gorgeous eyes on me full of heat, and that was it.

Sometimes I wonder at the difference he's brought to my life. I never knew that one person could make such a change in another.

I don't remember much of my parents, apart from the constant recriminations and accusations. I presume that they loved each other once, and hopefully they loved me, but I can't recall any of that. My childhood had been spent moving from care home to care home, so that by the time I was eighteen, the mould had been set. I wouldn't let anyone close, and if they offered I would take, but never give. I had been a selfish and cold man.

Dylan changed everything. I've never known love the way that he gives it, and the only real way to describe it is … steadfast. He's just always there loving me, and it warms areas of me that I never knew were cold. I know if I need him to talk to, if I wake in the night from one of my bad dreams and reach for him, or if I just need to be near him, he will always be there. Because he loves me.

What has been more of a revelation is that I want to do the same for him. I had given my previous lovers anything they wanted, as long as it wasn't a part of me, but him I want to give everything to, and the stubborn bastard won't take anything. I had tried to buy him expensive presents, but he didn't want them. He needed something more, and I found myself giving it to him, and in the process finding bits of myself that I had forgotten

I find that I *can* care because I have Dylan, and I love him fiercely beyond any of my previous barriers. I can be open, because I want him to know all of me, knowing that I won't get all of him if I don't. I can be warm, because I'm filled with the need to touch him all the time and make him happy, and I can be gentle because that's how I am with him. *Only* him though. I haven't suddenly become a soppy twat for anyone else.

The sweetest and most precious time to me is when we lie in bed, and I can feel all his warm, naked skin wrapped around me. It's ironic that I'd previously thought the only use for a man in my bed was to fuck, and now I've discovered a hitherto unknown need to cuddle.

I suppose what he does best is to encourage me to be the best, because he loves me. Maybe at its finest, that's what love should be.

Dylan

A supermarket at Christmas is perhaps the very definition of hell. Hot air pumps out of the vents, Christmas music plays cheerily, and hundreds of people are crammed into the place, armed with trolleys and an almost rabid desire to fill them. It often puzzles me that although supermarkets are only closed for two days over the holidays, people still act as if they're preparing for Armageddon.

I wander past a couple who are operating two trollies which are already filled to the brim and having an argument in hissing tones. Then I look back, not even bothering to suppress a smile at my shadow, who is currently leaning on a trolley and staring into space in a decidedly glazed manner. I suppose I can't blame him. This is Gabe's first experience of supermarket shopping. Before I'd moved in with him, the only things he had delivered were takeaways, booze and men. I'm still surprised I hadn't discovered cobwebs in his cupboards.

I, however, love cooking and entertaining, and it's become common for us to spend a portion of our weekends having friends over for dinner. I'd wondered whether he'd miss his old club days and picking up men. Instead, he seems to flourish, embracing our life with enthusiasm and joy.

This is the reason why we're now standing in Sainsbury's; because instead of going to my parents' house for Christmas, we're spending it in our own home this year. I love to say those words *our home,* to the extent that Jude invented a shot game around it. Every time I used the words in conversation, we all had to down a shot. He and Gabe had got rip roaring drunk one night while I glared at them.

I'd always dreamt one day of having my own home and a partner to go with it. I had no idea I'd end up sharing that dream with a grumpy, sharp-tongued man who used to be my boss, but I couldn't imagine anyone better. Gabe in a relationship is so different from what I'd initially presumed he'd be.

I'd thought that I'd have to tread carefully and avoid any references to relationships, the way that I had when we started. Instead, he revels in our commitment. Whenever we're out, his hand finds mine, he introduced me as his partner at work as soon as we got back together, and he makes no secret of how much he loves me. In love, this once cold man is warm and funny, and somehow everything I ever wanted.

I'd wondered whether he would struggle with me moving in with him, as he'd never lived with anyone before. In fact, we did have some teething troubles, in that I'm very messy, and Gabe likes a level of tidiness only really embraced in the armed forces. I like colour, while he's more neutral than Switzerland, and I don't come fully awake until lunch, while he's up at five and raring to go.

Consequently, at first, we'd argued fiercely over every little thing, and I'd done what I've always done when stressed. I'd made for the door and got outside. Walking outdoors never fails to calm me, but I'd been shocked by how shaken Gabe was when I'd got back. He'd seized me as soon as I got through the door, and we'd had wild, make-up sex in the hallway. Afterwards, he'd confided that he thought I'd left him.

I'd been mortified that I'd not paid heed to the fact that he'd associate an argument between a couple as a disaster in action, because of the way his parents died. I didn't stop myself arguing with him because that wouldn't be healthy. However, I had learnt to tell him that I was going out for fresh air and would be back, and equally he'd learnt to trust in me.

I grab a couple of tins of chestnut puree and wander back to my beloved. He's graduated from staring into space, into now staring with fascination at the couple nearby, who seem to be in the throes of divorce by Christmas food shopping. They're arguing fiercely and with increasing volume. I chuck the tins into the trolley. "Don't stare," I mutter.

He looks at me, the usual wide, warm smile that he gives me filling his face. "It's fascinating. Reminds me a bit of that Jeremy Kyle Show that you made me watch the other day."

"The one where you swore every second that you were losing brain cells."

He laughs. "That's the one." He stares at me as I mark off another item on my list. "Are we done?"

I smile. "Ah, optimism, thy name is Gabriel Foster."

He slumps slightly and then brightens as the argument next to us escalates in noise. "Come on," I urge, grabbing his arm and forcing him onwards. "Behave, or I'll have to take the trolley off you."

"Hey," he says indignantly. "I bloody paid for this. It's mine."

"It was a deposit," I say patiently, fighting a smile. "You don't keep it, and really you don't want it."

"It would have come in handy the other night, when you and Jude showed a shocking inability to hold your alcohol."

I shake my head. "I was only slightly merry. We were celebrating our win at the pub quiz."

"Shame I couldn't join you. I was just at work, having to take your increasingly furtive phone calls and give you the answers."

"Only on military questions. We had the rest covered."

"My champion," he says, fluttering his eyelashes disgustingly. "I still think you owe me one."

I look at him flirtatiously and lean in, seeing his breathing pick up as I lean closer. "I'll give you one later."

He laughs out loud, his high-boned face full of warm appreciation. Two girls nearby sidle nearer, only to be disappointed when he hugs me close with one long arm flung over my shoulder. Completely ignoring an old couple's tuts of disapproval, he smiles at me. "Come on, Romeo, let's finish the shopping."

His good mood, however, has severely diminished by the time we leave the shop. "That's three hours of my life that I'll never get back," he mutters, slamming the boot of his car closed and leaning against the car, as I slot the trolley back into the row and extract his pound coin. I throw it to him and he catches it neatly, but stays where he is as I move towards him.

"What's up with you?" I ask curiously as I go to open the door, but then gasp as I'm flung against the door and he crowds in against me. "What are you doing?" I laugh. I take a quick look around, but we're in a dark corner parked up against a large bush. "Whatever you're thinking of, I want to make it quite clear that I have no wish to spend Christmas in jail for public indecency. If Jude has to bail us out, I will never forgive you, because he'll never forget it."

He laughs and then nuzzles my neck. "I just wanted you close for a second. I feel like I haven't seen you properly for a couple of days."

I melt against him. "It's been so busy lately," I murmur, pulling him close and hugging him tight, feeling the instant warm, free feeling that I have with him. The lift in my spirits that I get just from being near him. For a precious few seconds we enjoy the closeness, until the sound of a car alarm makes us break away. I run my fingers over his full, pink lips and lean in close. "Don't forget, I promised you carte blanche in the bedroom tonight."

His head shoots up, and an impossibly hot look crosses his face. "Fuck, I forgot."

The door beeps behind me, and before I can protest, he's thrusting me inside and has run around the car, getting into the driver's seat and starting the engine.

I start to laugh. "This would have been like 'The Dukes of Hazard', if you'd only rolled over the bumper."

"This is an Audi, you buffoon," he says indignantly, as I start laughing. "Oh yes, laugh it up," he promises me darkly. "You won't be laughing when I get you home."

Two hours later he pulls himself out of me with a groan and slumps on his back. One arm is flung over his eyes, and he's panting heavily. I roll closer to him, sweat and come sticky over me, and run my hand down his wet chest.

He chokes out a laugh. "Don't come near me," he groans. "I swear to God you're going to kill me, Dyl. I only have to be near you, and my cock's ready and raring to go. I don't actually think that I've got another fuck in me, and if my cock tells you differently just ignore him."

I laugh. "I would never argue with my best friend."

He raises his arm in contrast to his words, and I immediately nestle in close, resting my head on his shoulder and feeling his rumble of contentment run through our bodies. We lie together, content in the wreck that was once our bed. The pillows and duvet disappeared ages ago, and the fitted sheet is only hanging onto the bare mattress by one corner. Cold air washes over us from the window that Gabe had opened after our first bout.

After a bit I stir, something flickering at the edges of my brain. "What's the matter?" he asks sleepily.

"What time is it?"

"Where's your watch?"

"Over there somewhere with some of my clothes, or it could be on the stairs with the rest."

He laughs. "It's eleven thirty-five. Nearly Christmas Day, love. Shall I give you your present?" he finishes somewhat lecherously, putting my hand on his cock. "I'll give you a clue. You don't like it wrapped, and it's eight inches long."

"Shit!" I shout out, bolting upright. "Fucking shitbags. Shit! Shit! Shit!"

"*What?*" he asks, coming up on his elbows. "What's the matter?"

"Oh, nothing." I search for an explanation. "I'm just a bit hungry."

He stares at me. "Wow, you must be starving."

I laugh maniacally. "Yes, you know me when my blood sugar's down."

"I do," he says slowly. "Only it's usually a bit more Eeyore, and less Hannibal Lecter."

I scoff and get up quickly. I go over to my pile of clothes and start trying to sort out the tangle, before giving up and grabbing a pair of jeans and an old Massive Attack t-shirt from the wardrobe.

"Wait, where are you going?" he asks plaintively. He gestures to his cock. "Dylan, you're leaving me with this? You're a cruel man."

I shake my head. "I'm going to make us something to eat while you have a shower." I make flapping movements at the bathroom while he stares at me. "Come on. Chop chop." When he starts to move, I dart out of the room, only to backtrack and stick my head around the door. "Take as long as you like, providing you're downstairs at midnight."

"So take as long as I want, is actually twenty-five minutes," he says wryly.

"Just do it," I shout, and race downstairs as soon as I hear the shower start. I book it through the house, banging my shin painfully on a kitchen stool, before flinging open the back door.

Jude looks up from his position sitting on the bottom step. "You know, Dylan, we should do this every Christmas Eve."

"I'm *so* sorry."

"No, really," he breaks in. "Spending Christmas Eve sitting on your patio in the cold, listening to you shouting at Gabe to do it harder, and him yelling about how good you are is just perfect. I've already put it in my diary for next year."

I glance up at the open bedroom window. "Oh God, sorry babe."

He smirks. "It was hot, but it's so cold out here I couldn't even pop a stiffy."

"Do you have him?" I whisper, looking up at the open window again, worried that Gabe will look out.

He smiles and nudges the open box sitting next to his feet. "Fast asleep."

I tiptoe closer. "Thank you so much, Jude. I really appreciate it."

He smiles. "Anything for you babe, you know that."

"Was he good last night?"

He smirks. "No, he howled all night. It quite put Dean off his stride."

I look at him disapprovingly. "Something I'm entirely in favour of. Jude, he's one of the vainest people I've ever met. What you're doing with him is beyond me."

"Have you looked at him?" he says lightly.

"Yes, but not half as much as he looks at himself," I say tartly.

"He's so shallow. I know he's a model, but so are you, and you're nothing like him."

He shrugs. "Not everyone can have what you do, babe."

I shake my head. "Of course you can have the same as me. You just have to stop shagging total cock heads."

I hear Gabe shout my name, but stare at Jude. "Stay where you are."

"Gabe needs you."

"So do you. You're just not being quite as loud about it."

He laughs. "I'm fine. Dylan, come on, it's Christmas. Let's table the subject of my hot hook ups, and you just focus on your man."

"Are you okay?"

"I'm fine." Gabe shouts again, and he gives me a shove. "Go and give your man his Christmas present."

I look down at the box, seized by a sudden doubt. "Shit, what if he doesn't like him?"

"He'll love him. Don't be fucking ridiculous." He laughs and pulls me up the steps, before kissing my cheek and thrusting the box into my arms. "Merry Christmas," he whispers, and then he's gone, vanishing around the side of the house.

"Don't think we won't be revisiting this conversation," I shout out the door.

"Who are you talking to?" I hear Gabe's footsteps in the hall, and putting the box down gently, I race out and drape myself over the door frame.

"Wow, you look good," I try to say seductively, but obviously fail as he looks at me as if I've gone mad.

"I'm in pyjama pants and a t-shirt. It's hardly designer gear."

"You'd look good in a sack," I try again, but I'm interrupted by a tiny whine from the kitchen.

"What's that?" he immediately asks.

"Nothing," I say quickly. "Now go and wait in the lounge."

The noise comes again, but louder this time.

He stares at me, as the whine becomes a positive howl. "Are you killing our dinner now? Didn't we buy meat earlier in Sainsbury's that was already dead?"

"Oh God," I wilt. "Listen, I did something, but now I'm having massive second thoughts. You always said that you didn't want one, and who am I to try and change your mind? I thought it would be an amazing Christmas present, but I've actually just gone entirely against the things you said you didn't want."

"Dylan, I have no idea what you're -"

He breaks off as there's a small thud from the kitchen, the sound of pattering footsteps, and then a tiny Border Terrier puppy teeters into sight. He manoeuvres through my legs, and comes to a slightly drunken stop, looking up at Gabe.

"Oh my God," Gabe says faintly.

"Merry Christmas," I say in a hearty voice, and then sag. "Shit. Gabe, I'm so sorry. I'll take him back. Mum won't mind."

I break off as the biggest smile that I've ever seen crosses his face, and he bends down, picking up the tiny puppy in one large hand. He brings it up to his face and the two stare at each other.

I hold my breath as he brings him into his chest, lowering his face to sniff him. "Is this my Christmas present? Oh, he smells lovely," he exclaims, sounding uncannily like a seven-year-old.

"You like him?" I ask nervously.

He laughs, and the puppy startles. "Oh baby, I'm so sorry," he whispers, kissing the top of his head. "Daddy's sorry."

"*Daddy?*"

He flushes as if suddenly aware of what he said, and tries to glare at me. "That was an accident, Dylan. We will never speak of it again."

I laugh out loud. "Oh, we will indeed, Gabe. We will speak of it many, many times." I break off as he engulfs me in a massive hug, taking care not to squash the puppy.

"Thank you, Dylan."

I stroke his hair. "Do you really like him?" I ask softly. "You said you didn't want a dog, and I ignored that."

He kisses the side of my head, pushing his face into my neck. "I'm glad you did. I'm so glad you ignored every single one of my rules." He lifts his face, and to my amazement, his eyes are suspiciously shiny. "Because you did, I have a home again and a life, and fuck, most of all I have you, and you're everything to me. *Everything.*"

"It frightens you sometimes, doesn't it?" I whisper, hugging him close.

"A bit, but the thing is, if I give in to that fear I'll lose you, and having you is worth every second of being scared. I'm really learning," he says earnestly. "Every day I trust more."

"Trust *me?*" I'm slightly stung, but he shakes his head immediately.

"No, I always trust you. I mean I trust in the love, in the life that you give me, and because of this, every day I become a little less frightened that I'll be like him."

"You could never be him," I say fiercely. "You're too strong."

"Not always, but *we* are strong, Dylan. I trust that now."

The puppy breaks the tension by yawning loudly, showing a long, pink tongue and tiny teeth, and we laugh. Gabe holds him up to look at him and kisses his little nose. "You give me so much, Dylan. I can't ever repay that."

"You don't need to repay anything. We're not keeping score, but if we were, I'd have to say that I've never been so happy in my life, and it's because of you."

"I've never felt this before, and I know that I mess up sometimes, but you need to know that I'm always happy with you," he says affectionately.

"Not always. What about last Friday when I was wrapping presents, and inadvertently sliced open the leather sofa with the scissors?"

"Even then I was happy."

"And what about when I put diesel in the car, rather than petrol? You didn't sound very happy then."

"Don't push it, Dylan. I'm sure everyone's happiness has a limit."

I laugh. "Okay then happy chap, how about we name this puppy? Then we can get some food and sit with him in the lounge. We can open our presents then."

He looks up. "You can't have your main present yet. You get that tomorrow."

I'm instantly intrigued. "Any hints?"

He laughs. "No, I'm too busy naming my new baby." He looks at him considering, and the dog looks back, grinning lopsidedly. "With his scrunched up little face, I'm going to name him after that actor you're always slobbering over."

"I do not slobber," I say indignantly, and then pause before saying incredulously, "Do you mean Charlie Hunnam?"

He nods happily. "Yes, that's the one. We'll call him Charlie for short."

"I'm not sure Charlie Hunnam would be flattered, but good name, daddy."

"Shut up," he growls.

Gabe

I wake up the next morning with Dylan's warm body pressed against mine. He's still sleeping heavily, his arm a lax weight across my belly, and his warm breaths huffing softly into my shoulder. I take a long second to just look at him, at the high cheek boned face and full lips that I know better than my own face nowadays.

If anyone had told me a year ago that I would be happily settled down and not interested in anyone else, I would have laughed in their face. But that was before Dylan. I breathe in, inhaling the scent of sex on the sheets wrapped around us. It's the smell of us, and it stands for joy to me.

Then a howl rises up from downstairs, and I smile and untangle myself. Dylan had insisted last night that Charlie go to sleep in the kitchen. He'd bought a basket for the puppy, and we'd left him last night, curled up comfortably with a hot water bottle wrapped in a towel. Apparently, this replicated the warmth of the puppy pack he'd been sleeping in until recently.

I'd been down a couple of times in the night to let him out, enchanted by his tiny body, sturdy, little legs and indomitable spirit. He'd fallen back to sleep quickly each time, but now his patience is obviously at an end.

I pull on my pyjama trousers, making sure to transfer the little box from my jeans to my pyjama pocket, and pad downstairs. I open the door gingerly, not sure what to expect, but apart from a little puddle there isn't anything, so I pick him up and open the back door.

"Who's a good boy then," I croon. "So clever for your daddy." I break off and look behind me, but luckily the piss taking fool is still asleep, so I can indulge in endearments freely.

I set Charlie down and watch as he lollops around, tracking scents and snuffling happily. The garden is secure, so leaving the door open I go back inside and switch the machine on to make coffee, a job that I'd thankfully taken over from Dylan. The man fucks like a dream, but his coffee tastes like something crawled up and died in the cup.

Here more than anywhere in the house I can feel him. Before he moved in, I had a beautiful, highly expensive kitchen. It was lovely to look at, but empty. Now it's a warm, functional room that serves as the heart of the house. Herbs grow greenly on the windowsill, and photos are three deep on the fridge. He'd painted one wall a deep vibrant pink which I'd initially looked askance at, but then his mum gave us one of her stunning paintings, and the wall suddenly made sense.

The painting is an abstract, a gorgeous melange of greys and pinks and silvers, and it hangs on the wall over a large, deep, silver, velvet sofa which is insanely comfortable. It's where we sit most mornings having coffee before we leave for our day, and where I tend to set up shop in the evening, working on papers while he cooks and tells me about his day.

Charlie comes gambolling into the room, tripping over the

doorstep and landing in a heap. He gets up happily, before zipping over to his bowl and pushing it around the room.

"Okay, wait a second." I fill it with water and stand, watching him drink. A sudden thought occurs to me. "Hope you're good at travelling. We've got a long journey ahead of us, mate."

I feel nerves settle in my stomach at the thought of showing Dylan his present. *What if he doesn't like it? What if it's too much?*

I shake my head. It's totally too much, but I want to give him everything. The trouble is that he doesn't normally let me. He insists on splitting things fifty-fifty, despite me not needing the money, so instead I've put the money in a separate account that we can raid for holidays and household stuff.

I tap my fingers against the box in my pocket. I want to give it to him so badly that it's killing me to wait. I want to see my ring on his finger and have him take my name, no matter how caveman it is. I want our lives entangled so deeply we won't ever get free.

I'm not stupid. I see how men look at Dylan. He's so gorgeous it's not surprising men look, but what is surprising are my territorial impulses. It's sort of ironic that a man who spent most of his sexual encounters sharing men, should have this desire to punch anyone who so much as looks at my man. I used to have such modern ideas about marriage, insisting blithely that it was the creation of straight people. Now, I want nothing more than to grow old with him.

As if my thoughts have summoned him, I hear his footsteps and his arms come around me from behind. I lean into his warm embrace and smile.

"Mmm, Merry Christmas," he mumbles, the early morning hoarseness in his voice catching me in my nuts.

"Happy Christmas, baby." I turn around and take his mouth in a deep kiss, noticing happily the lust drunk look in his eyes when I pull back. "Less of that," I say smartly, standing back and pouring his coffee. I shove his mug towards him, and watch as he takes a grateful sip of the hot liquid. "We've got a busy day today."

He looks at me curiously. "Can I get some answers to some questions now?"

"Hmm, maybe."

He groans. "Okay, I'm fine with having Christmas dinner on Boxing Day, but I need to know why? Are we going somewhere?"

I reach up and brush his golden-brown hair away from his face. "We are going somewhere, but I'm not telling you where."

Charlie prances up, and Dylan bends to pick him up, crooning nonsense to him and laughing as a tiny pink tongue washes his face. He shoots a look at me. "Are we taking him, because I don't think he'll stay on his own? Oh shit, has this thrown a spanner in the works?"

I pull them both into my arms. "Of course we're taking Charlie Hunnam. He's part of our family."

He laughs. "Jesus, I really wish that sentence was real."

I huff, and he raises his head and kisses me, but before it can get too heated, I pull back and smack his tight arse lightly. "No more. Take your coffee and go and get ready. You're fine in jeans, but make sure you wear something warm. We'll eat on the way."

An hour later, Charlie is lying in his basket on the back seat. We'd only driven ten minutes down the road before he fell asleep. Dylan looks back at him. "Mum said he was good in the car."

I shoot him a look. "Is that what they were doing in London on Tuesday?"

He nods. "Yeah. I got him from a litter on the next farm along from ours. They brought him with them, and he's been staying with Jude for the last couple of nights."

He reaches out and fiddles with the Bluetooth and his phone, until the sound of Wham's 'Last Christmas' drifts through the car. I groan. "*More* Christmas music."

"It is actually Christmas Day now. It's obligatory to play George and Andrew."

"I'm not sure that it's obligatory, but it's certainly torturous."

He sniffs. "Keep whining, Gabe, and the next song will be Cliff

Richard's 'Mistletoe and Wine'." I shut my mouth with an audible snap, and he nods. "Yeah, I thought so."

We drive, talking easily about anything and everything, mixed with his increasingly desperate guesses as to where we're going. We stop for lunch at a little pub and to let Charlie have a run, and then finally, after four hours, I flip the indicator and draw the car over to the side of the road.

He'd been dozing lightly, and I'd left him alone, very aware of the long hours that he's been putting in over the lead up to the holidays. He's now an editorial assistant, and I can see him going far. That mix of keen intelligence, his eye for detail, along with his natural warmth and ability to inspire loyalty, will see him well. I still miss him at the office, but it's a concrete fact that I get more work done now.

The sudden quiet wakes him up, and his eyelids flutter. I smile at him, and then before he can look around, I reach out and deftly slide the blindfold over his eyes.

"What the fuck?" he mutters. "Gabe, what are you doing?" His full lips smirk. "Oh, is *this* my Christmas present? Are we role playing? I can see it now. You're the hunky kidnapper, and I'm the naughty hostage drawn to you against my will."

I laugh. "You should try writing novels, rather than reading them."

He pouts. "Disappointing, but I'm rolling with the blow." He straightens his shoulders. "Okay, hit me with it. Why are we miles away from home in an unknown destination, and one of us is blindfolded in a sadly non-sexual manner?"

I shift in my seat. Something about that blindfold hits me in my groin – the slash of red across his face that seems to highlight his full, cock-sucking lips. I make a mental note to keep the blindfold, then bring my attention back to where it should be.

"Because I don't want you to see where we are," I say briskly, starting the engine again and pulling out onto the road.

"Oh, so it's somewhere I know," he immediately exclaims, and I smile.

"Shut the fuck up and stop guessing. We're nearly there."

The car crests the hill, and my whole sight is filled with the grey-blue mass of the sea. Seagulls fly overhead, and I see Dylan cock his head at their unmistakable cawing, but he says nothing. Looking left and right I drive slowly until I see the turn I'm looking for. I flick on the indicator, and try hard to fight down an attack of nerves. This has the potential to either be amazing or go horribly wrong. I smile, because that's life with Dylan. It's sort of a chicken and egg scenario. Which came first, my intense feelings or intense life experiences?

"You alright?" he asks quietly, reaching over and laying his warm hand on my thigh. I feel the weight of it, which seems to always magically ground me and set me free at the same time.

"Why?"

"Because your breathing just got really fast, and I can hear you vibrating from over here."

I pull the car to a stop and start talking really quickly. "Okay we're here, and I really need you to remember one thing. I love you more than anything, and all I want to do is see you happy." I stroke his face. "You also have to remember that anything I give you for the rest of our lives, will never balance the scales of what you give me every day."

"Oh God," he smirks. "You've bought me something really fucking expensive, haven't you?"

I hum and haw. "Price isn't the point."

He shakes his head. "Yes, I guessed right."

I push the door open. "Enough talk. You have to keep the blindfold on. I'll come around and lead you out."

I step out, lifting Charlie down, who immediately pootles off to water a few bushes. I pause for a second inhaling the scent of the sea greedily, and then race around to let Dylan out. He straightens next to me and stands still.

The air is full of the sound of the sea, and heavy with the fragrance of salt and a deep pine resin, and he sniffs deeply. "I know that smell," he says, and a silence falls before I reach back and untie the blindfold. It falls away and he looks up, stilling at what he's seeing.

We're standing on a gravelled drive, looking at a white-washed cottage. Two storeys with large windows, it seems to huddle comfortingly over us. It's obviously rundown, but still has a great deal of charm, and I'd fallen in love with it when I viewed it a couple of months ago with his mum. I'd walked the empty rooms with their stunning views of the sea, and I'd known with a bone-deep certainty that this was meant to be ours. I pay attention to these feelings now, as they'd led me to Dylan in the first place.

He looks around. "This is Mr Peter's cottage," he finally says. "It's been empty for a few years. Why are we here?" He turns to me with his beautiful green eyes full of questions.

I hold out my hand, and he puts his own into it instantly, and something about that gesture touches me deep inside. Then I raise it palm up, and reaching into my pocket I pull out a red box tied with white ribbon and put it into his palm. Swallowing hard, I try a smile. "Merry Christmas?"

There's a choked silence for a long second, then he opens the box to reveal a silver key on a naked Santa key chain. "Oh my God," he says quietly. "Is this real?" He looks at me. "Do people really do things like this?"

I examine his face intently. "If I said this was your Christmas present, on a scale of one to ten how angry would you be?"

That seems to stop him in his tracks. "You think I'm angry?"

I stare at him. "That's sort of the reaction I was anticipating."

He suddenly gives me that slow, sweet smile that I love. "You're the most contrary man that I've ever met, Gabe. You foresaw that I would lose my shit if you did something, and yet you went ahead and did it anyway. Why?"

I shrug. "I kind of like it when you lose your temper." He laughs, and I hasten on. "It's just that I wanted to give you something no one else would. A present that would really mean something to you. So I thought about it, and I realised that by being with me you're waving goodbye for a long time to moving near your whole family, and I don't want you to completely cut yourself off from being with them."

He turns to me, his expression soft. "Sweetheart, *you're* my family. You have to know that by now. I've given up nothing at all to be with you. Instead, I've gained everything."

I pull him to me. "But that home was mine first. I love that you love it, and I adore the way it's become our home, but I wanted us to have something that was ours from the beginning. Something we can make into our home here. I want you to be near your family and have everything."

He wraps his arms around me and hugs me to him, and I smell the familiar scent of his Tom Ford aftershave, which never fails to warm and excite me. "Gabe, we could have nothing, no home, no money, nothing, and I would still have everything because I have you." I swallow hard, and he smiles, reading my mood as always and lightening the atmosphere. "And Charlie Hunnam of course. Now *that's* my idea of a real threesome."

Before I can glare at him, the puppy staggers towards us, dragging a stick that's too big for him. Dylan looks fondly at him. "Just like your daddy, Charlie. Always wanting a big stick in your mouth." I laugh, and he throws his arms around me. "Thank you," he says fiercely. "I love it. I fucking *love* it. I've always loved this house."

"I know," I say smugly.

"How?"

"Your mum. She said that when you were little, you announced that you'd live in it one day."

"There you go," he says, smiling. "Dylan has presentiment. Let it be known far and wide that Dylan is a seer."

"Let it be known far and wide that Dylan is now talking about himself in the third person, and add that earlier on, he guessed his Christmas present was a golden dildo."

He snorts out a disgusting laugh. "That still would have been an epic present." He laughs suddenly and whirls around. "I can't believe we own this. I can't believe you did this for me."

I stay him for a second. "I would do this and more for you, Dylan. I would do anything for you," I say earnestly, and he smiles lovingly.

"Luckily for you, I'll never ask for everything. All I'll ever need from you, is *you*."

He reaches up and kisses me deeply, sending his tongue languorously over mine. I grab his head and pull him closer, feeling the familiar heat rise and twine around us.

He pulls away panting, with his eyes blown. "Let's christen the house," he says hoarsely, reaching down and stroking my cock, making me grunt and shove against him.

I pull back. "Shall I carry you over the threshold?"

He shakes his head. "Twat." Then he moves towards the house shouting something about not asking his brother Ben for a house-warming present, and did I remember his fondness for miniature alcohol.

I stare after him, then push my hands into my pockets, feeling the tiny ring box with the tips of my fingers. He has no idea of the way that my thoughts have turned to permanence. I know we're in it for forever, but I need visual proof on his finger.

No one should ever look to me for love advice because I have done everything wrong that could be done. Yet still, I have ended up with this wonderful man who will walk by my side for the rest of our lives. Maybe my luck has changed. I don't know about that, but what I do know, is that I will spend the rest of my life treating him properly and making him keep trusting me. I will spend the rest of my life with him.

I tap the box again. *Soon* I think, my old wolfish grin appearing, the way it does before I facilitate a deal. *Soon, love.*

The End

THANK YOU

My husband. I wouldn't be able to write if it wasn't for him. His absolute confidence in me has given me the confidence to *be* me. His warped sense of humour has also helped.

My boys who have maintained a sense of humour about having to talk to the back of their mum's head, and the way that dinner can sometimes be a bit of a lottery when I'm writing.

My mum and dad who have managed to be very proud in a vague sense, about books that I've forbidden them to read.

Leslie Copeland who is a brilliant beta reader. I loved the whole process of working with her so much, and I think that we both learnt things. I learnt how awesome it is to have an amazing beta reader, and she learnt that commas are the wallflowers at my school discos!

Natasha Snow for another fantastic cover. She totally nailed it on the first go, and I'm so in love with it. This is my second time of working with her, and again it's been an extremely positive and exciting experience. I look forward to her emails because they're like little presents.

Lastly thanks to you, the readers, for taking a chance on this book. I hope that you enjoyed reading it as much as I enjoyed writing it. If you want to know how Gabe's proposal happened (hint – it doesn't go the way that he plans) you can find the short story on my website.

I never knew until I wrote my first book how important reviews are. So if you have time, please consider leaving a review on Amazon or Goodreads or any other review sites. I can promise you that I read every one, good or bad, and value all of them. When I've been struggling with writing, sometimes going back and reading the reviews makes it better.

CONNECT WITH LILY

Website: www.lilymortonauthor.com
This has lots of information and some fun features, including some extra short stories.

If you'd like to be the first to know about my book releases and have access to extra content, you can sign up for my newsletter here

I'd love to hear from you, so if you want to say hello or have any questions, please contact me and I'll get back to you:
Email: lilymorton1@outlook.com

If you fancy hearing the latest news and interacting with other readers do head over and join my Facebook group. It's a fun group and I share all the latest news about my books there as well as some exclusive short stories.
www.facebook.com/groups/SnarkSquad/

ALSO BY LILY MORTON

Mixed Messages Series

Rule Breaker

Deal Maker

Risk Taker

Finding Home Series

Oz

Milo

Other Novels

The Summer of Us

Short Stories

Best Love

3 Dates

Printed in Great Britain
by Amazon

67589681R00170